A Reckless Moon

Dianne Warren

A Reckless Moon

and other stories

RAINCOAST BOOKS

Vancouver

Polestar Books and Raincoast Books gratefully acknowledge the support of the Government of Canada through the Book Publishing Industry Development Program, the Canada Council and the Department of Canadian Heritage. We also acknowledge the assistance of the Province of British Columbia through the British Columbia Arts Council.

Edited by Barbara Kuhne
Text design by Sari Naworynski

National Library of Canada Cataloguing in Publication Data

Warren, Dianne, 1950-
  Reckless moon and other stories

ISBN 1-55192-455-2

I. Title.
PS8595.A778R42 2002   C813'.54   C2001-911685-3
PR9199.3.W366R42 2002

Library of Congress Catalogue Number: 2002102364

Raincoast Books   In the United States:
9050 Shaughnessy Street   Publishers Group West
Vancouver, British Columbia   1700 Fourth Street
Canada, V6P 6E5   Berkeley, California
www.raincoast.com   94710

At Raincoast Books we are committed to protecting the environment and to the responsible use of natural resources. We are acting on this commitment by working with suppliers and printers to phase out our use of paper produced from ancient forest. This book is one step towards that goal. It is printed on 100% ancient-forest-free paper (100% post-consumer recycled), processed chlorine- and acid-free, and supplied by New Leaf Paper. It is printed with vegetable-based inks. For further information, visit our website at *www.raincoast.com*. We are working with Markets Initiative (*www.oldgrowthfree.com*) on this project.

1 2 3 4 5 6 7 8 9 10

Printed and bound in Canada by Friesens.

For Bruce.

Contents

Hawk's Landing

Edna Carlberg's sister-in-law, the widow of Clayton Carlberg, arrived from Canada on a hot day in the first part of August. Edna was in the garden when she saw the small car coming down the steep hill, heading, she thought, for the ferry. She'd completely forgotten about the letter that had arrived a month ago from her sister-in-law explaining that she was coming to make a dedication in the boys' memories at the Alliance Church in Covey. When the car turned in toward the lodge, Edna assumed the driver was stopping, like so many others, for reassurance that the ferry was not far, and that ascent out of the river valley on the other side was going to be possible. There ought to be a sign, Edna thought, warning those tourists who looked at a map and decided it would be an adventure to take a ferry instead of a bridge across the Missouri. When people called with inquiries about the lodge, when the ad was still in the *Montana Vacation Guide*, Edna was careful to warn them about the road. Sometimes she scared them off.

The lone occupant of the car, whom Edna didn't recognize as they'd met only once and that had been years ago, pulled up in front of the lodge. She stepped out of the car and stared at the monstrous, dilapidated building and the badly weathered sign that identified it as "Stony Landing Lodge." Edna, who had no illusions about the sorry state of the lodge, could just imagine what the middle-aged woman in pink shorts and sandals was thinking. She jabbed her spade into the ground and began walking the short distance from the garden, knowing she was a sight in her rubber boots and her straw sombrero with the pompoms around the brim, but not bothered in the slightest because she believed the woman to be a stranger.

"Hello there," she said when she was close enough for the woman to hear. "You must be looking for the ferry. It's just down the road, not a quarter of a mile. I hope you're not having car trouble. That road's a disgrace. I'm surprised you didn't turn around and go back."

"Edna?" the woman said.

For a brief moment Edna thought the woman must be a former guest, and then she remembered the letter, the one from her brother Clayton's wife. Edna hadn't known what to think or what to tell her mother so she'd filed the letter away, and when she didn't hear from Clayton's wife again she assumed she wasn't coming and forgot about it. Now here she was, Hildie Carlberg, expecting some kind of welcome and Edna was completely unprepared. She quickly decided there was nothing she could do but be herself. Pretenses were out of the question, considering how she looked in the sombrero and her garden clothes. She stuck out her hand, dirt and all.

"Hildie," she said. "It's nice to see you again after all these years."

Hildie shook her hand in a self-conscious way and stammered something that sounded like "How do you do," although Edna couldn't be certain Hildie had uttered words at all. The sounds might have been sounds of pain, or perhaps terror. Yes, terror, Edna decided, when Hildie managed to steady her voice and say, "How can I possibly get back up that road?"

It was on the tip of Edna's tongue to say something sarcastic about rusty cars and human skeletons littering the river valley, but she didn't. Instead, she said, "It's not as bad as it looks. We haven't lost anyone in here yet." Then she apologized for looking the way she did and admitted she'd forgotten Hildie was coming. She invited Hildie to sit on the porch in the shade while she went inside to get

Mrs. Carlberg, and motioned her toward the dozen or so wooden Adirondack chairs that were lined up deck-style beneath the windows. They hadn't seen paint for ten years and now they were blackened with mildew.

"Don't worry about the porch," Edna said. "It looks like it's going to fall off and slide down the hill any second, but it isn't."

Edna went inside wondering where they would put Hildie to sleep if she was planning to stay over, which she probably was, because now Edna remembered something about a dedication in the church. That would no doubt have to happen on a Sunday and it was only Thursday. More importantly, Edna wondered how she was going to handle her mother, who had never accepted or acknowledged that her two sons were both dead. She said things like, "I wonder if we'll hear from the boys at Christmas this year," no matter how many times Edna said, "Mother, you know they're gone. We have the obituaries from the paper." Edna had learned to live with her mother's nonsense, but the old woman's denial of the boys' deaths was bound to be a problem with Clayton's widow planning a memorial of some kind.

Edna went to the kitchen, quickly tried to scrub the dirt out from under her fingernails, then gave up and got a pitcher of lemonade from the fridge. She took a tray and three matching glasses from the cupboard. They were pretty glasses with little yellow lemons painted on them, a reflection of the contrasts Edna lived with every day. In spite of the disrepair, the lodge was filled with tasteful and interesting objects that her father had purchased when he had money and a vision of himself as a kind of ranch-land ambassador offering frontier and comfort in the same package.

Edna set the tray on the counter and went to the bedroom where her mother was supposed to be having her afternoon nap. She found her lying on top of the covers, awake, staring up at the ceiling.

"I thought I heard a truck in the yard," her mother said.

"A car," Edna corrected her.

"Not guests," her mother said.

"Well, yes," Edna said.

Her mother sat up. "You know, Edna," she said, "I had a feeling we might see guests, what with the good weather we've been having. We'll have to open up one of the wings. I was thinking east would be best, because you get the morning sun."

"Not that kind of guest," Edna said. "More the family kind."

"Family?" her mother said. "What family?"

"Hildie. Clayton's wife. The Canadian."

"Hildie?"

"She did write and say she was coming," Edna said. "I forgot to tell you, I guess. But anyway, she's here. She came all the way across that road in a little car. It's a wonder she made it."

"So," Mrs. Carlberg said. "Hildie. I'll be."

Edna stood in front of the mirror above the dresser and took off her straw hat. Her mother was always telling her how silly she looked in the hat, but Edna insisted the pompoms kept the mosquitoes away from her face with their constant motion.

Mrs. Carlberg said, "I suppose you let her see you in that hat."

Edna ignored her. She picked up a brush and ran it through her hair, then realized there wasn't much use, what with the garden dirt and the clothes she had on, and she couldn't very well keep Hildie waiting on the porch while she had a bath and changed. "She's in a bit of shock, I think," Edna said. "From the road and the look of the place."

"Pass me my sneakers," Mrs. Carlberg said.

Edna went to the big oak closet where her mother's running shoes had been neatly placed. She picked them up, hesitated, and said, very carefully, "I think she's come about a memorial of some kind, for the boys."

"Hurry up, Edna," Mrs. Carlberg said. "Bring me those sneakers. What are you waiting for? It's rude to keep guests waiting."

"Did you hear me, Mother?" Edna asked. "What I said about the boys."

"Of course I heard you," her mother said. "Now are you going to bring me those shoes or not?"

Edna took the old woman her shoes.

"She's on the porch, you say?" her mother said, tying up her laces, then standing and panting from the effort. Before Edna could answer she was off, heading through the lounge, past the field-stone fireplace, toward the front door.

"I'll just get the lemonade," Edna said, mostly to herself. She went to the kitchen, picked up the tray and carried it to the porch, where her mother had already seated herself next to Hildie. Hildie looked at Edna with dismay when she stepped through the screen door. Edna could guess why.

"Edna," Mrs. Carlberg said, "this girl has come all the way down from Canada to visit, and she hasn't brought the boys with her. What do you say about that?"

Edna said, as casually as she could, "Let's talk about something else. We'll deal with that little problem later."

"Well, I just can't believe it," her mother said. "I don't know what's wrong with those two. They never write and now Clayton has sent his wife down here alone, over that terrible road. I can't understand it."

"Later, Mother, please." Edna put the tray down, sighing in a way that said *long-suffering,* so that Hildie would know lunacy was not a common denominator here.

"Have some lemonade," Edna said, pouring. "It'll cool you off. There's beer in the fridge, but it's too early in the day for ladies like us." She laughed, but no one laughed with her. Hildie sat, not saying a word. Mrs. Carlberg had that puzzled look on her face, the one she got when she was confused and was working hard to put things in their proper order.

Edna's brothers, "the boys," had moved to Canada when they were young and now they were both dead, having died of sudden heart attacks just months apart. That's how their father had died, too, and his father before him. Edna and her mother remained summer and winter in the old man's hunting and fishing lodge, which sat tucked into the hills, overlooking the Missouri River, reminding the few who passed by on their way to the ferry that failure is the shadow of ambition. The lodge, known by the locals as Old Stony, hadn't hosted more than a handful of guests in recent years, and had seen none in eighteen months. Edna and Mrs. Carlberg (also referred to as Old Stony, although never to her face) had tried to keep the place going after the old man died, but once weather and age began to take their toll on the building, the upkeep had become onerous.

In truth, the lodge had never been much of a success. The road in was the main problem. Old Carlberg had had a loose promise from the county that the road would be upgraded, but getting action had turned out to be a battle, and when he died the promise was forgotten. And he had built the lodge too big, with a full second storey over the main floor and two single-storey wings, one at each end of the lounge. There were far too many rooms to fill. The guests, never more than a few at a time even in the good years, left feeling vaguely depressed. There was just too much emptiness in the place. Although the guests usually claimed to enjoy their stay and wrote compliments in the guest book, they rarely recommended the place to their friends.

After Mr. Carlberg died, Edna and her mother decided they would add family tourism to their business repertoire. In the first years after his death, when the lodge still looked new, they did host a few summer tourists, lured by the ad in the vacation guide and the opportunity to use the four-wheel drive in their Jeep Cherokees. But as the years passed, the grey paint peeled and the windows cracked, and Old Stony began to take on the appearance of a disaster. Then the river flooded one spring and came right up to the front porch, and when the water receded the land settled and the porch pulled away from the main building and sank a good foot on the east side. That was it for guests. Even those who had come expressly to visit the lodge took one look and decided to head for Havre or Great Falls, in search of a Best Western.

Mrs. Carlberg and Edna stopped advertising and sold off the horses so they wouldn't have to buy feed. They boarded up the wings to make the place easier to heat, which they had always done after Christmas, but now they left them boarded up when spring came. When a whole tourist season went by without guests, and then a hunting season, they boarded up the stairwell to the second storey, keeping open only the lounge with its field-stone fireplace, the huge kitchen and the master bedroom, which Mr. Carlberg had decorated as though it were his private chamber. It contained a hand-made four-poster bed with a cattle drive carved into the headboard, an antique rocking chair made from buffalo horns, and a small Charlie Russell painting on the wall above the bed, the real value of which neither Mrs. Carlberg nor Edna knew.

The two of them, Edna and her mother, shared the master bedroom. Mrs. Carlberg slept in the four-poster and Edna on a single bed under the window. Edna liked to sleep with the curtains open so she could see the stars, which were multitudinous on a clear night. Although the lodge had eaten up the savings over the years and given almost nothing back, Edna and her mother were not in dire straits, thanks to the old man's insurance policy and a small share they still held in his lumber business. They lived a life they were used to, although Edna understood that it would soon be coming to an end, even if her mother was not prepared to admit it.

Edna looked at her mother, whose lemonade was untouched. She was staring down at her running shoes and kicking at a loose board on the porch. Hildie took a nervous sip of her lemonade and looked off in the direction of the river. Edna saw that the ferry was coming toward them from where it had been docked on the other side.

"That's the ferry coming across," Edna said.

"Oh," said Hildie. "It's not very big, is it?"

"There isn't much need for a big one," Edna said. "Is there, Mother?"

"Is there what?" Mrs. Carlberg asked.

"Ferry," Edna said. "I was telling Hildie there isn't any need for a big ferry."

"Of course there isn't," her mother snapped. "Is someone saying we need a bigger ferry?"

"Never mind," Edna said. "I'm sorry I mentioned it."

The ferry disappeared behind the hill to the east where the landing was, and where the ferryman lived. He had probably seen the car, Edna thought, and was coming to collect it, never suspecting that the Carlberg women might have company.

She finished her lemonade, trying to think of something to say to break the silence that descended. Then Mrs. Carlberg broke it by saying, "Well, I'll be damned," and for emphasis she added, "I'll just be Goddamned." Hildie turned white, even whiter than she was already, as though she'd just looked the devil squarely in the eye. Edna noticed that she began to play with the little gold cross that hung around her neck.

The ferryman's grandson was thirteen years old and small for his age. He was living with his grandparents for the summer because his mother, their youngest child, was single and the boy was a handful. He'd had a few encounters with the law in Lewistown, south of the river, where he lived with his mother during the school year. The scrapes he got into were not serious, but his mother was worried they would lead to bolder, more dangerous crimes. When Mrs. Carlberg caught him in the lodge once in the middle of the night, Edna convinced her that the boy was mixed up, living with his grandparents in the middle of nowhere, hardly ever getting to town where his friends were, so Mrs. Carlberg had agreed not to tell the boy's grandparents. Instead, Edna had convinced her to give the boy the three-wheel all-terrain vehicle that they'd purchased years before and no one used. It would give him something to do, Edna said, and keep his mind off trouble. Now the boy tore through the hills all day like a demon, reckless beyond normal for a boy his age, but, according to his grandfather, happy as a pig in shit. His grandfather, the ferryman, couldn't understand why the boy had no interest in horses (he and his wife kept several in a small pasture near the ferry landing), but he said he was grateful to the Carlberg women for keeping the boy busy with something, even if he was determined to break his neck, the way he was going at it. The ferryman was philosophical about children, boys in particular. When Edna asked him if he was worried about his grandson's reckless nature, he shrugged and said, "Some of them make it and some of them don't."

Edna had known the ferryman, whose name was Hawk, all her life. They'd both grown up in Havre, before her father sold off most of his lumber business and built the lodge. It was her father who'd got Hawk the job as ferryman when the previous ferryman got so old it wasn't safe to let him continue. He'd fallen asleep on one particular crossing and crashed the ferry into the landing going full speed, causing considerable damage and sending a dog overboard. Luckily, the dog was a retriever so the flight into the Missouri was more bewildering than injurious.

The old ferryman wept when they told him his time was up. Then Mr. Carlberg threw him a big send-off at the lodge and the local ranchers chipped in and bought him his own engraved bar stool in the Covey Hotel. He moved on happily enough, and Hawk and his family moved into the aluminum-sided trailer on the riverbank.

Edna was one of the few people who knew that Hawk's mother had not called him Hawk when he was a baby, she'd called him Antoine, after a favourite uncle whose mother was French Canadian. He'd hated Antoine almost from the minute he understood it was his name, and grabbed the first opportunity to rid himself of it. That came when he flew off the roof of the school in first grade and made a successful landing in the school yard below. He'd known the boys, Ward and Clayton (they had "run together," as Mrs. Carlberg put it), before old Carlberg moved the family out to the newly constructed lodge in 1956. A few years later, when Hawk was only nineteen, he married Nancy, who was an aspiring trick rider he'd met and made pregnant at a rodeo in South Dakota. About the same time, Ward and Clayton headed for Saskatchewan to work on the pipeline, not wanting anything to do with the old man's dream or the life he had planned for them.

Edna, being a few years younger, was not ready to leave the nest. And unlike her brothers, she shared her father's belief that the lodge would eventually render the dividends it promised. She was prepared to work hard and wait for the payoff. Then she discovered the lodge offered something even better than money, and that kept her going for years.

When she was twenty, a look passed between her and an out-of-state duck hunter when she placed his dessert in front of him. Although she was relatively inexperienced, she knew instantly what the look meant, and what to do about it. She discovered she was able to decipher with not much more than a glance which of the hunters could meet her two conditions: discretion, and an enthusiasm that matched her own. She became a phantom, stealing undetected through the lodge to the bed of a waiting stranger who was drunk on the kill and, sometimes, her father's Scotch. In summer, when the fishermen came, she dared her lovers to meet her on the riverbank for a swim in the dark water. Sometimes they did. If the river was high there was a dangerous current and the sex afterward was all the better.

Edna had no false notions that these liaisons were anything other than what they were, and for years she had no desire for them to be anything else. Then, when she was closer to forty than thirty, she fell in love with a hunter who had come back three years in a row. She dared to believe he had come for her, and it was a grave and humiliating mistake. She found herself in a conversation she'd never had before, one motivated by a man's need to tell her he was married, happily so. In spite of the inner strength she'd always thought she had in spades, she was devastated. She loathed her disappointment, and was frightened by the idea that loneliness could come upon you and make you blind. She resolved to give up her encounters, but in the end her resolution was without meaning because the old man died and the entries in the guest book began to dwindle.

Edna eventually got over the hurt, and she accepted passion as a thing of the past, about which she was able to have fond memories. She did allow herself to wonder, only rarely but once in a while, whether the lodge, which had once offered so much, was the reason she now slept in a single bed across the room from her mother. And she allowed herself to feel just an inkling of regret whenever she glimpsed Hawk's grandson, the small and reckless boy, zipping around on the three-wheeler.

The day Hildie Carlberg arrived, when they were still sitting on the porch with their lemonade, Hawk's grandson roared into the yard like an angry hornet. He circled the lodge twice, throwing out clumps of dirt and clay as he navigated the corners, then flipped himself right over trying to climb straight up the steep hill west of the lodge and lay still.

"The silly bugger," said Mrs. Carlberg. "What's he done now? Knocked himself out cold, it looks to me."

Edna jumped up and ran the few hundred yards to where the boy was lying. He was pale, the colour drained from his face. He had a scrape on the side of his head where, Edna surmised, he'd landed on a rock, but there was no swelling, at least not yet. She picked him up and was amazed at how heavy he was for his size, and then she thought maybe all boys were solid, no matter what their size, how would she know anything about that, having never held one in her arms. Hawk's grandson was warm and smelled of sweat and grass – boy smells, she thought. She staggered back toward the lodge, trying not to panic. This was what you feared living out here, an accident. She began to talk to the boy.

"You're all right, Sonny," she said, "You'll be all right. We'll just get a cold cloth on that head, some ice to keep the swelling down. It's all right, honey. It wasn't a big rock. You'll be okay, honey." She didn't notice that she'd switched from calling him Sonny, which was his name, to honey. She was thinking how she would never forgive herself if he wasn't all right, because she had talked her mother into giving him the three-wheeler. A philosophy like Hawk's – some of them make it and some of them don't – would not be a comfort.

When Edna reached the porch, Hildie and Mrs. Carlberg were standing at the top of the steps looking concerned, but neither of them looked like she was about to do anything to help.

"Is he all right?" asked Hildie, although it was obvious he was hurt.

"Knocked himself silly, hasn't he?" said Mrs. Carlberg. "I knew he would, the way he drives that thing."

"Get some ice, Mother," Edna said. "It's all I can think of to do right now, put some ice on his head."

Her mother opened the door so Edna could carry the boy inside, then she bustled off to the kitchen for the ice. Edna struggled to the big leather couch in front of the fireplace and laid the boy on it. Mrs. Carlberg came back with ice cubes in a tea towel, and Edna gently touched the bundle to the goose egg that was beginning to form on the side of the boy's head. Her sister-in-law stood over her watching, looking like a terrified bird, and Mrs. Carlberg disappeared into the kitchen again, this time to phone Nancy and Hawk and tell them what had happened. She came back minutes later and reported that there was no answer, but then the boy started to stir and Edna said, "Honey? Are you all right? Does it hurt anywhere?"

The boy opened his eyes.

Edna heard Hildie say, "Praise the Lord." She could see that the boy was studying her, trying to figure out what had happened.

"Sonny?" she asked. "Do you know where you are?"

She put her hand on his forehead and brushed his hair back. He let her, and she felt a wave of caring and relief that his eyes were open, even though he hadn't yet spoken.

"Does it hurt?" Edna asked.

The boy shook his head, but Edna could see that it did hurt.

"Get your painkillers, Mother," Edna said, and her mother bustled off again, this time to the bedroom, and returned with a prescription bottle. Edna took out one of the large yellow capsules, bit off a small piece of it, and placed it on the boy's tongue. Hildie still had her lemonade in her hand. She handed it to Edna, who helped the boy lift his head and held the glass to his lips until he swallowed obediently.

"I hope he can handle that," Mrs. Carlberg said. She turned to the boy. "What did you think you were doing anyway, driving like a maniac? You should know better, out here miles from a hospital."

"You're one to talk," Edna said sharply to her mother.

"He could have a concussion," Hildie said. "We should keep him awake. That's what they do."

The boy sat up and swung his feet over onto the floor. He still looked dazed, although his colour was coming back. Edna sat down beside him.

"You just sit here for a while," Edna said. "Make sure you're all right." She placed her hand on his knee. He didn't seem to mind.

"Do you feel sick?" she asked him. She knew that was a sign of concussion. "Do you think you might throw up?"

He shook his head.

"Well, that's good then," Edna said. "You just need a few minutes to get yourself straightened around, get the cobwebs out and the world back right side up."

The couch sat in front of the fireplace. The old man's chess set was on the hearth not far from their feet. Edna could see the boy looking at it. She counted, and saw that five of the hand-carved pieces were now missing, all pawns. The pawns were jack rabbits and each had a distinctive pose. She wondered when her mother would notice. Luckily, she knew nothing about chess so had no idea how many rabbits were supposed to be on the board.

"What about the three-wheeler?" the boy asked, as though he had just remembered what happened. "Is it wrecked?"

"I don't think it's wrecked," Edna said, "although I must say I didn't pay much attention to it, with you lying in the dirt not moving. I can't say the three-wheeler was my first concern."

"I'm going to check," the boy said standing up, but Edna pulled him back down and said she would check, if he was that worried about it. She made him promise to stay put, and she walked out to where the three-wheeler was tipped over on the side of the hill. She managed to get it flipped upright, then she started it and drove it back to the lodge. It seemed to be undamaged. The boy was waiting on the porch when she pulled up and stopped.

"It's okay," Edna said. "No problems that I can see."

The boy stepped down off the porch and climbed onto the three-wheeler.

"Why don't you let me drive you home in the truck?" Edna said. "You can pick it up tomorrow."

"I'm okay," the boy said.

"You go straight home then," Edna said. "That was one of mother's painkillers I gave you. It might make you sleepy." It occurred to her that maybe she shouldn't have given it to him, because of what Hildie had said, about keeping him awake. The boy took off, and not toward home either, the other way.

Hildie and her mother were watching through the screen door.

"I told him to stay put," Mrs. Carlberg said, "but he wouldn't listen, would he? Silly bugger."

"I hope he's all right," Hildie said. "They must make them tough out here. I always told Clayton, 'You must come from awful tough stock down in Montana,' and then he up and died. He was watching a hockey game on TV and he died, just like that. I couldn't believe it. I still can't."

Edna looked at Hildie through the screen door. She felt bad that she hadn't remembered Hildie's letter and been prepared for her.

"Well," Edna said, opening the door and stepping into the lodge. "Don't worry about the boy. Let's worry about getting a bed fixed up."

"Bed?" Mrs. Carlberg said. "Is she staying?"

"Of course she is," Edna said.

"I hope you have room for me," Hildie said. Edna thought Hildie was turning out to be a little slow, the place was obviously the size of a horse barn, but maybe Hildie had noticed most of the lodge was boarded up. She probably had.

Edna said, "This place calls itself a guest lodge, it ought to have an extra bed. You can bring your bags in and we'll cook up a nice big supper to celebrate. Clayton's wife from Canada – this *is* something to celebrate." She was thinking her mother had a point, the east wing was sunny, but the upstairs might be in better shape as far as mice and cobwebs went.

"Mother," she said, "try to call Nancy again and tell her what happened. Hawk can track the boy down and make sure he's all right." She turned to her sister-in-law and gave directions to the bathroom, which was off the kitchen. "Make yourself comfortable while I get your room fixed up." She was trying to remember where the wrecking bar was so she could tear down the boards covering the stairwell. "I'm looking forward to a good talk," she said. "We don't get much company out here, and we want to know all about the boys, what they did in Canada. And I hope you brought pictures."

"Yes, I did," said Hildie. She went out to the car to get her bag.

Edna's mother came back in, saying that she'd got Nancy on the phone, and Nancy had been out in the garden earlier, and she'd get Hawk to saddle a horse and go looking for Sonny.

"Good," said Edna. "I'll feel better when they've got him at home and can keep an eye on him."

"Nancy says she's got slugs in the tomatoes," Mrs. Carlberg said. "I told her to lay down crushed egg shells. Did you notice slugs in the tomatoes?"

"We don't have tomatoes this year," Edna said.

"Why not?" her mother wanted to know. "I like a good tomato."

"The plants froze," Edna said. She was still trying to remember where the wrecking bar was.

"I like Nancy," her mother said.

"Good. Fine. I'm glad you like Nancy."

"She's kept her figure. She does aerobics in front of the TV, you know. That's why she looks so smart."

"I have more important things on my mind than Nancy's figure," Edna said. "I wish I could be more organized about where I put the tools."

"I heard you call that boy honey," her mother said. "Don't you think I didn't hear you call him that."

"I didn't call him honey," Edna said.

"It's not normal, at your age," Mrs. Carlberg said. "Anyway, he's a boy, and a wild one at that. You didn't catch me calling Ward and Clayton honey."

Edna wondered what was wrong with calling a child honey, although she didn't remember calling him that.

She went out back to the shed to look for the wrecking bar, thinking that was the most likely place for it to be, which probably meant it wouldn't be there. When she came back inside (*with* the wrecking bar, surprise, surprise) she found her mother pulling pots and pans out of the cupboards. That was a good sign. Her mother had enjoyed cooking for the guests and Edna hoped that cooking for her daughter-in-law would make her happy in some way, even if she insisted Hildie was putting on an act when she called herself a widow.

"What have you got in mind for supper?" Edna asked.

"You just worry about getting a room fixed up," her mother said. "I'll worry about food. Since when did you have an opinion on the meals anyway?"

"Fine," Edna said. So her mother was cooperating. Good. She left her to take care of supper and headed for the stairwell to tear down the boards.

Hildie had come with a tape recorder. What she wanted, she explained after supper, was for Mrs. Carlberg to tell stories about the Carlbergs for the Canadian branch of the family. It seemed funny to Edna, the realization that there was a Canadian branch, but she supposed there was. In fact, there were now more Carlbergs in Canada than there were in Montana, thanks to the fact that Edna had never married and had children.

"I don't know much about Clayton's family," Hildie said. "His ancestors. His childhood. Whatever you want to tell me, really."

Hildie's mini-tape recorder was lying on the table. Mrs. Carlberg was looking at it as though it was something that had got inside by accident and needed killing. Hawk had stopped by after supper to tell Edna and Mrs. Carlberg that he'd been able to track Sonny down earlier and had ordered him back to the trailer for Nancy to check him out. He seemed to be okay, Hawk said, although he had a humdinger of an egg on the side of his head. Edna had invited Hawk in for coffee so he could meet Clayton's wife, and now they were sitting at the big kitchen table. It was not quite dark. There was a pale sunset behind the hills, which you could see through the window above the kitchen sink.

"Mrs. Carlberg," Hildie asked, "would you do that for me? Tell me about the Carlbergs."

"You can just ask Clayton yourself," Mrs. Carlberg said. "He'll tell you what he wants to. Or ask Ward. He was always the talkative one."

Edna was looking at the photo album Hildie had put together especially for the trip. She and her mother were in a few of the earliest pictures, taken at Clayton and Hildie's wedding. Edna and Mrs. Carlberg had driven up to Canada, just the two of them, after Mrs. Carlberg had had a huge row with the old man over his refusal to come along. They'd attended the ceremony and then had turned around and driven home again because there were guests to be fed at the lodge. Edna guiltily remembered that her mother had wanted to stay for a few days, but she'd sided with her father and insisted they had to go back. The lodge was everything in those days, the hen about to lay a golden egg. Ward and Clayton had never ventured south of the border again as far as Edna knew, although nothing had been said, and two Christmas cards arrived from Saskatchewan every year with a few lines scribbled about the weather and good health.

Hildie's photographs moved from the wedding through three decades of the boys standing in front of their houses or their cars, with Hildie, with each other, sitting in lawn chairs or at picnic tables on various holidays, their hair growing lighter and thinner over the years, but they looked good, Edna thought, both of them fit and handsome. They didn't look like the type to get taken by heart failure, but neither had their father. The photos of Clayton and Hildie included their two daughters, whose names were Sandy and Lynn, and eventually Sandy's babies, Hildie's grandchildren, who were now three and five, she informed them, and cute as little buttons.

"Look here, Mother," Edna said. "You have two great-grandchildren. Imagine."

Mrs. Carlberg was refusing to show interest. She was still staring at the tape recorder. Edna decided to leave her alone. She'd been pleasant enough at supper, all through the cooking and the meal and the washing up afterward.

"Lynn has a boyfriend," Hildie said, "but they're not engaged yet. They're both going to school, and I suppose they want to finish before they commit themselves."

"How come Ward never got married?" Edna asked.

"I don't know," Hildie said. "I think Ward was happy enough to be on his own. He was a private sort of person, in spite of his outgoing nature. I guess you know that."

"It's not too late," Mrs. Carlberg said.

So she was listening after all, Edna thought. Hawk looked at Edna and Hildie and winked, and for the first time Edna saw a little smile cross Hildie's face, just a flicker.

Edna turned to the last page of the photo album and realized she was looking at pictures of her brothers' grave markers. She couldn't say she felt grief when she saw the headstones, but somehow silence seemed right and she looked at the photos for several minutes, letting it sink in that her brothers were truly dead and buried. Hawk was looking too.

"The graveyard is lovely," Hildie said when she saw what pictures they were looking at. "I think you'd approve."

Hawk said, "Hard to believe, isn't it?"

"Well," Edna said, closing the album. "Thank you for bringing this with you."

"You can keep it," Hildie said. "I had copies made. I thought you might want some photos."

"Yes. Thank you," Edna said again. She was wondering whether some kind of reunion could have come about if the boys hadn't died. She wished they hadn't died, and that they were all sitting at the big table, along with Clayton's children and grandchildren. How stupid and careless, she thought, to let people you love get away. But there was no sense thinking about that, no sense beating yourself up. She'd long ago got used to the boys being absent. It was never spoken about by her parents as anything out of the ordinary, so she hadn't thought of it that way. Only now she thought it was out of the ordinary.

Hawk stood and said he'd best be getting home to check on that wild grandson and see if he was still conscious or if he'd died in the middle of his chess match with Nancy.

"Nancy knows how to play chess?" Mrs. Carlberg said.

"She claims to," Hawk said, "although I don't know, she might be just moving those pieces around and pretending."

"I'll bet she knows," Mrs. Carlberg said. "I'll just bet she does."

Hawk told them he'd locked up the three-wheeler for a few days, so Sonny'd be forced to stay put. Edna wondered if it was possible Hawk didn't know about Sonny's night-time wandering, which was always on foot, or if Hawk was like her and simply listened and waited.

"I'll walk you out to the truck," Edna said, and they left the kitchen and stepped out into the summer evening, which was a perfect temperature and relatively free of mosquitoes. She wanted to ask Hawk what he thought of her life, but instead she started to laugh.

"What's so funny?" he wanted to know.

"Oh nothing," Edna said. "It's just, I was going to ask you if you think I live a strange existence out here, but then I thought, how in the world would you know?"

He laughed too. "You're right about that. Anyway, I don't have opinions on people's lives. I make a point not to. People talk when they're crossing the river. I figure it's best to stay neutral."

Edna said she thought that sounded prudent, then she said, "So isn't this something, Clayton's wife showing up? I don't have a clue what I'm going to do with her until Sunday, but anyway, it was nice of her to bring the photographs. And she's got this idea about some kind of memorial in the Alliance Church. She's got a pair of silver candlesticks with her, with the boys' names engraved, and she wants to make a dedication. I guess she doesn't realize the Alliance Church in Covey doesn't even know Ward and Clayton Carlberg ever existed. But it's up to her. And maybe the church will be glad to have a new pair of candlesticks, no matter whose names are on them. I suppose we'll be expected to go."

Hawk climbed into his truck and sat there with the door open.

"Nancy's kind of enjoying the boy being here," he said. "They get along like a house on fire."

"That's good," Edna said.

A silence hung between them for a minute, but not a bad one. Hawk closed the truck door and started the motor.

Edna went back inside to the kitchen, where her mother had disappeared. Hildie was still seated at the table. The photo album and the black tape recorder were in front of her. She looked exhausted and Edna felt sorry for her.

"You probably want to go to bed," Edna said. "I can see that you're tired."

"I am tired," Hildie said. "Driving can make you tired."

Edna didn't think it was the driving, but that was all right. It was nice of Hildie to blame it on the driving.

"People have their troubles, don't they?" Hildie said.

"What do you mean?" Edna asked.

"Your mother told me about the boy, Sonny," Hildie said. "How he was hanging around with a bad lot and getting in trouble. I don't know if I could have survived if one of my children had turned out bad. The worry would be unbearable. But if that's the Lord's plan for you, you just carry on, don't you? I'll pray for the boy, tonight. That's all you can do. Pray and put your troubles in the Lord's hands."

Edna didn't point out the flaw in Hildie's logic: if everything was a part of the Lord's plan, then He was the one giving you the troubles in the first place and you were already in His hands. But it was the kind of thinking there was no point arguing with.

"And all you can do if you're tired is go to bed," Edna said. She walked upstairs with Hildie even though she'd already shown her to her room, which had not been in too bad shape, dusty and a bit stale-smelling, but not as bad as what it could have been. There'd been no sign of mice, at least, and that had been her biggest worry, that mice would have taken over the whole upstairs, even though she'd placed out poison before she'd sealed it off. She had given Hildie a room at the top of the stairs. There were six other rooms upstairs, and she hadn't even opened the doors to see what was in them, she'd been so busy just getting the one clean and ready and airing it out. She hadn't bothered with the upstairs bathroom, and she apologized to Hildie for the inconvenience, but Hildie said she didn't mind and was just glad to have a bed. Edna told Hildie she would leave the stairwell light on so she could find her way to the main floor bathroom if she needed to, and she said good night and went back downstairs. She passed the boards that had covered the entrance and were now stacked along the east wall in the lounge, on top of a pile of fibreglass insulation. She'd decided to leave the boards and insulation there, thinking she would seal off the upstairs again after Hildie left.

Mrs. Carlberg was in bed already, pretending to be asleep. Edna knew she was awake because she always snored when she was sleeping. Mrs. Carlberg had pulled the curtains closed and Edna opened them again, just to see if her mother would be driven to argue, and they could talk for a few minutes. But she didn't say anything, so Edna crawled into bed and lay looking at the stars.

Finally she said, "I don't think you should have told Hildie about Sonny. She'll misjudge him." When there was no answer she said, "Anyway, I'm glad Hildie brought the photograph album. Wasn't that something, seeing pictures of Ward and Clayton?" She didn't really expect a response from her mother, but Mrs. Carlberg said, "I'll just bet Nancy knows how to play chess like a Russian."

"What do you care whether Nancy can play chess or not?" Edna asked.

"Your father always said playing chess was a sign of intelligence."

"What is this thing you've got about Nancy lately?" Edna asked, but that was it, that was all her mother would say.

Edna woke up at three in the morning and heard Sonny come in the back door, which they never locked at night, and make his way through the kitchen and into the lounge. He was all right then, Edna thought, none the worse for wear after his bump on the head. She crept out of her bed and stood in the doorway to the kitchen, listening.

Edna knew, or had known at one time, the exact location of every creak in the pine floor, and it amused her to listen to the boy as he prowled around in the dark. Her mother was snoring away in the four-poster across the room, which was a good thing for Sonny's sake, because the boy had had his one chance as far as she was concerned. Edna wondered at his tenacity. The time Mrs. Carlberg caught him she'd scared the bejesus out of him by waving a shotgun around. It wasn't loaded, but Sonny hadn't known that.

Edna heard a creak and knew Sonny was over by the south wall where the front window faced the river. She hoped he'd see the stack of boards; if he stumbled on them they'd be sure to make a racket. She held her breath, then remembered she'd left a light on for Hildie.

Another creak. He was by the stairwell now, and a new thought came to Edna. What if he decided to go upstairs out of curiosity when he noticed the boards had been removed, and what if he opened the door to the first bedroom on the left, where Hildie was sleeping, or trying to sleep, already expecting something bad to befall her? That would be the last straw, a juvenile delinquent standing in her doorway, or maybe she'd think the old place had a ghost. Oh, Edna was mean, almost wishing for such excitement.

But no. A metal clank, quickly stifled. Sonny was by the fireplace, where the chess set was sitting on the stone hearth. He'd stay there for a bit now, Edna knew, and then she'd hear him in the kitchen again on his way out. She crawled back into her bed, remembering the long-ago, delicious thrill of almost being caught.

Mrs. Carlberg snorted in her sleep, and the snoring stopped. Edna tried to decide if her mother was awake. If she was, she'd surely hear Sonny on his way out. *Quickly*, she thought. *Now. Hurry, hurry.* A minute passed, maybe two, and she heard him cross the kitchen linoleum and slip out the back door. Edna waited for her mother to give some indication that she'd heard the soft, quick footsteps, but her snoring started up again, and then a coyote yipped close by, and another answered from up in the hills somewhere. Edna lay there until she knew Sonny was home again, with Hawk and Nancy. She rolled onto her side and slept, satisfied.

The next morning, Friday, Edna was in the bedroom putting away laundry when her mother came in and said, "You should just hear what that silly arse of a woman is saying out there, that Hildie."

"What do you mean?" Edna asked.

"She's been on the phone for half an hour talking to the Alliance Church in Covey. I don't know what she's up to, and I don't know why she's come."

"You do know, Mother," Edna said. "She's come about a dedication for the boys. She's explained."

"The Alliance Church yet. I've never had a conversation with one of those people in my life and I don't intend to."

"She's explained that, too. She belongs to some church that I've never heard of, but the Alliance Church is acceptable to her. Besides, lots of people you know go to that church. You don't know what you're talking about."

"I'm not saying a word into that tape machine. I don't care what you say."

"You don't have to," Edna said. "It's up to you. Only you might enjoy telling the story of the lumber yard and the lodge, and how you and father met and so on. All of that."

"One of the boys can tell it. They know as much as I do."

Edna wanted to scream but she didn't say a word. She was beginning to see a nastiness in her mother that she didn't like. She saw it in old people sometimes and wondered why they were so sharp with the people they depended on. Were they that certain you weren't going anywhere?

When she got to the kitchen, where Hildie was sitting at the table with the telephone and a pad of paper, Hildie said, "Does she have Alzheimer's? I was just wondering."

"I don't have a clue," Edna said. Then she said, "No, she doesn't. She's just old, that's all."

Edna saw the tape recorder on the table and said, "I don't know how far you're going to get with that."

"I'm not sure where the photo album got to," Hildie said. "Your mother asked about it and I said I didn't know."

"Mother asked about the photo album?" That was surprising.

"Yes, she did," Hildie said, "But I don't know where it is. I thought you might know. I told your mother you probably put it somewhere."

Edna thought back. The photo album had not been on the table when she got up in the morning, she was sure of it. She'd seen the tape recorder when she set the breakfast dishes, and she was sure the album had not been there. She remembered that Sonny had been in the lodge the night before, but what would Sonny want with a photo album?

"It'll turn up," Edna said. "Mother probably put it away and can't remember where."

The telephone rang. It was for Hildie. Edna handed her the phone. Hildie listened for a minute, then said, "I see. Well, thank you then." She put the receiver down and began to sniffle.

"What is it?" Edna asked. She got the box of tissues off the top of the fridge and handed it to Hildie, who took one and blew her nose.

"I don't know why the Lord wanted me to come here," Hildie said.

"Excuse me?" Edna said.

"They said no at the Alliance Church," Hildie said. "They said it didn't make sense to have a dedication for people they'd never heard of."

"Oh," Edna said. She sat down with Hildie at the table. "I'm sorry."

"Would you mind phoning them?" Hildie asked. "Maybe they'd look on this differently if a local person talked to them."

"I couldn't do that," Edna said. She didn't give any explanation. She just didn't feel like phoning the Alliance Church, or any church at all, and how could she say that to Hildie, who was still sniffling in a way that Edna was beginning to find tiresome.

"I didn't want to come here, you know," Hildie said. "Pardon me, but I'm just being honest. Clayton never really forgave you, but the Lord wanted me to come here, so I did. And now I have to look for the reason. I have to trust Him."

Edna definitely couldn't say what she was thinking now, which was that her mother had been right when she called Hildie a silly arse of a woman. Instead Edna said, "Maybe the reason was to bring mother that photo album. Maybe the Lord made it go missing to take your mind off the other, the candlesticks and the dedication." She wondered where the hell that had come from, and was pleased with herself when Hildie instantly perked up. Hildie blew her nose again and said, "Yes, you're probably right. It's sometimes difficult to understand His plan."

Hildie spent the rest of the morning outside, walking along the riverbank and up into the hills behind the lodge.

"What is she doing out there?" Edna's mother wanted to know.

"How should I know?" Edna said. "Looking for arrowheads."

When Hildie finally came in for lunch, Mrs. Carlberg asked, "Did you find any?"

"Any what?" Hildie asked.

"Arrowheads," Mrs. Carlberg said.

"I wasn't looking for arrowheads," Hildie said. "I was looking for something else."

They were saved from having to ask what when the telephone rang. Mrs. Carlberg answered it. She spoke for a few minutes and hung up.

"That was Nancy," she announced. "We're invited for a barbecue tonight, if we're not busy. Are we busy, Edna?"

"What do you think?" Edna said.

"Good, because I said we'd come. And that includes you," she said to Hildie.

"Oh my," Hildie said. "I'm not sure."

"What do you mean you're not sure?" Mrs. Carlberg said. "Have you got other plans?"

"Of course not," Hildie said. "It's just … well, the problems with the boy. Maybe they don't need the trouble of an extra person."

"Never mind that," Mrs. Carlberg said. "Nancy has him wrapped around her little finger. She's good with kids, isn't she, Edna?"

"Yes, Mother," Edna said. "The amazing Nancy is wonderful in every way."

"If you'll excuse me," Hildie said, "I think I'll go and lie down for a bit." She took several tissues from the box on the fridge and left the room.

"What's the matter with her?" Mrs. Carlberg asked.

"I guess the Alliance Church doesn't like the Carlbergs any more than you like them," Edna said. "They won't let Hildie make her dedication. Now she's trying to figure how it all fits into the Lord's plan for her."

"They're a crazy lot, those people," Mrs. Carlberg said. "I've always maintained that."

"Did Nancy say if we should bring anything?" Edna asked.

"I'm sure Nancy will have everything taken care of," her mother said. "She sets a nice table, does Nancy. Not to mention her needle-work."

Edna had known that telling Hildie about Sonny would turn out to be a bad idea. They were sitting at Nancy's picnic table on the screened-in deck Hawk had built onto the side of the trailer, and Edna wanted to give both her mother and Hildie a good kick – her mother for not keeping her mouth shut, and Hildie because Edna was sick and tired of her "Lord this" and "Lord that." Sonny was staring at Hildie defiantly. It was clear his staring made her nervous. She kept fingering her little gold cross.

It had all begun when Hildie asked if she could say grace before they ate. After the food blessing, which no one minded, she asked the Lord to "help Sonny find his way to the light, Amen." You could have heard a pin drop. Edna almost choked with embarrassment. Hawk and Nancy were polite, though, and didn't say a word. After the Amen, Nancy began to pass the serving dishes as though nothing had happened.

Or maybe it had begun before that, when Nancy offered them a glass of her chokecherry wine. Hildie, of course, turned it down, which was fine, but then she looked positively wretched when everyone else had a glass. She was probably afraid, Edna thought, that they would all lose their moral faculties under the influence, assuming they had any in the first place.

Edna glanced over at Sonny. He was still staring at Hildie. Hildie was picking her way through the meal, trying to eat but not getting very far. Out of pure meanness, Edna asked Nancy if she could have another glass of wine, and then Nancy and Mrs. Carlberg had one as well. Hawk said he wasn't much of a wine drinker, no offence to Nancy and her wine-making, and got himself a beer instead.

They were just finishing dessert when Hawk noticed a dust trail on the road across the river, and a pick-up truck emerged and came winding down toward the ferry crossing.

"That looks like Barry Moss," Hawk said. "Wonder where he's going." He stood up to leave, and he asked Hildie if she wanted to go along, to get a good look at the Missouri.

"She's like a sheet of glass tonight," Hawk said. "Pretty as a picture."

Hildie said, "No thank you. I'm not much for boats and water."

"I wouldn't exactly call this a boat," Hawk said. "More like a raft with a motor. Anyway, it's on a cable. It can't go anywhere. One side to the other, that's about it."

"Thanks," Hildie said, "but I'll just wait here." She was looking at Hawk's empty beer bottle.

Edna decided to go along with Hawk, mostly to get away from Hildie before she strangled her. The river was only 300 yards wide at the crossing, and it took them just minutes to get to the south side and dock. Barry got out of the cab as soon as he was on the ferry. He told Hawk and Edna about a rancher they knew who had recently lost his arm in a farm accident. Hawk shook his head and said, "You don't say," and "I'll be damned." There was time for a few words about the weather, and they were on the north side again. Barry got in his truck and drove off. Hawk shut the ferry down and made sure it was tied fast, then he and Edna walked the short distance back to the trailer, where all hell had broken loose.

Apparently Mrs. Carlberg had been telling Nancy about how Clayton and Ward had sent Hildie all that way on her own, and why in the world hadn't they thought to come with her, and Hildie had said, "Mrs. Carlberg, Clayton and Ward are no longer with us. You know that."

"I don't know that," Mrs. Carlberg said.

"Yes, you do," Hildie said. "You saw the photographs of the grave markers."

"What photographs?" Mrs. Carlberg asked.

"The ones in the photo album," Hildie said. At that point she looked at Sonny, who had stretched out in a lounge chair to read a comic book.

"There's no photo album," Mrs. Carlberg said. "You made that up. If there's a photo album with grave markers in it, let's see you produce it for all of us to see."

Had Edna not been walking up from the ferry with Hawk, she would have known at that moment that it was her mother who had taken the photo album, and the reason would have been clear to her: Mrs. Carlberg was getting rid of the evidence. But Hildie didn't have Mrs. Carlberg figured out and, besides, she'd already made up her mind about where the photo album had disappeared to, so she said, "I can't produce it, because Sonny has it. Don't you, Sonny?"

Sonny looked up from his comic book. "I don't have any photograph book," he said. "Why would I have it?"

Hildie said, "You took it last night. And the Lord will forgive you if you give it back."

Sonny said, "I don't have it." He threw the comic down and was about to storm out but Nancy grabbed him and said, "Wait a minute, buster, let's get to the bottom of this."

Then Hildie said to Nancy, "He was in the lodge last night. I saw him. It was three in the morning and everyone else was asleep. I didn't say anything because he left right away. And in the morning the photograph album was gone. I thought he might have thrown it outside somewhere, but I looked around and couldn't find it. Unless he threw it in the river."

Nancy said, "Is this true, Sonny, what she's saying?"

"I was there," Sonny said, "but I didn't steal any photograph album."

Then Mrs. Carlberg got into the picture and said, "You little bugger. I told you not to come back when I caught you sneaking around the last time."

"You caught him in the lodge before?" Nancy said.

Mrs. Carlberg said, "I wanted to tell you, but I let Edna talk me out of it."

There was a long silence and then Nancy drew back her hand and walloped Sonny a good one on the side of the head, where he already had the goose egg, and that's when Hawk and Edna walked through the door, right as Nancy hit Sonny. It was a shocking thing to witness, to just walk through a door and see a grown woman hit a boy as hard as she could. Mrs. Carlberg jumped as though she was the one who'd been hit. She made a sound like a cat being stepped on.

"What the hell's going on here?" Hawk said.

Sonny broke away from Nancy and managed to escape out the door.

"What happened?" Hawk asked again.

Nancy was shaken. Without saying anything, she sat down on a chair and put her head in hands.

Hildie finally said, "I told Nancy that I saw Sonny in the lodge last night, and that he took the photograph album."

"You saw him?" Edna said.

"Yes," Hildie said.

"The silly bugger," Mrs. Carlberg said, "he had it coming," and Edna told her to please shut up, all they needed was her two cents worth at this particular time. Edna decided they had best go home and let Nancy and Hawk deal with Sonny. She was sorry Nancy had found out about Sonny being in the lodge because now, in all likelihood, he would not be back.

On the way home Hildie said she was leaving in the morning. Edna did not respond, other than to say, "The weather's supposed to be good, so you won't have to worry about the road." She'd been planning to follow Hildie in the truck, but had changed her mind. She didn't care if Hildie got hung up in the ruts somewhere and had to walk ten miles.

Mrs. Carlberg was quiet. As they pulled up in front of the lodge, she said, "I didn't mean for her to hit him like that." She sounded guilty and Edna detected it right away.

"It's too late now, isn't it?" Edna said.

When they got inside the lodge, Hildie went up to her room and brought the candlesticks down. "What should I do with these?" she asked.

Mrs. Carlberg said, "You can put them on the fireplace mantle, if that's dedication enough for you." Then she went to bed.

Edna decided to have a bath to calm her nerves. Half an hour later, when she emerged from the steaming bathroom, she heard a vehicle go by, heading north in the direction of Covey. She looked out the window to try and see who it was, but it was too dark. She could see the ferry's lights on the opposite bank and she thought Barry Moss must have gone by on his way home while she had the bath water running.

Edna crawled into her bed under the window. Her mother wasn't sleeping, there was no snoring. There was a lot of sighing though, and eventually Edna saw her mother's form rise and sit on the edge of the four-poster bed. Edna sat up and switched on her bedside light.

"What's the matter, Mother?" she asked. "Do you need a painkiller?"

Her mother had that look on her face, the puzzled one, and Edna knew her question hadn't registered.

"Mother?" Edna asked again. "Should I get you a glass of water?"

Mrs. Carlberg got down on her knees beside the bed. For a brief, ridiculous moment Edna thought her mother was going to say a prayer. But then she reached under the mattress and pulled out the photo album. She sat down on the edge of her bed and ran her fingers over the cover. "We're not going to be here much longer, are we, Edna?" she said. She opened the album and flipped through a few pages, then closed it again. She looked up and her eye rested on the Charlie Russell painting. "I'd like to give that Hildie a present before she leaves," she said. "I think I'll give her that little cowboy painting, if it's all right with you."

Edna nodded. She was speechless.

"I suppose I could say a few words into her tape machine, although I don't know what," Mrs. Carlberg said. "Do you know what she's done with it?"

Edna found her voice. "As far as I know it's still in the kitchen," she said.

Mrs. Carlberg got up and took the painting off the wall. "I might as well," she said, and she went to the kitchen in her nightgown.

The ferry was docked across the river because Sonny had taken it there. Edna and Hawk were standing on the north bank in the dark, watching. Hawk figured Sonny was getting set to take off for Lewistown, but so far he was still on the ferry. They could see him in the lights, sitting on the railing, smoking a cigarette. He'd taken Hawk's sixteen-foot motor boat across with him too, trailing it behind the ferry on a rope tied to the bow. The three-wheeler was still locked up in the shed behind the trailer.

Edna had driven down to the ferry landing to bail Sonny out of trouble and to apologize to Hawk and Nancy for her mother, and for Hildie, even though Hildie was sleeping and didn't yet know her mother-in-law had taken the photo album. Edna had left her mother sitting at the kitchen table, fiddling with the tape recorder. She had no idea what her mother was going to say once she got started; Hildie might be sorry she'd asked. Edna had brought Sonny a peace offering in a shopping bag – what was left of the old man's chess set – and had already called across to him that they'd found the photo album, and that Hildie was leaving and good riddance, but he hadn't answered.

"It's a long walk to Lewistown," Hawk said. "Maybe he's having second thoughts." He asked Edna, "Have you got a boat up there in working order?"

Edna shook her head. They'd sold off all but one, and when the motor died the summer before, they hadn't bothered to replace it.

"Then I guess there's nothing to do but hurry up and wait," Hawk said.

It was Nancy that Edna had heard passing on her way north. She was planning to cross the Missouri on the bridge fifty miles to the west. It was a long trip around, but she figured she could get to Lewistown before Sonny did and maybe head him off before he got himself into trouble.

"You know what Nancy's planning to do when she catches up to him?" Hawk asked Edna.

Edna didn't answer. She thought she knew, but it turned out she was wrong.

"She says she's going to take him to Disneyland," Hawk said. "I told her he's too old for Disneyland, but Nancy said, 'The trouble with that boy is he's never been a child.' She tried to talk me into coming, too, but I've got no interest in Disneyland."

Hawk coughed from deep in his chest. "Do you think he's too old for Disneyland?" he said.

"You're never too old for Disneyland," Edna said. "At least according to those ads on TV. Maybe I should take mother. She's not going to last that much longer. I doubt if we'll spend another winter out here."

"Well anyway," Hawk said, "I'm not going. Somebody's got to keep the ferry running."

They watched as Sonny tossed his cigarette in the water and got down off the railing. He went into the engine room, rummaged around and came out again. He was carrying something.

"What's he got?" Edna asked.

"I can't tell," Hawk said. They watched as Sonny stepped onto the shore, and then they couldn't see him as well because he was out of the light.

"What's he doing?" Edna asked.

"Little bugger's trying to loosen the clamps on the cable." Hawk walked out onto the ferry approach, as close to the river's edge as he could get. "Sonny," he yelled. "Quit messing with that cable. You're out of trouble now as far as I can see, but if you let that ferry go sliding down the river you'll be in mighty big trouble."

Edna followed Hawk onto the approach and watched Sonny struggle with the cable. She felt the same thrill she'd felt when she snuck through the lodge in the night, the one she always felt when Sonny was creeping around in the dark, stealing rabbits from the chess set. It was the thrill of doing something bad, even though you knew better.

Hawk said, "Jesus H. Christ." Then he said, "I don't think he can get it. He's not strong enough."

Sonny threw down the wrench and went back onto the ferry and into the engine room. He emerged with something else – it looked like a small saw – and Hawk started to laugh, not loud enough for Sonny to hear, but quietly, to himself.

"What is it?" Edna asked.

"A hack saw," Hawk said. "He's going to try to cut the cable. It'll take him till Christmas with that thing."

They heard the sound of a vehicle coming from the north. It was Barry Moss, on his way home. He pulled up and turned the truck engine off. "What's going on?" he asked, stepping out of the cab.

"Might be a while before I can get you across," Hawk said. "There's a little problem with the cable on the other side. Sonny's over there working on it."

"Sonny's working on it?" Barry asked.

"He's not getting anywhere fast," Hawk said. "Why don't you come in for a beer?"

"I just might," Barry said.

Hawk asked Edna if she wanted to come in and she said she'd stay outside for a while and keep her eye on Sonny. Hawk and Barry walked back to the trailer.

Edna emptied the old man's chess set out of the shopping bag. The pieces rolled around in the dirt. She picked up the white king, a wolf on its haunches, beautifully carved out of soapstone, and threw it in the direction of the ferry.

"Hey Sonny," she yelled. "Catch."

She didn't know whether he heard her or not. It didn't matter. The wolf landed in the river and sank. One by one, Edna threw all the chess pieces into the river. Sonny noticed her throwing things and looked up, then he went back to work on the cable. When the last piece was at the bottom of the Missouri, Edna picked up the wooden chessboard and threw it sidearm, as though she were trying to skip a flat rock. It hit the water on an angle and disappeared and she thought it had sunk, but it bobbed to the top and floated away in the slow current. She took off her socks and shoes and slipped into the river. She swam to the other side, fighting the current all the way so she wouldn't end up downstream, and hoisted herself onto the ferry, thankful the water was low because she wasn't the swimmer that she used to be. She lay on her stomach gasping for air, her cheek against the worn planks. They smelled of motor oil and diesel. She listened to the thin, raspy sound of the saw, then it stopped. She lifted her head and saw Sonny looking at her.

"Don't mind me," Edna said to him, still struggling to catch her breath. "I'm just here for the ride."

Sonny lit a cigarette. He stuck it in the side of his mouth and went back to sawing at the cable.

Tuxedo

Once, when we were still students and before Zoe married Chuck the trumpet player, Zoe's father crawled into bed with me. Six months ago, I found out there were others, or at least one other. I learned this from Zoe, who called and woke me from a sound sleep on a Saturday morning. We'd been out the night before and I had a headache. I'd slept all night with a wet facecloth over my eyes.

"Claire?" Zoe said. "Are you awake?"

"Barely," I said.

"You won't believe this," she said. Then she told me her father had been caught in a hotel room with a high school girl, one of his patients. The police were investigating and his licence to practice had been suspended by the College of Physicians and Surgeons. It was in the local paper, she said, on the third page, right next to a story about the arsonist who was burning down the city one building at a time.

"Where are you?" I asked, not quite able to take in this news.

"I'm at Lenore's," Zoe said. Lenore was her mother. "Can you come over? She talks to you. She thinks you're sensible."

"I'm on my way," I said. "But I won't know what to say."

I should not have been surprised by this news about Zoe's father. I should even have expected that some such story would eventually surface, but I had convinced myself that when he lay beside me for those few minutes, he had meant no harm. Whenever I saw him after that, he displayed no signs of guilt or even acknowledgement. He treated me like he always had, in an aloof and slightly patronizing manner. His strange behaviour, then, had had something to do with commiseration, his need for comfort after the death of a baby in his care. I was satisfied with my explanation, however implausible, because it allowed me to forget about the incident, or at least to pretend nothing of consequence had happened.

When I arrived at Lenore's house after the call from Zoe, I expected to find Lenore in pieces, but it was Zoe who was falling apart. She was pacing like an animal and I could see she had already been on a rampage. Bits of broken china were scattered on the dining room floor, and a brass lamp lay overturned and sprawling. Lenore, surprisingly, was calm.

"She's been like this for hours," Lenore said to me. "I don't know what to say to her. I wish Chuck were here."

Zoe raged at her mother. "You do know what to say. Say that you're not going to behave like a total jellyfish. Say what you know is true. He's guilty."

"I can't say that when I don't know for sure," Lenore said. "Think of all the times men get accused by vengeful women and it ruins their careers. Especially successful men like your father. I know it looks bad, but I'm waiting to learn more. I'm not going to convict him on the information in the newspaper."

Zoe looked around for something else to throw, then she suddenly slumped into a dining room chair and dropped her head to the tabletop. "Your life with him was miserable," she said. "Why are you trying so hard to be reasonable?"

Lenore went to Zoe and put an arm across her shoulder. "The man's career is at stake," Lenore said.

"What about my career?" Zoe asked. "His timing is impeccable, isn't it? What are the chances people won't make a connection between the last names." She was talking about her art gallery. She had just found a space in the warehouse district and was in the process of negotiating a lease from the bank.

Lenore patted Zoe's shoulder. "This has nothing to do with you, dear," she said. "No one will make the connection. Don't you worry about that. Besides, we can still hope there's nothing to this." She patted Zoe again, then went to the closet for her jacket.

"Where are you going?" Zoe asked.

"To see his lawyer," Lenore said.

"Oh good," Zoe said. "That nice man who did you out of everything. The one who advised him to 'accumulate debt' so he'd have less to negotiate with."

Lenore said, rather coolly, "I feel some responsibility to get the facts, Zoe," and then she left.

After she was gone, I asked Zoe if she wanted me to make fresh coffee.

"I want a drink," Zoe said.

"Where's Chuck?" I asked as I searched the cabinets for liquor.

"Out of town," she said.

"I know that," I said. "Where out of town?"

"I'm not sure," Zoe said. "Anyway, what does it matter? If he's not here, he's not here."

"You must have a phone number," I said. "Can't you call him?" She ignored me.

I found a bottle of Glenfiddich and got a couple of glasses from the cupboard, but then Zoe wouldn't drink it because it was her father's, left behind when he moved out. She took the top off the bottle and emptied the contents onto the carpet.

"He's guilty," Zoe said.

"I know," I said. I didn't say how I knew.

"I'm changing my name," Zoe said. "I refuse to have his name." She asked me to get her the phone book. I did, and she quickly flipped the book open and pointed. The tip of her finger landed on the name Klumpp.

"Zoe Klumpp," she said. "How does that sound?"

"Fine," I said. "But why not just use Chuck's name? People do that, you know."

"Gallerie Fuse," she said. "Owner, Zoe Klumpp."

"It has a ring," I said. "I guess."

There was a cup of cold coffee on the table in front of Zoe and she picked it up and poured it on the newspaper, which was still lying open on page three. I got a cloth from the sink and wiped it up, so it wouldn't stain Lenore's table. As I did so, I read the article about the arsonist. It said the city was bringing in federal investigators. The fires were increasing in frequency; no cause for public alarm though. I threw the soggy paper out, then went to the closet and got a dustpan. I started to pick up the broken china.

"Will Lenore want to repair any of this?" I asked. "Should we save the pieces?"

"Stop it," Zoe said. "I don't need anyone to clean up after me."

"I don't mind," I said. I felt guilty somehow, like maybe I could have prevented this.

"You're acting like Lenore," Zoe said. "That's what Lenore is doing right now. She's out trying to clean up someone else's mess. She won't be able to this time, though." Zoe got up and took the broom away from me. "You might as well go," she said. "I'll clean up before she gets back. Don't worry."

I had an appointment to get the oil changed in my car so I left. I could see Zoe picking up the china as I walked by the window on my way to the street.

At quarter past six, the day of Zoe's official opening, I parked illegally in a bus lane and ran up the block to the dry cleaner's, thinking it would be locked up tight – after-hours on a Friday – but it wasn't. A bell jingled when I opened the door. It was dark inside the old brick building and I couldn't see right away, but I heard a voice say, "Claire, right? The tuxedo."

"That's right," I said. My eyes adjusted and I realized that all the lights had been turned off except for the one above the cash register. I saw a man at the counter, holding my tuxedo in a clear plastic bag.

"I'm late," I said. "I thought you'd be closed."

"Normally, I would be," he said. "I was waiting for you."

I looked at him. He was an older man, handsome for his age.

"I wanted to see what the woman who wears a tuxedo looks

like," he said. "And you sounded desperate when you phoned. Must be a big event."

"It is, sort of," I said. "My friend's new art gallery. Her first show. The opening's tonight. I bought the tuxedo secondhand, through an ad in the paper."

"An art gallery opening. I thought it would be something like that." He handed me the tuxedo. "So you're one of those artsy types, are you?" he said.

"Me? No. I was an architecture student for a while, but that's not very artsy. About as close as I'll get, though. Anyway, I'm glad you waited. Thank you. I had to get to the bank. They're transferring all the savings accounts over to some kind of new account and I had to sign something. 'Absolutely by the end of today,' this woman told me when she phoned for the tenth time."

"Or what?" the dry cleaner asked.

"Or I wouldn't get my name in the draw for a cell phone, for one thing. And then I got behind a guy who was holding up traffic to get a parking spot, and all I could do was wait because he was really big and mean-looking. But never mind that. I really appreciate you waiting for me. How much do I owe you?"

"Nothing."

"Nothing?"

"Like I said, a woman who wears a tuxedo … it gave me something to think about while I was waiting. No charge."

I was embarrassed.

"I can't just take it," I said. "This is a business. I expect to pay."

"Not much of a business," he said. "Writing's on the wall for dry cleaning. I've sold the place. This is my last day. My last day as a dry cleaner. When I walk out the door tonight, that's it. Finito. Goodbye dry cleaning business."

"You're kidding," I said.

"So, no charge. You're my last customer. And absolutely fitting that you would be collecting a tuxedo. It's poetic."

"Okay then," I said. "Well, thanks." I turned to leave.

"Wait a minute," he said. "I'll walk out with you. You can witness me closing the door for the last time."

He came around the counter and I followed him to the door, the tuxedo draped over my arm.

"How long have you owned the place?" I asked.

"Seventeen years," he said.

"Aren't you sad then?" I asked as we stepped outside. He pulled the door shut, turned the lock and slipped the key in his pocket.

"No," he said. "Not a bit. Like I said, writing's on the wall. I feel sorry for the guy who bought it. He should have gone into computers. That's what my son's doing. The dry cleaner's was supposed to be his, but he's bought a computer business instead. Smart kid. So, what time's the party?"

"Seven," I said.

"Too bad. I'd ask you to go for a drink with me, to commemorate the occasion."

"Oh," I said. "Too bad." I was tempted to go with him. "Maybe I could be late for the opening," I said. "Probably no one would notice."

"Better not be," he said. "You might miss something."

I saw that he had a nice smile, boyish and charming, and white teeth. I wondered how old he was.

"Another time, maybe," he said.

"Sure," I heard myself say, "another time." I was thinking he wasn't really serious, because he didn't know my phone number. Or did he? Maybe I'd left it when I dropped off the tuxedo.

"Well then," he said, "I think I'll go and order myself a couple of double something-or-others. Have fun at the party."

"I will," I said. Then I added, because I'd been saying it to people all day, "Stop by my friend's art gallery tonight, if you're interested. Corner of Rose and 7th. Low rent district. Gallerie Fuse. If you say it fast it sounds like 'Re-fuse', as in, say no. Or garbage. That works too."

"Re-fuse. That's clever. Catchy." He turned and walked down the sidewalk. I thought I should say something else, like "good luck" maybe, because it was his last day as a dry cleaner, but then I saw a city bus coming. I quickly got in my car, tossing the tuxedo in the back seat, and pulled ahead just in time, as the bus roared up behind me. When I came to a red light at the next intersection, the bus came to a stop alongside me and the driver motioned for me to roll down the passenger window. For some reason I complied.

"Stay out of the bus lanes," the driver yelled at me, obviously not caring about public relations. He was a big man too, like the guy I'd encountered on my way to pick up the tuxedo.

"Sorry," I said. "I was in a hurry."

"That's your problem," the driver said. "Just obey the law, or next time you won't get off so easy."

I rolled my window back up. Get off so easy? What did he mean by that? He sounded like he was threatening me. When the light turned green I sped through the intersection to try to get well ahead of the bus, resolving to take a self-defence course.

Zoe's inaugural show was a ceramics exhibition. The artworks were odd little figurines: boney, clown-like characters sitting in alleyways, surrounded by garbage, gaunt cats and coloured shapes that looked like patio lights. You might be tempted to call them cute if the figures didn't look so pathetic.

I had already heard how Lenore and the artist, whose name was Robin, had broken half a dozen of the pieces while they were installing them on display pedestals around the room. Some of the damage was minor – a couple of bases chipped, the head knocked off one of the figures – but three pieces had been smashed beyond repair. Zoe had tried to get Robin and Lenore to leave so she could install the show herself, but Lenore wanted to be helpful and the artist was bent on milking every minute out of the exhibition experience. He was a recent art school graduate, although not an especially young one.

After they finally got the show up, Zoe found out that Lenore, who was helping her in the gallery as a kind of girl Friday, had forgotten to mail the invitations. About the time I was picking up my dry cleaning, Zoe found them, stamped and ready to go, in a drawer in her desk. As a result, the only people who showed up for the opening were friends with healthy appetites for hors d'oeuvres and wine, and there was not one potential customer in the lot. The artist didn't seem to care, but Zoe had been counting on a few red dots to help with next month's rent on the space. She tied into the wine with a vengeance. Lenore, who was on edge to begin with, felt so bad about the invitations and the broken pieces that she spent most of the evening in the washroom crying.

Which is where she was when I arrived. Zoe gave me a drunken explanation of what had happened with the invitations (printed with her new name, Zoe Klumpp), and then pointed to the washroom, from which Lenore had still not emerged. I waited for Zoe to say something about my tuxedo. She didn't seem to notice. It was as though I always dressed in such a dramatic fashion, which was hardly the case.

I looked around the room for Chuck but didn't see him. Zoe had been hoping he'd be in town. She thought he could maybe throw together a band at the last minute to play at the opening. When I asked about Chuck, she said his road trip had been extended.

"And I'm not complaining," she said. "Work is work." That was the thing about being married to a musician. If Chuck did happen to be available on a weekend, it wasn't good. It meant he was unemployed.

Lenore finally came out of the washroom. I was about to call hello to her when she bumped into a pedestal and sent another ceramic piece crashing to the concrete floor. Luckily, Robin was outside at the time having a smoke. Zoe quickly scooped up the pieces. Lenore started to cry again, and Zoe said, "Mother, the stress is getting to you. Go home now. *Please* call a cab and go home." Lenore – who had never worked a day in her life because Zoe's father wouldn't have it – agreed; she had been feeling the pressure, all the planning and then the fiasco with the invitations, not to mention her life in general. I wasn't sure if she was referring to her obvious distress at finding herself alone as she approached her sixth decade, or to the ugly charges against Zoe's father, which to my knowledge were still unresolved.

I helped Zoe move the empty pedestal into the back room.

"Chuck is always talking about how musicians get off the ground or they don't," Zoe said. "This opening definitely did not get off the ground. I hope that doesn't portend failure. Gallerie De-fuse, Gallerie Sputter-to-an-early-death."

"It takes a while for word to get out," I said, trying to sound optimistic.

When Robin came back inside, Lenore apologized to him. He was so drunk he didn't realize she was telling him she'd broken *another* piece, and he waved her away, saying "No problem, no problemo," which made Lenore feel a little better. Zoe started looking through the phone book for a cab number, and Lenore turned to me and said, "Don't you look nice, dear. So ... black and white. That's a tuxedo, isn't it?" I was glad someone had noticed after all the trouble I'd gone to. I decided to offer Lenore a ride home, thinking that would be a discreet way to leave. I told Zoe to forget the cab. Just then, as Lenore and I were about to leave, the dry cleaner came through the door.

I was taken by surprise and had no idea what to say. He also was wearing a tuxedo. When he entered the small room Zoe's friends stopped talking and stared, as though a famous movie star had dropped in, someone of the Robert Redford vintage. There was a stillness in the room, a kind of pause, then the conversation started up again as though a conductor had raised his stick and said, This is it, dress rehearsal's over, it's the real thing. Clearly, the dry cleaner in a tuxedo made a much bigger impact than I did.

"Hi," I finally stammered.

"This is a friend of yours, dear?" Lenore said, stepping up to be introduced. Her eyes were still red from crying and she sounded like she had a cold.

I said, "Yes," and then I had to say to the dry cleaner, "but I don't know your name ..."

"Marcus," he said. "Marcus Brandt." I introduced Zoe and her mother. Zoe managed to pull herself together and behave like a proper art dealer, showing him around the gallery.

I was stunned that he'd turned up. Lenore and I stood side by side and watched. All eyes followed Marcus and Zoe around the room. Marcus appeared to be interested in Robin's work. After looking at the show and talking briefly to Robin (who also managed to pull himself together), Marcus bought a piece. He wrote Zoe a cheque and she offered him a glass of wine, but he said he had another commitment. He made arrangements to pick up his piece after the show was over. He shook my hand before leaving.

"Thank you for inviting me," he said. "I enjoyed the exhibition. Is that what you call it, an exhibition?" I nodded. Marcus turned to Zoe and Lenore. "Good luck with the gallery. You should do well. Good location for this sort of thing." Then he left.

Zoe looked at me accusingly. "Who would have guessed?" she said.

"What do you mean?" I asked.

"Next time, I'm just going to give you the invitations and you can hand them out to your posh friends."

"I think that was just an accident," I said. "I had no idea he would actually come."

Zoe placed a red dot on the tag next to the sold item.

Robin staggered over and stared at the dot as though it were sacred. Then he turned melancholy over the broken sculptures, which he now claimed were among the best he had ever done. Zoe quickly decided the evening was over.

The party moved to a brew pub down the street. I was ready to go home and I offered Lenore a ride.

"He's very good-looking," she said when we were in the car.

"Who?"

"Your friend. The one who bought the little sculpture. How do you know him? He's quite a bit older than you, isn't he. More my age, I'd say."

"Through someone at work," I said. It was simpler to say that than to explain about the dry cleaning.

"I don't suppose you know if he's married?"

I felt sorry for Lenore because of the way she asked the question, as though she was thinking "just my luck" before she even knew the answer.

"I don't know if he's married," I said. "I don't know him that well."

"Never mind," Lenore said. "I would never have asked if I hadn't had too many glasses of wine. One is my limit. I get silly after that."

I waited a few minutes, then casually asked Lenore if there was any news. She knew right away what I meant.

"No," she said. "The police are still investigating. They're waiting for others to come forward. They say if he's guilty, chances are this girl is not the only one. I suppose they're right, although I can't bear to think he has a history of this."

"I can understand that," I said.

I dropped Zoe's mother off at her big, empty house and drove home, contemplating the dry cleaner and thinking about the night Zoe's father had got into bed with me. I wondered whether I should be the one to come forward – whether that would do any good or just do a lot of harm, because I'd kept it to myself for so long, and because someone might make more of it than what I'd decided it was.

This is what happened. I'd been planning to sleep over at Zoe's house. We'd been out at a party and had had too much to drink. I had my own apartment, or rather room in a student boarding house, but it seemed like too much trouble to go home. Lenore was away somewhere, visiting relatives in another city. Zoe and I sat in the family room for a while, flipping channels on the television and talking about people who had been at the party. We laughed a lot, usually at someone else's expense, but sometimes at our own.

We heard the front door and it was Zoe's father. He joined us in the family room and told us he'd just delivered a premature baby, and it had died. He showed us how tiny the baby was by cradling something invisible in his hands, and he said it had everything a human being needs to live, but it was just too small. We didn't feel like laughing anymore. Zoe's father poured us each a brandy, which I didn't like but drank anyway, because it was an occasion for something like brandy. Zoe finished her drink quickly, then went down the hall, to the washroom, I supposed. Her father and I were left alone, awkwardly. My eye rested on the baby grand piano, for no particular reason, but he noticed.

"Do you play?" he asked.

"Badly," I said. "Grade five or six, I can't remember which, and then I quit. Mrs. Bartowsky. She got mad at me once because I touched her drapes. They were that flocked stuff you just had to touch. You couldn't stop yourself."

He got up, crossed the room and sat on the piano bench. "Come here," he said. "I'll show you something."

I stood behind him, not really wanting a piano lesson and wishing I could just go to bed. He opened a book of sonatinas and said, "Do you want the left hand or the right?"

"Excuse me?" I asked, not understanding.

"You play one hand, I'll play the other," he said.

"Oh," I said. "Well, I'd better take the right hand then. I read that better."

I sat down on the right side of him and after a few awkward starts on my part, we stumbled through the sonatina. It sounded surprisingly good.

"See," he said.

Zoe had by this time come back and her father noticed her standing in the doorway.

"Zoe refused to take lessons," he said matter-of-factly.

"That's right," she said, just as matter-of-factly. It was no secret that they didn't get along very well. "I'm going to bed," she said.

"Me too," I said quickly. I had placed my brandy on a coaster on top of the piano. I finished it, then Zoe and I headed down the hall to bed. I was to sleep in the spare bedroom, which was across the hall from Zoe's room. The master bedroom was on another level.

"That fucking piano," Zoe said. "He thinks he could have been a concert pianist. As if. He plays about as well as any other Leila Fletcher graduate. You'd think he'd know that."

"Yeah well," I said, "it is kind of fun. Like doing a crossword puzzle."

"Exactly," she said. "But he believes that if he weren't imprisoned by his life of responsibility, he could be playing for adoring audiences. He's a complete idiot."

I thought she was being a bit hard on him but I kept that to myself. We said good night and went to bed. I was just about to drop off to sleep when I heard the door open. At first I thought it was Zoe, but in the light from the hallway I could see it was her father, clad only in a pair of boxer shorts. He closed the door quietly, then lifted up the covers and crawled into the double bed with me.

Zoe's father lay on his back beside me and I didn't know what to do. I wondered if he knew I was there. Maybe he thought I was in Zoe's room. Maybe he slept in the spare room when he got home late, or maybe he slept there when Lenore was away. I coughed. He didn't move or say anything.

It had to be some kind of mistake. After all, he was Zoe's father and Lenore's husband. And a doctor, and everyone knew they took all kinds of oaths having to do with ethics. I lay there for a while, hardly daring to breathe, and then I left. I slipped out of the bed, found my clothes on the floor and carried them to the bathroom. I got dressed and went home.

And that was it. It didn't seem like anything I should tell Zoe about. Where her father spent the rest of the night, I have no idea, and if Zoe wondered why I wasn't in the spare room in the morning, she didn't ask. I came up with the dying baby explanation, and then I forgot about it.

But that's not true. I didn't forget about it. At the strangest times a picture of Zoe's father would pop into my head, the doctor standing there in his boxer shorts.

A few days after Zoe's opening, Marcus stopped by the gallery again, this time with a few friends. Zoe was alone in the gallery at the time. She said they looked like Shriners, but she couldn't say what she meant by that. It might have been the way they dressed, she said.

"What do you mean?" I asked. "They were wearing plaid pants? Clown suits? What?"

She couldn't remember exactly how they were dressed. Maybe, she said, it was the way they talked to one another, like they were in a club of some kind.

They didn't buy anything, although Marcus encouraged them to. Zoe said he told her to say hello to me, which she didn't seem to think was out of the ordinary. She was assuming, like Lenore, that my knowing him had something to do with my job. I worked for an insurance company, in the communications department. I encountered all kinds of people every day.

I knew that Marcus would call me. I decided he must have my phone number from when I left the tuxedo at the dry cleaners, and if he didn't he could easily figure it out from the phone book. When he called, we decided to meet in front of the old CN hotel downtown, which had a quiet lounge where you could sit and talk. It was a nice evening in July. A few storm clouds were building on the horizon, but they looked like the kind that probably wouldn't amount to much. On the way to the hotel I stopped at an ATM for money but it wouldn't give me any. My chequing account was bare, and I couldn't remember the correct sub number for my new savings account, the one that had made me late the day I picked up my tuxedo, when Marcus was still a dry cleaner.

"Never mind," Marcus said later, when I told him. "I think I can afford to buy you a drink."

We sat down at a table next to the window, where you could see people walking by on the street. We ordered drinks. Marcus said, "There's something I want to ask you."

"What's that?" I asked.

"Are you involved with anyone?"

"No," I said. "Are you?"

"That's not an easy question to answer," he said.

"I guess I know what that means," I said.

"No, you don't," he said. He paused and then continued. "I *am* married," he said, "but I'm separated. The question was, 'am I involved,' and of course I'm still involved with my wife. We've spent almost thirty years together and raised two sons. So it's complicated."

I wasn't sure what to say, or what exactly he was saying.

"We respect each other deeply," Marcus said. "All those years, and you can't begin to imagine what she went through. I was in the police force before I went into the dry cleaning business. We had a young family then. I quit, finally, because I didn't want them to live with the constant worry. Most people don't understand how hard the force is on wives and children, or the number of marriages that don't last. I suppose it was already too late when I quit."

I didn't say anything. I was taking in that he used to be a policeman. From policeman to dry cleaner was quite a career change.

"We're still good friends," he said.

"Oh," I said. I was confused about what he was telling me and why. "Did she work in the dry cleaners too?" I asked. It was all I could think of.

Marcus laughed. "No," he said. "She's a psychologist. She has her own practice."

"Wow," I said.

"We live together," he said. "But we have an understanding. Do you know what I'm saying?"

"You live together?"

"Yes," Marcus said. "We support one another, in a manner of speaking. We're an old habit. But we're not man and wife anymore."

"I see," I said.

"I want to be honest with you," Marcus said. "We've talked about living apart, but we haven't done anything about it. Because this arrangement seems to be working, I guess. We see other people. Like I said, we're good friends. Probably better friends than when we were a couple."

"That's amazing," I said. "Do your children know? That you've separated?"

Marcus laughed again. He seemed to think my questions were funny. "They're not children anymore," he said. "And yes, they know. We couldn't live in the same house and pretend. Neither of us is any good at that."

When our drinks arrived, I said, "Here's to your last day as a dry cleaner." We toasted the end of the dry cleaning business and the future of computers, for Marcus' son's sake. I asked Marcus if he had a picture of his wife. Because of what he'd told me, it didn't seem inappropriate. He took out his wallet and showed me a photo.

The woman, Marcus' wife, was striking. She was wearing a tailored white shirt in the picture and had her long salt-and-pepper hair pulled back, away from her face. She had full red lips. The photo could have been cut from a classy magazine ad for expensive perfume.

"She's beautiful," I said. "Gorgeous. What's her name?"

"Annabel," Marcus said. Then he handed me pictures of his sons. Both of them looked close to me in age.

"That's Rob," Marcus said, "the one in the computer business. And Marcus Junior. M. J., we call him, to keep the two of us straight. He and his girlfriend are getting married next month. I bought that little sculpture from your friend's art gallery for them. They like things that are different. They have a baby, a little girl. They weren't sure, at first, if they wanted to get married, but now they've decided. They're ready to commit." I looked at the pictures, then handed them back. I wasn't really interested in the sons.

"I don't have any pictures," I said.

"You will someday," Marcus said.

When we got back to our cars, Marcus kissed me on the cheek. I'd been expecting more. Later, I realized it was all part of his idea of courtship. We met for drinks twice more in the next week and each time he kissed me on the cheek before I got in my car to drive home. He moved slowly. Anticipation was important.

Robin was giving Zoe trouble. The show was over and the piece Marcus had bought was the only one that sold. Robin had decided Zoe should pay him for the broken pieces as well. Zoe didn't have an insurance policy because she couldn't afford it yet, and because she was planning to show only her friends, for a while at least, she had assumed that insurance wouldn't be necessary.

"You really ought to have insurance," Lenore said. "Even if your friends don't sue you, there's the arsonist. You just never know what can happen." Lenore looked at me. "Shouldn't she have insurance, Claire? You tell her."

We'd just finished lunch at Earl's, on the deck – me and Zoe and Lenore. It was packed, as it always was on a hot day, and we'd had to sit in the smoking section. The umbrellas were up to provide a bit of shade. The only empty table was next to us. It had a Reserved card on it.

"She should," I said. "But I'm no expert."

"You work for an insurance company," Lenore said. "You should know something."

"I'm a community relations type," I said. "It's totally different. I don't even have insurance. Let's hope the arsonist doesn't decide to burn down my apartment block."

"Never mind," Zoe said. "I can't afford insurance. I looked into it. The question is, what am I going to do about Robin? I don't have a dime."

"What about Chuck?" I asked.

"Get serious," she said. "He has less money than I do."

"Okay then, what about your father?" It came out before I thought.

"My father is a pig," Zoe said. "He's the last person I'd ask. Anyway, you know who's going to get his money now. That asshole lawyer."

"Don't talk like that," Lenore said. "He did one good thing. We had you together. I just wish I could pay you for the pieces. I'm the one who broke them."

"Not all of them," Zoe said. "I refuse to pay Robin for the pieces he broke himself. It's ridiculous. He says he wasn't the artist when he broke them, he was the installer. So the artist should still be paid for the pieces. And what are they anyway? Precious little objects. I never should have agreed to show them. The next show's different. Wait and see."

"I can lend you money," I said.

"Really?"

"Consider it an investment in your gallery. When you start selling things, you can pay me back."

"God, that would be a life saver," Zoe said. "I figure I owe him nine hundred dollars. That's for three pieces."

"The ones I broke," said Lenore. "I feel so guilty."

"I can manage that," I said. "Pay me when you can."

I noticed a woman coming toward us, heading for the reserved table. She was tall, wearing a floppy hat, and she looked familiar. When she was seated under the umbrella she took her hat off. I recognized her as Marcus' wife. I was about to write Zoe a cheque, but my pen stopped in mid-air.

"What?" Zoe wanted to know.

"Nothing," I said. I finished writing the cheque.

Zoe leaned across the table. "You were staring at that woman," she whispered. "Who is she?"

"No one," I whispered back. "I just think she's striking, like a model."

"Too old," Zoe whispered.

"Too old," Lenore said aloud. "I am too old, aren't I?"

"We weren't talking about you, Mother," Zoe said.

"I know," Lenore said. "But that's how I feel. You don't need me anymore, and even if you did, I couldn't be much help to you. I've proved that, haven't I? What good on this Earth is an old divorced woman?"

"Mother," Zoe said, "you're feeling sorry for yourself and you're whining. Stop it before it gets irritating."

I thought Zoe was being too hard on her. "You'll meet someone else before long," I said. I wasn't sure if that was the right thing to say or not. Lenore had a tenuous hold on her emotions these days. It wasn't hard to make her cry by saying the wrong thing. I wondered who the woman, Annabel, was waiting for, and hoped it wasn't Marcus.

"I would like to meet someone," Lenore said.

"Well, not here, today," Zoe said, signalling the waitress for the bill. "We have to get back to the gallery and get the new show up. Photographs this time. Wait until you see them. This woman's serious, not an amateur like Robin." She handed me some invitations to the opening. "Hand them out," she said. "You're my best contact for sales."

Lenore said to me, "What about that friend of yours?"

"What friend?" I asked.

"The man in the tuxedo. I can't remember his name. Mario, I think it was. Or Marco."

"Something like that," I said. Annabel was sitting by herself. She could hear every word of our conversation.

"The man who bought something, you remember. He was so elegant. Be sure to ask him. I don't suppose you ever found out if he's married."

"I don't know," I stammered, trying to come up with a way to change the subject.

"I could look in the records at the gallery, although even if I knew his name, I wouldn't do anything about it. I wouldn't know how."

The waitress appeared with the bill.

"I'll get it," I said, grabbing it. I knew Zoe and Lenore would argue with me, and I hoped that would steer Lenore away from the subject of Marcus.

"You're not paying the bill on top of lending me money," Zoe said.

"Never mind," I said. "You can get it next time. Can't she Lenore? Seems fair to me."

"I'll get it next time," Lenore said. "I might sell the house. It's too big for me. I was just kind of waiting ..." She trailed off.

"Waiting for what?" Zoe asked.

"Nothing," Lenore said. "I don't know."

Zoe stood up to leave. I stayed put. "Aren't you coming?" Zoe asked.

"Go ahead," I said. "I want another coffee."

"Can I call you tonight?" Lenore asked me. "There's something I want to talk to you about."

"Of course," I said. "You can always call me. You know that."

After Zoe and Lenore left, I thought maybe I had made a mistake in staying. I didn't know what I would do if it turned out Annabel was waiting for Marcus. I was just deciding to leave after all, when I heard her voice.

"Excuse me."

I looked at her, terrified.

"Sorry to disturb your thoughts," Annabel said, "but are you using your ashtray? There isn't one on my table."

I handed her the ashtray.

"Thank you. Like I said, sorry to disturb you. I hate to invade someone's privacy, but I'm a smoker. You know how we are."

It was a joke. I laughed. Then Annabel saw the person she was waiting for, not Marcus, another woman. Annabel waved. I looked away. How could I leave now? Two women were bound to talk. I ordered a coffee, decaf, and tried to look like I was lost in thought.

I listened for the word Marcus. That was what I wanted to hear, his name, spoken by his wife. But Annabel wasn't talking about Marcus. She was talking about a Greek restaurateur – the one who owned Athene's – who had apparently asked her out on date.

"We were in the restaurant a week ago – me, M. J. and Cynthia, and the baby. The baby was a gem all evening, cooing and gooing and being an absolute darling. Tim – the owner, the one I'm telling you about – made quite a fuss over her. Late in the evening, after a couple of bottles of wine, I was walking around the restaurant with the baby and he asked me if I was married. I said no – that's not really a lie, is it? – and he said, 'Neither am I'. Then he said, 'Would you like to go for a drink some night?' and I said, 'Why not?'"

At that point Annabel's friend interrupted to ask how old he was.

"I don't know," Annabel said. "Younger than I am, definitely, but not really young. Forty-five maybe. Anyway, I wrote my phone number on a business card, and as I was writing he was fussing over the baby and making her laugh, and I thought, this is nice, a man who likes babies. Maybe he was thinking the same about me. Maybe Greek men are attracted to maternalism."

"Especially in older women," the friend said. "You probably reminded him of his mother."

They both laughed. I wondered why they were laughing. It was hardly a complimentary thing to say. But then, I'd noticed this before. Older women at lunch or dinner, laughing their heads off. Too bad Lenore couldn't find someone to laugh with. It occurred to me I had never known Lenore to go out with women her own age. I wasn't sure she ever went out, unless it was with Zoe.

"Of course I never expected to hear from him," Annabel continued, "but the other evening at about dinnertime he called and asked if I wanted to meet him that night, after he closed the restaurant. I said yes, and he said he'd call me later; hopefully he'd be able to get away a bit early, by eleven or so. Then after I hung up the phone – we're getting to the funny part, well not exactly funny, but significant, you'll know what I mean in a minute – I decided I'd have a bath, do my toenails, dig out some sexy underwear, which I did. And then I decided if I was going out that late, I'd better have a nap so I wouldn't fall asleep on the poor guy. I lay down on the couch and closed my eyes and the next thing I knew I was waking up and it was one-thirty in the morning. I'd missed his call, slept right through it. Can you believe it?"

Annabel's friend said, "Oh my God, Annabel, what did you do?"

Annabel said, "I checked my answering service, and sure enough, he had called several times. I felt awful. And by then it was almost two o'clock so I couldn't call him."

"Have you heard from him since then?"

"No," Annabel said. "I guess I'll call him and apologize, but the truth is, I probably would have backed out anyway."

"Really?"

"I think so." Annabel laughed again. "Well, that's what he gets for wanting to date an older woman, isn't it?"

I snuck another look at Annabel. When her friend caught my eye, I decided it was time to leave. It was too obvious that I was eavesdropping. As I was leaving, I heard Annabel say, "Normally, I would not encourage that sort of attention. But it was the baby. He was so interested in the baby."

"I have a feeling it was the two bottles of wine," her friend said, and they laughed again, and then I was out of earshot.

I couldn't get Annabel out of my head – her story, the toenails and the lace underwear. In the middle of the afternoon, I closed my office door and phoned Marcus.

"I want you to come over tonight," I said. It was clear what I meant.

Marcus said, "Are you sure?"

"Yes," I said. "Definitely. Without a doubt."

"Good then," he said.

We talked for a bit, about nothing in particular. He sounded pleased. We both did. It was as though we'd reached an understanding after a time of uncertainty.

I left work early to get ready for him. I had a bath, shaved my legs and painted my toenails amber. I had to make a special trip to the The Bay cosmetic counter for nail polish, and decided to buy new underwear at the same time, black lace. I felt like a harem girl in preparation. The hours of waiting were an aphrodisiac.

When Marcus finally arrived, he was carrying a bottle of champagne and two delicate fluted glasses. I wondered where he'd got the glasses, if he'd bought them especially, or if he'd taken them from the china cabinet at home. He uncorked the champagne, then handed me a glass.

"I went to Kenya once," he said.

"Kenya," I said. "What were you doing in Kenya?" My voice sounded like someone else's. I felt like another person, not myself. It was thrilling.

"Shhh," Marcus said. The bottle was upright in his hand. Champagne bubbles hissed their way up the neck. "Don't talk," he said. "Listen."

"It's just that you have so many secrets," I said.

"I don't have any secrets," Marcus said. "I'm an open book."

My hand, the one holding the delicate glass, began to tremble. I was almost relieved when the telephone rang. I remembered that Lenore was supposed to call.

"Don't get it," Marcus said.

"I'd better," I said. "But I'll say I'm in the middle of something." I answered the phone. It was someone named Susan.

"From the bank?" she said, as though she was asking me. "And how are you tonight?"

"Fine," I said, looking at Marcus and the open champagne bottle in his hand.

"I'm just calling to ask how you're making out with the new account?"

"The new account?" I said.

"The Special Plus. Any problems?"

"Well, now that you mention it, I've been having trouble at the ATM."

"Didn't they tell you at the bank?" Susan asked.

"Tell me what?"

"The new sub number won't be activated until next Monday. You have to go into the bank or use the Teleservice until then."

"Oh," I said. "Well, that explains the problem, I guess."

"No problems, other than that?" Susan asked.

"No," I said. "Look, I'm kind of busy here ..."

"I'll let you go then," Susan said. "Good luck on the draw."

"The draw?"

"The phone. They put your name in a draw for a new phone, remember? Maybe you'll win and that will make up for your trouble. You have yourself a good evening now."

"Yeah. Thanks." I hung up. "That was Susan," I said to Marcus. "From the bank."

"Come here," Marcus said.

I did.

"Now, where were we?"

I held up my glass.

"No more talking," he said. "Just listen." He began pouring, filling my glass slowly. "A man in Kenya told me this. Swahili is a very romantic language. When you pour a glass of wine, you're saying, 'I'm filling this glass with wine,' but that's not really what you're saying in Swahili. You're really saying, 'I can't get enough of beauty, and beauty is a woman. I can't get enough of this beautiful woman.'"

"You're kidding me," I said, self-conscious and intrigued at the same time, watching my glass, watching the bubbly, almost clear liquid rise. No man my own age would even dream of engaging in this type of foreplay.

"No," Marcus said. "It's true."

"Then it's a lovely story," I said.

When my glass was full I lifted it to my lips, feeling diaphanous and light-headed before I'd had even a drop. When Marcus touched my shoulder, I felt my breath catch in my throat. I dropped my glass and it broke softly on the carpet. When he kissed my neck I heard a moaning that I knew was mine, but it was a sound I had never made before. I'm speaking a new language, I thought.

"Swahili," I murmured. "It must be Swahili."

"Yes," he said. "Yes, I believe it is."

The phone rang again. This time I didn't answer it.

Lenore called me at work a few days later and said she had, just *had* to see me, and Zoe mustn't know.

"I've done something terrible," Lenore said.

"Whatever it is," I said, "I'm sure it's not terrible." I was thinking Lenore wasn't capable of doing terrible things. If she were, she would be a different person, possibly a happier one. She suggested we meet in the park for lunch, across the street from my office building. There was a hot dog stand on the corner. You had your choice of all-beef, chicken or tofu.

We bought our hot dogs and found a place to sit on a bench near the war memorial. There were several kids on skateboards, trying to do tricks on the marble steps that led up to the statue of the unknown soldier. One of them was a girl. You didn't see girl skateboarders very often. She was wearing a T-shirt with GIRLS RULE written on it. I took a bite of my tofu dog and Lenore confessed the terrible thing she'd done.

"I called that friend of yours," she said.

"What friend?" I asked.

"You know. Marcus. The man in the tuxedo who bought one of Robin's sculptures. I got his name from Zoe's records in the gallery."

I had my mouth full of tofu dog and hot peppers, and I almost choked. "You called him?" I managed to say. "What for?"

"You should know the answer to that," Lenore said. "I called him because I'm lonely, and he's handsome, and I gathered from you and Zoe and your friends that calling a man and inviting him for a drink is an acceptable thing to do these days. Of course it's nothing I've done before and consequently I wasn't very good at it."

I watched as the girl skateboarder spun around the statue, building up speed, and then soared into the air, bypassing the marble steps on her way down. She flipped the board out from under her feet, tried to grab it in the air, missed and landed in a heap at the bottom of the stairs. The board crashed down beside her, upside down, wheels still spinning.

"Fuck man," she said. "That hurt." When she saw Lenore and me watching she said, "Sorry. Excuse the language." She reached into the pocket of her oversized pants and fished out a pack of cigarettes. Without testing her limbs, she lit up.

"I hope that girl is all right," Lenore said. "I think they'd be better at those tricks if they didn't wear such big pants. They must get in the way."

"What did he say?" I asked.

"Who?" Lenore wanted to know.

"Marcus," I said. "What did Marcus say when you called him?"

"Well," Lenore said. "It was humiliating, I can tell you that. He said he was seeing someone. I said, 'That's all right. I'm very modern. We could have a drink and I wouldn't care if you were otherwise attached.' Then he said he was flattered, but no. He said it quite resolutely, I thought, and then I said something utterly awful like, 'Thank you anyway, for your consideration,' and I hung up. Isn't that humiliating? I can't go to Zoe's opening on Friday night, because he might be there and I just couldn't face him."

I didn't know what to say. This was a complication. I couldn't tell Lenore I was the person Marcus was seeing, and now I'd never be able to appear with Marcus in public because Lenore would wonder why I hadn't told her sooner. I was glad, though, that Marcus had admitted he was seeing someone.

"I wish I were dead," Lenore said.

"No, you don't," I said.

"You're right," Lenore said. "I don't. I'm not that defeated."

The girl on the skateboard tossed her cigarette butt aside and lifted herself onto her feet. She inspected her shins, checked her board for damage, then headed off down the sidewalk. Apparently these crashes were just a part of the sport.

"Don't you think skateboarding is amazing?" I said to Lenore.

"You're trying to change the subject," she said. "You're embarrassed for me."

"No," I said. "I mean it. It's amazing how skateboarders claim a public space. It's kind of like freedom of speech. These kids are trying to tell us something; I'm just not sure what it is. Maybe they don't know either."

Lenore looked at me as though I were crazy.

"If it makes you feel any better," I said, "I think Marcus is married. I know he told you he was seeing someone, but I'm pretty sure he's married."

Lenore thought for a minute. "You know what I hate about marriage?" she said. "You can't wish for anything. When I was young, before I got married, I used to dream about things. The future, where I wanted to live or travel, adventures even. Then I met Zoe's father and we had Zoe and my time was taken up with living our lives together. I didn't think much about what I wanted. I had it, I suppose. After Zoe grew up and moved out, I started wishing again, only it wasn't like before, because every wish had to be measured against what I knew about Zoe's father – he doesn't like to travel in countries where he doesn't speak the language; he has no desire to own a cottage at the lake; he hates living in a mess so house renovations are out. There was no pleasure in dreaming about anything, unless it was some little thing that he had no opinion on. Maybe that's why women shop so much. They buy things like clothes or lamps, say, that their husbands have no opinions on, and it keeps them from wishing for things that might affect their husbands' lives. 'I think I'll buy some lawn furniture,' is less troubling than, 'I think we should go and live *en Provence* for a year.'"

I hardly knew what to say. I wanted to say it didn't have to be like that, but how did I know? Maybe she was right.

"What about Zoe and Chuck?" I said. "That doesn't describe their marriage."

"Nothing describes Zoe and Chuck's marriage," she said. "It barely exists."

"That's really depressing," I said.

"I don't know why I was even thinking of another man," Lenore said. "I should know better. I'm glad it worked out this way."

I folded up my empty hot dog wrapper and tossed it in the trash.

We sat quietly for a few minutes and then Lenore said, "Maybe I should take him back."

"Who?" I said.

"Zoe's father," she said.

"Is that what he wants?" I asked.

"It would help his case, if it goes to trial," Lenore said. "He hasn't asked, not in so many words. He's too proud. But I know he's waiting for me to make the suggestion."

"God, Lenore," I said. I didn't want to say anything else. I didn't want to have an opinion. The consequences were too dire.

"We used to play the piano together," she said. "He'd play the right hand and I'd play the left. Or sometimes we'd switch. Neither of us could play particularly well, but together we could play fairly complicated pieces. Maybe we could do that again."

"I think I'd better get back to work," I said, beginning to feel quite ill. "Anyway, you didn't do anything terrible. Calling Marcus, I mean. Don't worry about it."

"Promise you won't tell Zoe," Lenore said. "Not about Marcus, or the other thing. She's so impatient with me these days. I know she claims to hate her father, but sometimes I think she believes it's all my fault."

"She probably feels a bit helpless," I said. "Just like the rest of us."

We left it at that.

Lenore didn't come to Zoe's opening. She claimed to have the flu, and Zoe took her word that she did. I didn't know whether or not Marcus would show up, or how I was supposed to behave if he did come through the door. Would I let on there was something between us? I thought not, because Zoe would be sure to tell Lenore and then I would feel badly for not being completely honest with her. I hoped he wouldn't come, but on the other hand I kept watching the door, waiting for him to come through it with aplomb, like he had the last time.

I had no idea how Zoe had put together her invitation list, but several well-heeled couples stopped in for a glass of wine and a look at the black-and-white photographs on the walls. A woman in a body-hugging royal blue dress stood out from the others, partly because her dress was so tight and partly because she erupted every few minutes in a loud demand for Zoe's attention. There were also Zoe's friends (including Robin), and lots of art students. The artist was there, of course, a woman named Catherine something or other. She was about my age and hopelessly awkward with Zoe's guests. She hid in the back room for most of the evening and Zoe kept going to get her so she could introduce her to potential buyers. She was obsessed with the arsonist, who had struck again the night before. Whenever Zoe introduced Catherine to a guest, she asked about the arsonist instead of talking about her work. She seemed to think someone might have inside information on the investigators' progress.

"Fire is the ultimate destroyer," I heard her say several times. "Just the idea of fire. Do you know what I mean?" People said they did, but they obviously thought she was a bit wacky. Whenever Catherine saw a chance, she retired to the back room again.

I wandered around and looked at the photographs. I couldn't tell what they were photographs of. There were hard edges in many shades of black and grey, and shapes that seemed to represent buildings. I tried to make something of them but the shapes were dark and fuzzy, and whenever I'd try to put them together, they'd get lost in the muddle and disappear. I didn't see how Zoe could expect to sell these photographs, or why she had chosen to display them if her intention was to earn a living. I was looking at one particularly obscure photograph when Zoe came and stood beside me.

"You should talk to Catherine," she said. "You two have something in common."

"What's that?" I asked.

"Catherine was an architect, before she gave it up to become an artist," Zoe said.

"I was never an architect," I said. It irritated me whenever Zoe brought up my short-lived studies in architecture, as though they gave me some kind of legitimacy. "I don't know anything about architecture," I said, "so don't try to get me to talk to her. It's humiliating to have to tell people I flunked out."

She gave me one of those looks she usually reserved for Lenore. "Anyway," she said, "you must be able to see how architecture informs her work."

"I can't see anything in these photographs," I said.

"Catherine believes modernism has destroyed the built environment for the common person," Zoe said.

"There you go," I said. "I can't even remember what modernism is. Or maybe I didn't get that far."

"Stop pretending," Zoe said. "You know more than you let on."

"Tell me this," I said. "Why is she so interested in the arsonist? It's completely weird. Hey, maybe it's her. Wouldn't that be a twist?"

"Yeah," Zoe said, giving up on me. "That's it. Probably."

The woman in the tight dress called Zoe's name from across the room and Zoe motioned that she'd be there in a minute. "By the way, did I tell you Chuck's gone missing?" she asked me.

"What do you mean, missing?"

"I haven't heard from him in a month. I have no idea where he is."

"God," I said. "Do you think something's happened to him? Surely you would have heard."

"That's what I figure," Zoe said. "So no, I don't think anything's happened to him. I think he's gone on a permanent road trip, that's what I think."

"You mean he's left you?"

"You make it sound so pathetic."

"But that's what you're saying."

"I suppose," she said. "Anyway, I thought you'd like to know."

The woman called Zoe's name again.

"She'd better buy something," Zoe said. "She's been a pain in the ass all night and I'd hate to think I've been nice to her for nothing." She crossed the room to see what the woman wanted.

Several people decided to leave about then, and I noticed that Catherine grabbed the opportunity to escape. She looked like a person without a ticket trying to sneak in with a crowd, only she was sneaking out. I watched as she purposefully avoided Zoe and managed to get away relatively unnoticed. As she hurried by me I saw that her mascara was smeared, and I remembered Lenore crying in the bathroom all night at the first opening. You wouldn't think receptions at art galleries could turn out to be such tearjerkers.

An hour or so later, when the place was cleared out except for the hangers on – Robin and company – the bell on the door jangled.

"Guess who," Zoe said.

I turned and looked. It was Marcus. He crossed the room, kissed me on the lips and draped his arm over my shoulder. Zoe tried to cover up her dismay but she didn't do a very good job of it. Marcus wandered around and looked at the show and then he said to me, "These are interesting, aren't they? Which one do you fancy? I'll buy it for you."

"You don't have to do that," I said.

"I want to. Really."

I pointed to a photograph that was mostly black, with just a bit of light illuminating something that looked like a beam. I didn't particularly like it – I didn't like any of them – but I was willing to help Zoe's sales.

"Done," Marcus said.

He paid for it, and Zoe placed a sold dot on the wall. That made three. The woman in the tight blue dress had, in the end, bought two photographs. Things were looking up. Marcus whispered to me, "Put it somewhere you can see it when you're lying in bed. That would make me happy."

"Christ, woman," Zoe said to me later, when Marcus was out of earshot. "You're just chock full of surprises."

"Don't tell Lenore," I said to Zoe.

"Why not?" Zoe wanted to know. "Have you got something to hide?"

"I just don't want her to know," I said.

She told Lenore anyway, the very next day, although it came out in a roundabout way so maybe she didn't set out to tell her. She went over to Lenore's to see how she was because she thought she had the flu, and to tell her about Chuck. Lenore responded by accusing Zoe of being a less than dutiful wife and said it was her own fault that Chuck had decided not to bother coming home.

This surprised Zoe because she'd always had the impression Lenore thought Chuck was pretty much useless. It began to make sense, though, when Lenore confessed that she was taking Zoe's father back. Zoe was furious and said she'd never set foot in the house or even speak to Lenore again if she did something that stupid. While they were in the midst of swapping these miserable confidences – and I can only guess how the conversation developed – Zoe told Lenore about me and Marcus.

When Zoe told me that Lenore knew, I called and asked Lenore if I could take her to lunch. I wanted to explain. She said no, she was busy.

"Tomorrow then," I said. "Or the day after. It doesn't matter to me."

"I don't think so," Lenore said, and then she hung up on me.

I tried not to take it personally. I could understand why she wouldn't want to see me, not just because of Marcus, but because she couldn't put herself in the position of having to justify her decision to take Zoe's father back. I wondered if maybe she'd been encouraged by someone from Zoe's father's social group, the wife of another doctor, maybe. I did hope she had someone to talk to. It all just seemed like a mess to me, and I hoped for Lenore's sake that the allegations would be resolved soon, one way or the other.

A few weeks later I was shocked to receive an invitation to M. J. and Cynthia's wedding. When it arrived in the mail, I told Marcus no, absolutely not. "Not on your life," I said. "Nothing in the world could convince me." But then Marcus told me Annabel wasn't going to be there. She had been called away on business.

"To Germany," Marcus said. "She's being given an award for some research she did. M. J. and Cynthia wanted to postpone the wedding, but Annabel insisted they carry on because the plans were already made. She was willing to miss the awards ceremony, but M. J. convinced her she had to go. It's a very prestigious award, a once-in-a-lifetime thing. Anyway, none of us values marriage as an institution much. The wedding is just a party really, a gathering of friends."

I said it wasn't just Annabel, it was Marcus' sons and their friends and relatives, just the idea of meeting people from his other life. But then Marcus acted hurt and implied that I wasn't comfortable with the openness of his relationship with Annabel. He made me feel old-fashioned, which seemed ridiculous considering our respective ages, and so I said I would go to the reception, although not the wedding, because Marcus had a role to play during the ceremony and I didn't want to have anything to do with that.

I said no to wearing the tuxedo at first, too; my better judgement told me it would be inappropriate. But Marcus said he liked me in the tuxedo. And the wedding was a coming out party in a way, he said, the two of us appearing in public as a couple. The tuxedo, he reminded me, was the cause of our meeting in the first place. I said I would wear it.

The wedding was in the CN hotel downtown, the same one where Marcus and I had met in the lounge and he'd shown me Annabel's picture. Because I had not gone to the wedding ceremony, I told Marcus I'd meet him in the hotel lobby. When I got there, he was waiting for me. He was wearing a pale blue suit. That was the first warning that the tuxedo was a mistake. My foolishness was confirmed when we walked into the banquet room. There were no more than thirty people at the reception and they all seemed to be dressed in pale colours, even the men. I heard a voice from a stupid old movie saying, "I thought it was a costume ball": Gene Wilder dressed as a chicken.

It got worse. I was to be seated for the meal at the head table, next to Marcus. By the time I understood this, it was too late. Marcus was already introducing me to the bride and groom, the attendants (one of whom was Rob, Marcus' other son), and the bride's parents. Then I realized he was introducing me to Annabel. She also was sitting at the head table, although at the end opposite from where we were to sit. The room faded briefly, but I pulled myself together.

Marcus introduced her as his "dear Annabel," and she was friendly enough, and shook my hand and said, "Nice to meet you." She had her long hair in a braid and again she looked quite beautiful, her red lips perfectly shaped. She was wearing a plain, sophisticated mint green dress. As the mother of the bride, she couldn't have dressed more appropriately. I managed to stammer, "How do you do," and then Marcus led me to our seats.

The table was covered with a cream-coloured cloth. Red rose petals were scattered loosely, and there were several candles burning in very tall ceramic holders. Too many candles, I thought; I could see myself knocking one over when I reached for a wine glass, which I was planning to do as soon as possible.

"You didn't tell me," I said to Marcus.

"Tell you what?" he asked.

"That Annabel would be here."

"I'm sorry," he said. "I didn't think. She cancelled the trip to Europe at the last minute."

"And you didn't tell me that I'd be expected to sit here," I said. "I wouldn't have come."

"That's why I didn't tell you," Marcus said. He squeezed my shoulder and smiled. "You should be more self-confident," he said. "You can hold your own. I know you can. Now enjoy yourself. They're all wondering who Marcus' sexy new girlfriend is."

"I feel like a freak," I said.

"You look wonderful," he said.

I made it through the meal and the speeches and toasts in a kind of numbed state. When Zoe quizzed me afterward I couldn't even tell her what we'd had for dinner.

"Seafood?" she asked. "Chicken? Roast beef?"

I had no idea. I told her I drank too much wine and felt like Alice, getting bigger and becoming more of a spectacle with every swallow.

"Wouldn't it have been funny," I said, "if I'd burst into tears and filled up the room? Ha ha."

After the plates were cleared away, most of the people from the head table, including the bride and groom, moved to the end of the room where the grand piano was. A classical pianist was playing tasteful after-dinner music. Marcus excused himself.

"Where are you going?" I said, terrified of being left alone.

"I'll be right back," he said. "Don't worry."

I remained where I was, poured myself another glass of wine, and waited for Marcus to return. Fifteen minutes passed. He'd obviously been sidetracked. Annabel appeared and sat down next to me in Marcus' empty chair. I thought I would die.

"So. This is a kettle of fish, isn't it?" she said.

"I guess it is," I said.

"Don't be smart with me," Annabel said. "I wouldn't advise it."

"I wasn't," I said. "It's just … well, it's awkward, isn't it?"

She looked at me like I was out of my mind. "What did you think it would be?" she asked.

"I don't know," I said. "For one thing, I didn't think you'd be here."

"Why not? It's my son's wedding."

"Europe," I said. "Marcus said you'd be in Germany."

"Marcus said that."

Marcus came back and sat down on my other side.

"Who's using my name in vain?" he said.

"Christ, Marcus," Annabel said. "You have about as much common sense as a slug."

"Now Annabel," Marcus said.

"So I was to be in Europe, was I? That's what you told her."

"You mentioned it," he said. "At one point."

She turned to me again. "This happens with men sometimes, you know. You might think he's too … shall we say, virile for a woman his own age. But it's the opposite. He needs something a little special to get him started. Not that you're anything special, from what I can see. Although you do seem to like costumes."

"Now Annabel," Marcus said.

"Now Annabel what?" she said.

I couldn't help watching her mouth, her lovely red lips.

There was a half empty glass of wine near her hand on the table, left by one of the groom's attendants. "What the hell," she said, picking up the glass. I thought she was planning to toss it at him but she lifted it to her lips and drained it. When she set the glass down, there was a perfect red lipstick mark on the rim.

I felt dizzy. I stood up and swayed forward, from the wine I thought, too much wine.

I heard Marcus trying to calm Annabel.

"My dear Annabel," I heard him say.

I swayed dangerously close to the candles on the table.

"I'm getting bloody tired of this," she said. She looked up at me. I tried to focus. "I suppose you think you're the first," she said. She turned to Marcus. "I hope you're not planning to move this one in with us."

I could feel myself swaying closer and closer to the candles. She said to me, "Did he mention that he moved one of you in with us once? His so-called bookkeeper. Her apartment block was sold and torn down, poor thing. What could he do?"

My hair was on fire. I could smell it. I slapped at the side of my face, sending sparks and burnt hair to the cream-coloured tablecloth. Neither Marcus nor Annabel seemed to notice.

"My hair's on fire," I said.

Annabel looked up. "You're right, it is," she said. She stood, picked up a jug of water and emptied its contents over my head.

"There," she said. "It's out."

She left and walked toward the piano, calling, "Do you do requests? I have a request."

I looked at Marcus. I thought sure I'd see remorse, uneasiness at least; but I didn't. What I saw was satisfaction. Marcus was enjoying himself. When the pianist began playing Annabel's request I knew it was my exit cue, even though I didn't recognize the tune.

The swinging doors through which the servers had carried the food were closer than the main entrance to the banquet room, so I went that way. Several kitchen workers, many of them Asian, stared as I made my way past the rows of stainless steel countertops toward the far end of the room. I heard murmurings in a language that was foreign to me, Korean perhaps, or Cantonese. I passed through another set of swinging doors and down a staircase, and finally I was in the hotel lobby.

There was a full-length mirror by the elevators and I walked over and looked at myself. My hair and jacket were soaking wet. One side of my face was framed with ragged burned hair. I started to laugh. I said to myself, "Well, at least you learned a few words of

Swahili. That's something." Then I realized Marcus' story about Kenya was probably bogus, and all I was left with was the thought that I was standing in the lobby of a nice old hotel, the only one in the whole city that had retained the elegance of a former time, and I was wearing a second-hand tuxedo and my hair was burnt and dripping.

The following Wednesday I got a call at work telling me I had won the phone.

"What phone?" I asked.

"The one at the bank," a voice said. "We put your name in a draw and you won."

At noon, I went to the bank, which was in a strip mall and was identified by a neon sign advertising term deposits.

I approached a teller. "Hi," I said. "I guess I won the phone."

"Lorna," the teller called over her shoulder loudly. "We have our winner."

It was noon and the bank was crowded. Everyone was looking at me. I thought, this is why it never pays to win anything.

A woman in a suit, the manager no doubt, came from her office carrying a box.

"Congratulations," she said to me. She handed me the box. It was an ordinary telephone.

"And how have you been enjoying your Special Plus account?"

"Fine," I said. "But I thought it was a cell phone."

"No," the manager said. "It does have a speaker function though. I find that handy. But seriously, has the new account been of benefit?"

I said, "Thanks. Really. But I'm in a rush." I hurried out of the bank with my new phone, a completely useless object since I already had one.

When I got home to my apartment, there was a voice message from Marcus. I deleted it without listening to what he had to say. I tried to picture him in the blue suit, looking like a Shriner from my father's generation, and was relatively successful. I decided to go out. I checked the paper and saw that all the early movies had started. Dinner then. Athene's popped into my head.

It was a bizarre place. The white plaster statues around the room were Greek in their origins, but there was a camp-style fireplace in the middle of the room, and the walls were filled with photographs of cowboys and hunting parties. There were even a few stuffed birds on the counter near the till.

There were three or four couples having late dinners, and several men sat in a booth by the kitchen. They were wearing suits and speaking Greek. I kept my eye on them, trying to listen and catch names. One of them might be the owner. Tim, she'd said his name was. I worked on my spinach and feta pizza, and my half litre of red wine, and listened.

Apparently, I am no good at eavesdropping. I noticed the whole table of men looking at me, and then one of them stood and came to my table.

"Are you enjoying your meal?" he asked.

"Yes, very much," I stammered.

"Very good," he said. "This is your first time in the restaurant?"

"Yes," I said, "that's right."

"You're not meeting anyone?" he asked, pouring the last of the wine from the carafe into my glass.

"No," I answered. "I was, you know, working late, and stopped on my way home."

"You don't mind dining alone?" he asked.

"I don't mind," I said.

He called to the waitress. "Another half litre of wine for the lady, on the house."

"Oh, that's not necessary," I said.

"My pleasure," said the man. "My name is Tim. Welcome to Athene's."

"Pleased to meet you," I said.

"I like to keep my customers happy," Tim said. "That way, they come back."

"Well," I said. "Thank you then."

"My pleasure," he said again, and returned to his table.

The waitress returned with a fresh carafe and placed it on my table.

"Enjoy," she said, in a voice that clearly meant something else. When she passed Tim on her way to the kitchen she said something to him in Greek. I wondered if she was his wife. The waitress went through the swinging doors into the kitchen, and then Tim got up and followed her. I could hear them shouting at each other. The men at the booth laughed. One of them looked at me and said something, and they laughed again. I wanted to leave, but what to do about the wine? I felt like I had to finish it.

I remembered I'd picked up a newspaper and retrieved it from my bag. I skimmed the front page and a headline caught my eye: "Prominent local doctor charged." I read the article, trying to take it in. Four other women had come forward. There were many charges going back several years, and a conviction would probably result in jail time. Poor Lenore, I thought. The encounters, if that's what they were called, had to have occurred in the years they were married, maybe even while Zoe was still in high school. According to the dates, I would not have been the first.

I finished the wine quickly, put the newspaper in my bag and went to the till. When Tim, who was still sitting in the booth, saw me paying my bill he once again approached. In Greek, he shooed the waitress away.

"You enjoyed the meal?" he asked.

"Yes," I said, and thanked him again for the wine.

"Maybe you'd like to go for a drink sometime," he said casually, putting the money I handed him into the till.

"No," I said quickly. "I mean, I have a friend."

"Of course," he said, handing me my change. "I understand."

Then I said, "I hope your wife didn't mind about the wine."

Tim looked at the waitress, who was clearing my table. "She's not my wife," he said.

"Oh," I said.

"I'm a widower," Tim said. "My wife died a year ago."

"Oh," I said. "I'm sorry."

"Never mind," Tim said. "I shouldn't have asked. It gets lonely here. I work all the time. I see people come in and I think it would be nice to have a life outside the restaurant."

"I'm sorry," I said again. I believed he was telling me the truth about his wife, although I couldn't help but think he was a little impulsive, even for a man who is desperately alone.

When I got home, there was another phone message, from Zoe this time. All she said was, "Call me immediately." There was urgency, not just in the words, but in her voice.

It was possible, I thought, that she would surprise me. It was possible she'd found out Chuck really was missing, or that something terrible had happened to him. It was possible her gallery had burned to the ground, a victim of the arsonist. I figured, though, that she was calling to tell me what I already knew: her father was guilty. I deleted the message, had a sobering bath and went to bed. I lay there with the lights on and stared at Catherine's photograph, my gift from Marcus, which was now on the wall at the foot of my bed. The photograph began to make sense in a grievous kind of way, as things often do when you're resigned to them.

Bone Garden

Dixie Carmichael drives her new white Acura south toward Regina and tries to keep her headache in check by popping a couple of 222s with codeine. She takes the last two capsules in the foil package, then selects a soothing Garth Brooks CD from the pile on the seat beside her. She's glad she made the decision to drive her own car and wonders if she's a perpetrator of corporate crime for not obeying the rule, which states, more or less, that employees on government business will drive government-issue Chevy Cavaliers. This trip, Dixie said to hell with it. She couldn't stand the thought of three hours to Saskatoon for a two-hour meeting and then the trip home again in generic discomfort.

She tries to drive all the way without stopping, but the 222s make her drowsy and she decides she'd better grab a coffee. She pulls into a roadside gas station at St. Pierre just as the sun is beginning to set and parks in front of the coffee shop. Then, instead of going inside, she walks the short distance into town to get some air and stretch her legs. A cold wind reminds her that it's the end of October.

She comes to a store with a sign that reads DOT'S FAMILY FOODS. A bell jangles as she opens the door and steps inside, and a middle-aged woman comes from the back, where the family apparently lives.

"What can I do for you?" the woman asks.

"Just browsing," Dixie says.

The woman gives her a look that says browsing is an odd thing to do in this store, so Dixie says, "Actually, I need a pair of gloves. There's a real chill in the air."

"Gloves and mitts are next to the cooler," the woman says, pointing.

Besides the usual basic food stuffs, the shelves are stocked with canning and freezing supplies, birthday and sympathy cards, embroidery thread, knitting needles, grey work socks, plaid flannel shirts and industrial strength cleaning supplies, all in a space not much bigger than someone's living room. Dixie supposes that these items comprise the necessities of life in St. Pierre.

The only gloves she sees are nylon Ski-Doo type gloves. Although she doesn't want them, she now feels she should buy something so she picks out a pair of navy blue ones and tries them on. They're too big, but it doesn't matter because she's not planning to wear them.

"These ought to keep me warm," Dixie says, and then thinks to ask, "Do you have anything for a killer headache?"

The woman reaches up to a high shelf behind the counter and retrieves a bottle of Extra Strength Tylenol. "I'll get you a glass of water," she says.

"That's all right," Dixie says, but the woman is already on her way through the door to the living quarters.

As she waits, Dixie scans the rows of gum packets and chocolate bars in the case under the countertop. She sees a box of beaded rosaries tucked into the corner next to the Oh Henrys. She was not raised Catholic and has always been curious about things like rosaries and crucifixes. When the woman returns with a glass of water, Dixie opens the bottle of Tylenol, pulls out the cotton and shakes two capsules into her hand. She casually asks the woman for one of the rosaries, thinking she might hang it from the mirror in her car.

"I hope I didn't disturb your dinner," Dixie says as the woman rings up the sale.

"Doesn't matter," the woman says. "We're always open, only I tell people it better be an emergency if they knock on my door at two o'clock in the morning. It happens. You wouldn't believe how often."

Dixie says, "You're just like a social worker then, on call all the time."

The woman says. "Now there's a profession I have no use for."

"I know what you mean," Dixie says. This attitude toward her chosen line of work is nothing new to her, although she doesn't completely understand it.

A child begins to wail in the back and the woman excuses herself. Dixie says good night and leaves with her gloves and Tylenol and rosary beads in a plastic grocery bag.

As she closes the door, she notices several carved and painted wooden figures on display in the store window. A hand-lettered sign propped behind the figures says CARVED BY MR. WILLARD HASSEL, NOW DECEASED, NOT FOR SALE. She looks closely at them, at their quirky postures and their odd faces. She wonders if Mr. Willard Hassel has one of the little figures sitting on his headstone. She's tempted to find the graveyard, not just to look for the carving, but also because she likes graveyards. They make her think of the British Museum in London, which she visited as a teenager on a trip with an aunt. They saw the ancient peat bog man, petrified like an insect in amber. As her aunt shuddered and tried to move her along, Dixie stood for ages staring at the remains in their Plexiglas case. She found herself thinking about the individual, the particular human being, and she wondered who he was before some wise holy man decided to make a sacrifice of him, hit him over the head and then slit his throat. She imagined that someday her own bones might be dug up and put in a museum, and that someone might wonder about *her* life.

Dixie turns away from the store window and walks back to her car. It's getting too late in the day for a tour of the graveyard and her desire to see a carved gnome on Willard Hassel's headstone seems frivolous. When she gets to the gas station, she feels better from the fresh air. She decides she can drive again without a cup of coffee, but just as she's about to get into her car she recognizes someone through the plate glass window of the coffee shop, a teenaged boy named Moe, whose mother is on her caseload. She wonders what he's doing alone in St. Pierre, then tries to convince herself it doesn't matter, it's none of her business. Maybe it's not even him, she thinks. He turns his head slightly and she gets a better look. It is Moe, there's no doubt, and who is she kidding, of course he's her business. She can't drive away without at least asking him what he's doing here. She reluctantly locks her car again and goes inside for a chat with Moe, thinking that she should have picked a job where her clients were, say, bones, and asked nothing of her.

Carmen, already bored and restless and they've only just arrived, sits in a leather armchair in the Saskatoon hotel lobby while her mother checks them in. Carmen's ten-year-old brother Daniel has discovered a dish of peppermints on the registration counter and is filling his pockets. She contemplates going over and giving his hand a good slap but it seems like too much trouble and then everyone would know she's connected to him and her mother somehow.

Carmen isn't here in this hotel by choice. Her mother made her come. Carmen argued for days that she's old enough to stay home alone, but of course she lost the argument because she's only fifteen and now she's stuck here for the weekend, two hundred and fifty kilometres away from Moe, in nightmarish proximity to several teams of pre-pubescent basketball players, not to mention all the other weird people who are staying at the hotel. The lobby is like the set of a large-cast movie with too many extras wandering around waiting for their ten seconds in front of the camera. Carmen looks at all the costumes – the hairstyles, the hats, the clothing, everything from evening wear to sweat pants and running shoes – and thinks, no one's in charge, no one told the extras what to wear so they all just guessed and came in whatever they wanted. She decides the movie is a modern interpretation of Noah's ark. Instead of preserving all the animals in the world, God has given orders for the preservation of all manner of hats and shoes and hair colours.

Carmen picks up a *Cosmopolitan* magazine someone left in the chair next to her and flips through it, stopping when she comes to a quiz with the title "Measure Your Own A. Q.," which she discovers stands for Adventure Quotient. Mildly interesting, she thinks, and reads on, but the questions have nothing to do with real adventure. They're all about adventures with men and sex and they're completely transparent. Carmen puts the magazine back down and decides to make up her own quiz, not one about relationships, either.

Question One: Which person in this lobby has just eaten the eye of a newt? Carmen looks around and settles on a woman in a short, fake-leopard skirt. The woman has witchy-looking dyed black hair and deep red lipstick. She's such a perfect answer Carmen wonders if her subconscious saw the woman first, before she made up the question. She decides to close her eyes before she composes the next question, which ends up being, Which person in this lobby has AIDS? Carmen opens her eyes and she immediately spots an unusually thin man waiting for an elevator. Carmen's impressed. Maybe it's psychokinesis, this ability to imagine people before she sees them. She tries again. Question Three: Which person in this lobby believes in angels and harmonic convergence? Definitely the woman talking on the pay phone. She's middle-aged and looks as though she's into the spiritual thing in a big way. There's a stack of books piled on the floor at her feet. Carmen can't see any of the titles, but she's sure they're all New Age. She considers ambling past the woman just to check, but then the woman hangs up the phone, collects her books and disappears into the open courtyard, which is just beyond the lobby and the bank of elevators. Another question then. Question Four: Which person here hates her mother? That one's boring and way too easy.

Carmen's mother finally has the key to their room. She waves at Carmen, who worries for a moment that her mother is going to call her in a goofy voice. She doesn't, though, and they take the elevator up to the fifth floor. Carmen's mother has a map in her hand – a map of the hotel courtyard with all its dining areas and lounges and coffee bars.

"This is a very civilized hotel," Carmen's mother says, studying the map with her little pink reading glasses perched on the end of her nose. "Look here. There's even an English tearoom. I'll just bet they serve scones."

"I could get pretty excited about that," says Carmen.

"You don't even know what scones are," says her mother. "They're a kind of biscuit. Very good with jam. I wonder where the swimming pool is. Surely there's a swimming pool. I'm not very good at figuring these map things out."

Carmen grabs the map and finds it right off.

"Oh," says her mother. "Good. Maybe we can all go for a nice swim later on."

"I didn't bring my bathing suit," Carmen says.

Her mother looks at her over her glasses.

"I specifically reminded you to bring your suit," she says. "I don't know how you could have forgotten it."

"Maybe I didn't forget it," Carmen says. "Maybe I just didn't bring it."

Her mother sighs. Daniel wants to know if there's a water slide. Carmen says it doesn't say so on the map, and her mother assures Daniel he can have fun anyway, hotel swimming pools were considered a lot of fun before the advent of water slides. The elevator bell rings and the doors open.

"Maybe you can rent a bathing suit," Carmen's mother says to Carmen.

"As if I would wear a rented bathing suit," Carmen says. "That's disgusting." Carmen sticks her hand in Daniel's pocket and comes up with a handful of peppermints. Daniel glares at Carmen like he's willing to fight for the mints, then looks at their mother, who is holding the elevator doors for them, and changes his mind. Carmen slips the peppermints into her own pocket.

"Here," she says to Daniel, handing him her overnight bag. "Carry this into the room for me."

"Carry it yourself," Daniel says, but he takes it anyway.

The rooms in the hotel are in a circle around the perimeter of the building, and the courtyard on the main floor is open all the way to the skylights. While Carmen's mother and Daniel go inside to check out their room, Carmen stays in the hallway with the map. She decides that whoever designed this hotel was trying to create a kind of biosphere, like a space station, only the project went wrong so they turned it into a hotel instead. Below her, she can see trees and flowers, winding walkways and street lamps and park benches. There's even a stream of turquoise water snaking around the foliage and disappearing periodically under little footbridges along the path. There might be goldfish in the stream, Carmen thinks, seeing flashes of orange. Then she thinks, how could she see goldfish from way up here?

According to the map, the whole courtyard is divided into separate spaces, which are identified by coloured umbrellas. Carmen tries to pick them out. She finds the red umbrellas, which, the map says, indicate the family dining area. Then she finds the blue umbrellas, which complement the patio furniture scattered around the swimming pool deck. Green umbrellas surround the dance floor; pink, the English tearoom. There's a revolving lounge with a piano player, a formal dining room and a cappuccino bar, each with identifying umbrellas. From her vantage point, Carmen finds them all, the nooks and crannies of a world under glass, separated by flowerpots and trees and the too-bright turquoise blue snake. She looks up at the dome covering it all. Filtered light from outside mixes with cigarette smoke and artificial light, creating an unhealthy fog that hovers under the skylights. Carmen thinks she can detect the sound of running water, but decides it's the hum of fans, white noise that muffles any real sounds. A person could get murdered down there, she thinks, could scream and scream and no one would hear. Then Carmen hears the phone ring in their room. It's puzzling, how she can hear the phone so clearly when she's positive no one could hear her if she screamed.

Her mother picks up the phone and says hello. Carmen listens through the closed door and then she calls, "Who's on the phone? Is it for me?"

"Wrong number," her mother calls back.

"Are you sure?" Carmen says. "I told Moe to phone me."

"It was a wrong number, Carmen," her mother says, "and if Moe does phone it better not be collect. You're not allowed to accept the call if it is. Do you hear me?"

"I hear you," Carmen says. "So does everybody else for six blocks."

Moe is the reason Carmen's mother was so insistent Carmen come with her and Daniel. She tried to hide it by telling Carmen they'd make the weekend a family outing, but Carmen knows the real reason she's been dragged along. Her mother didn't want to leave her and Moe alone together. Her mother doesn't like Moe. He wears black T-shirts and boots and doesn't look like he's planning a career in international law, which Carmen's mother keeps pointing out is the career of the future, either that or computer programming. And she's worried Carmen might get pregnant. As if. Carmen and Moe don't even sleep together. Carmen thinks all that groping that goes on in cars and parking lots and the hallways at school is disgusting. She and Moe are joined in mind and spirit, they're not slaves to their bodies.

One night not long ago Carmen's mother came into her room at bedtime and said, "This is difficult for me, Carmen. I do not approve of Moe and I do not condone young people sleeping together. But I want to know if you need to talk to the doctor about birth control and sexually transmitted diseases. I don't want you dying of AIDS or ruining your life with a baby."

"Mother!" Carmen shrieked, and then she told her mother to get out of her room and mind her own business. If she needed birth control or anything else she would handle it herself, she wasn't stupid, she didn't need her mother holding her hand.

"I never should have let your father call you Carmen," her mother said. "I knew it would turn out to be a mistake."

"Oh right," Carmen said. "I'm a slut because my father named me after his favourite opera. That makes a lot of sense."

Her mother gave up and closed the door. Carmen put her head under the covers and that's how she fell asleep.

It's her mother's attitude toward Moe that Carmen gives as the main reason for hating her. She tells people she hates her father, too, because he moved to Vancouver and married a woman ten years younger than him and now has twin three-year-old girls, who are supposedly her half-sisters but she doesn't feel any connection to them at all. Twice a year her father sends airline tickets for her and Daniel, and then he asks Carmen to babysit the girls every second night while he and his new wife go out. "We like to take the chance while you're here," he tells her. "We don't trust many people with the girls." He pays her well, but that doesn't matter, it still bugs the hell out of her.

Although Carmen tries not to let on, she doesn't mind the new wife, Becky, or "Becks," as her father calls her. When Carmen showed Becky a picture of Moe last summer, she said she thought he was cute. Carmen inwardly snorted at the word cute, but still, Becky hadn't said he looked like a drug dealer or a neo-Nazi, so that earned her a few points. And she went out of her way to cook vegetarian things like tofu stir-fry and black bean stew for Carmen without lecturing on the importance of protein and iron. Carmen doesn't like Becky enough to want to move to Vancouver and live in the same house as her. If she did that, she'd have to babysit the twins all the time and she'd be half a continent away from Moe.

Carmen's mother opens the door to the hotel room and says, "We should grab a bite to eat before we have to leave for the game."

"Fine," says Carmen.

"Well. Don't you have to unpack a few things?"

"No."

"Don't you have to go to the bathroom or freshen up or comb your hair?"

"Jesus, Mother," Carmen says. "You are so Christly embarrassing."

In the family eating area, half an hour later, Carmen's mother checks her watch.

"Hurry up, Carmen," she says. "The bus is leaving for the gym in fifteen minutes."

"Big deal," Carmen says. She's hardly eaten anything.

"If you make us late, I will be extremely unhappy with you," her mother says.

"I could care less if we're late for the bus," Carmen says. "I don't want to go to a stupid basketball game anyway."

"Fine. Fine. Stay at the hotel then, if that's the way you feel."

"Give me the room key," says Carmen.

Her mother gives her a key and stands to leave. "Can you find your way to the room?" she asks.

"Of course I can. I'm not a child," Carmen says.

"Are you going to wish your brother good luck?"

"No," Carmen says. "Competitive sports aren't healthy."

"Oh for Pete's sake," her mother says. "I just don't know what to do with you. Come on, Daniel. We don't want to miss the bus."

Daniel says, "I'm glad you're not coming, Carmen, because I think you bring us bad luck."

"That's right," Carmen says. "I have the power of the evil eye, and don't you forget it."

Carmen's mother and brother finally leave her alone. She sits by herself under the huge red umbrella and plays with her French fries. She pretends she's making a brick wall and stacks fries until the wall topples. She hears dance music coming from somewhere. Even though she hates dance music, she wants to find it. She dumps half a bottle of ketchup over her fries, stirs, writes "Have a nice day" on a napkin and lays it over the mess on her plate. Then she goes searching.

Moe needs to see Carmen. It's not that they're inseparable or anything; up until now their friendship has been loose, the kind that finds its own way and falls into place when the time is right. When Carmen told him her mother was making her go to Saskatoon for the weekend, he thought, what's a few days? But now he has this longing that he doesn't understand. There's no explanation for its strength.

He sits in the coffee shop on the highway, trying to warm his hands around his coffee cup, and wonders what she's doing. He's already tried to call her a half dozen times. He tried the hotel every ten minutes until finally the operator said, yes, they've checked in, and put him through to their room. Carmen's mother answered, though, so Moe hung up. He tried again a few minutes later and the phone rang and rang and no one answered.

He didn't really plan to go to Carmen, it just kind of happened. He was walking along Albert Street, heading north to D. J.'s to play pool, and when a bus came along he got on it and when the stop for D. J.'s came up, he didn't get off. He rode the bus as far north as it would take him, and then he walked to the highway and right away he got a ride, except the guy who picked him up turned off at St. Pierre an hour later. Moe tried for ages to get another ride. Finally his hands got so cold he went into the coffee shop and ordered coffee and fries. Now here he sits. He's thinking about calling the hotel again from the pay phone, when who comes walking in but Dixie, his mother's case worker.

"Moe," she says, sitting down at the table with him and taking off her coat. "I thought that was you. What are you doing here?"

"Trying to get a ride to Saskatoon," he says. "Which way are you going?" He anticipates her answer, hoping she's going his way.

"Wrong direction," she says. "I'm on my way home. I'll give you a lift back if you want." Then she adds, "I don't think you should be standing out there on the highway at night."

Moe thinks for a minute, then decides he'll keep going. The waitress comes by with the coffee pot and a cup for Dixie.

"Does your mother know you're going to Saskatoon?" Dixie asks.

"Yeah," he lies. "I'm going to hook up with my girlfriend and her mother. They invited me for the weekend but they had to leave right after lunch. Her brother has a basketball tournament or something. I don't know. Maybe it's soccer."

"Where are you staying?" she asks, and he tells her the name of Carmen's hotel; he sees no reason to lie. He notices her looking at his hands wrapped around his coffee cup.

"Don't you have any gloves with you?" she asks.

"I forgot them," Moe says.

Dixie laughs. "You won't believe this," she says, "but I was just forced to buy these nylon things that I will never, ever wear. Don't ask me about it, it's a long, dumb story. They're too big for me. Maybe they'll fit you." She hands Moe the new gloves.

"Thanks," he says.

"Watch my coat, will you?" Dixie says. "I'm going to the washroom."

She takes her purse with her, but she leaves her keys on the table. Moe looks out the window and tries to remember what kind of car she drives – a new one, a white Honda of some kind. He sees it in the parking lot and thinks, I could take her car. The ease with which the idea came into his head surprises him. He's not a thief, has never stolen anything in his life.

The car is there, just outside the window. The keys are in front of him on the table. The desire to get to Carmen grows deeper as he looks at the keys, and suddenly a line is crossed and the desire is deeper than the fear of what will happen to him. His hand reaches over and picks up the keys. He tells himself, Dixie isn't a stranger, it wouldn't be as bad as taking a stranger's car, there's even a chance that she wouldn't call the police. He takes a five dollar bill out of his wallet and puts it on the table, stuffs the gloves in his jacket pockets and ducks out the door.

Dixie comes out of the washroom and sees that Moe is no longer sitting at the table. Through the window, she sees her car pulling onto the highway and heading north.

"Damn," she says. "Goddamn it to hell." She stands there, looking out into the growing darkness, and tries to decide what to do. She knows she should call the police immediately, but she also knows about Moe's clean record. He's not a bad kid and if she calls the police he'll become a bad kid, on paper and at school and in everybody's minds forever forward. She's seen it happen.

"Goddamn it," she says again.

"Something wrong?" A man seated at a table nearby is looking at her. She decides quickly. Everybody in this coffee shop is heading either north or south. There's a fifty-fifty chance and he looks harmless enough, an older man with grey hair, probably a business-man of some kind. "Yeah," she says. "I have to get to Saskatoon and I'm having car trouble. They can fix it here but it'll take a few days to get parts."

"I'm on my way back to Saskatoon," the man says. "I can give you a lift."

"No kidding," she says. "What good fortune."

"I'm just about to leave," the man says. "But I'll wait for you if you're not ready to go. I don't mind."

"Whenever you're ready," Dixie says.

"I'll meet you outside then," the man says.

Dixie can't believe it, cannot believe Moe stole her car. She shakes another couple of Tylenol capsules out of the bottle and downs them with what's left of her coffee. Then she picks up her coat, the grocery bag with the rosary beads in it, and the check. She notices the five dollar bill on the table and leaves it for a very large tip.

When she gets outside, Dixie sees that the man has pulled up to the door. He's driving a Cavalier.

"You must work for the government," she says as she gets in.

"Why do you say that?" he asks.

"The car," she says.

"Oh," he says, "I see. But no. I sell advertising."

"I have a splitting headache," she says. "I'm probably not going to be very good company."

"I sympathize," the man says. "Car trouble's enough to give anyone a headache."

"You have no idea the kind of day I've had," she says.

"I can imagine," the man says. "I've had a few bad ones myself."

The white Acura is out of sight, but Dixie knows it's up ahead with a young car thief at the wheel. She tries to stay really angry to keep from feeling humiliated. Or frightened. Who knows if the kid's ever driven on the highway?

"Damn," she says.

"I sympathize," the man says again.

Carmen follows the cobblestone pathway, which is not really cobblestone, but rather is indoor-outdoor carpet with a cobblestone pattern. Every so often the path splits and antique-looking signposts give directions – ironwork arrows pointing to the dance floor, the swimming pool, the exercise room. To enter each area you have to pass through a white iron gate with horse heads on either side. Carmen feels like she's in some kind of theme park, one of those places that line the highway in touristy parts of the country, the places her mother would always want to visit and her father wouldn't and they would argue and her mother would always win, even though

Carmen never wanted to stop and Daniel was too young to care one way or the other.

She follows the music to an elevated hardwood dance floor. Small bar tables are placed around the edge of the dance floor and the whole area is enclosed by a white fence, which is decorated with a string of pink and blue twinkle lights. Carmen suspects that she is not supposed to go inside the fence because of her age, but she wants to see what goes on here so she boldly opens the gate and steps inside. She picks a table close to the gate so that she can leave in a hurry if she sees a waiter walking officiously toward her.

What is going on here that Carmen thought she wanted to see isn't much. A young couple is sitting at one of the little tables sipping at pink drinks that look, from a distance, like Pepto-Bismol. The woman is wearing a tight sweater, a short flared skirt and very high heels. She says something to her companion, and they stand up. Carmen thinks if they leave and a waiter doesn't come right away, she'll go over and check out the half-finished drinks. They don't leave though. They prance to the middle of the dance floor and the woman curtseys to Carmen, then makes a great display of kicking off her high heels, which skid across the hardwood floor and come to a stop at Carmen's feet. Losers, Carmen thinks. She gives one of the shoes another kick and it slides off the dance floor and into a plant pot. "Hey," the woman says, but then she turns her attention to her partner, who is holding out his hand to her and making heavy eye contact. Their idiocy is confirmed when they begin doing some kind of salsa dance thing. Carmen decides to leave before she pukes. She slips the woman's other high heel into her backpack and goes out through the gate again.

Dixie tries to act like a person whose irritation is caused by her car breaking down. She doesn't tell the man that, in truth, the white Acura just ahead of them on the highway is her car, the first new car she's ever owned. When he gets too close to it Dixie says, "I hate to sound ungrateful, but I get really nervous travelling with someone else. Would you mind not following the car in front of us too close?" She doesn't think it would be a good thing for Moe to figure out she's in the car right behind him. He might panic and do something stupid, like pull off too quickly onto a grid road and roll, or decide a Hollywood-type high-speed chase is right up his alley. She doesn't think he'd do that, but then she didn't think he'd steal her car either. Dixie feels stupid asking the man to slow down. She herself can't stand nervous passengers who give advice. But the man is very polite and slows down a little.

"My wife is a nervous driver," the man says. "I think most women are. Because they don't have as much experience behind the wheel, I guess."

It kills Dixie to let that go by but she does in the interest of keeping up her pretext. And she's glad he mentioned a wife. Not that she's worried, but if he were the type to hit on a woman, he wouldn't be mentioning his wife.

"Maybe it's just natural," she says. "A genetic kind of thing."

"Oh, I don't think so," the man says. "I don't think that's it. I wouldn't go that far." Then he asks, "So what line of work are you in?"

"Social work," Dixie says. "I'm a social worker."

"Now there's an occupation that's never tempted me," the man says.

"Why's that?"

"Oh, I don't know. Too depressing, I guess. Too many hopeless cases. Take this woman who lives next door to my sister. Single, of course, on welfare, and she keeps having kids. That's the thing. She can't afford them but she keeps having kids." He looks at her. "Now what would you as a social worker do about a situation like that?"

Dixie is about to say she'd try to keep the kids from starving to death, but just at that moment a deer darts from the ditch onto the highway right in front of them. The deer freezes in the lights and Dixie can see it coming at her, can see it coming up over the hood and through the windshield, but the man swerves and manages, somehow, to miss it.

"Whew," he says when he has the car under control again. "That was a close call. Are you okay?"

She can still see the deer's big eyes looking at her through the windshield. "I'm not sure," she says.

"Do you want me to pull over for a minute?" the man asks.

"No," she says, "I'm all right. Just give me a minute to get my heart back in my chest."

"I'm really sorry about that," the man says. "You try to pay attention, but you can't see them. There's no way you can see them at this time of night. I'm really sorry."

"Forget about it," Dixie says. "At least we didn't hit it."

"That's right," the man says. "Thank God for that."

The revolving lounge promises more of interest than the dance floor, but Carmen figures that her chances of getting in are pretty slim. A hostess, an elegant middle-aged woman in a sequined dress, is seating people and Carmen just knows this woman would I.D. her. She finds a spot in the jungle of potted palms, pink hydrangeas and twenty-foot-high fig trees, crouches down and creeps forward until the lounge revolves just a few feet from her. She's well hidden in the greenery, which is humid and smells like a florist shop.

About a third of the lounge is an open platform. The rest of it is closed off by the bar and by the backs of a number of velour-upholstered booths. To step up to the lounge, people have to wait on the path until the platform revolves very slowly to the open side again, and then the hostess beckons them. There's a piano by the bar, which a woman in a black gown is playing, but it's impossible to make out the tune. The sound mixes with the music from the dance floor and the fans and the trickling of the water until it all becomes one homogenized din.

As the lounge revolves, Carmen can see what's going on only part of the time. She's especially interested in three women in their mid-twenties who are sitting at a table near the platform's edge. One of the women is pale and overweight. The other two, a blonde and a redhead, are vivacious and have career clothes and good haircuts. Carmen tries to make out what they're saying. If she really concentrates, she can do it. She can isolate their words and listen to their conversation for about half of each rotation.

What Carmen gathers is that the pale woman has just been fired from her secretarial job and she doesn't know why. She thinks it's because she's too shy, she isn't very good with the public. The blonde and the redhead, whose name Carmen gathers is Diana, appear to be concerned. They try to convince her that it's better she lost the job.

"It was a terrible place to work," the blonde says.

"Yeah," says Diana. "Your boss was a jerk. A real jerk. You don't need a job where you have to work for a jerk like that. Nobody does."

"And another thing," says the blonde. "The hours were way too long. There are labour standards, you know. You could probably phone somebody about him. I'll bet you could get him in big trouble if you wanted to. I would. If it was me, I'd phone somebody."

"You can make more money someplace else," says Diana. "After you get another job with higher pay, you'll be glad that creep fired you. I think you should get on the phone right now. Go use the phone in the lobby. Just phone and ask some questions or something," says Diana.

"It's too late," says the blonde woman. "They'll be closed. She'll have to call tomorrow."

"Oh yeah. Well, tomorrow's not too late." Diana looks at her friend who has been fired. "You are going to phone, aren't you? I mean, we know you're shy, but this is your chance to get that bastard in trouble."

"I don't know," says the woman. "I don't like to fight with people. I'll think about it, though."

"I hope you'll do more than think about it," Diana says. "I know I would if it were me."

They disappear from Carmen's view and when they come around again the pale woman is wiping her eyes vigorously with a tissue.

"Don't do it like that," Diana is saying to her. "You'll get make-up all over your face. Here. Like this." She shows her how to dab.

Carmen decides the blonde and the redhead are not really sympathetic at all. They're excited that the woman who's crying got herself fired; now they can give her advice and tell her what to do with her life. Carmen feels sorry for the woman, and feeling sorry makes her remember where she is and that she wants to be at home. If she were at home she might be talking to Moe. Sometimes at night when they're not together he calls her from a pay phone. He doesn't say much, he just checks in. Once he knocked on her bedroom window after she'd gone to bed and she snuck out and they went to the park, lay on their backs and looked at the stars and promised each other they would die before they'd ever work for computer companies.

Carmen tries lying on her back in the jungle of plants. She looks straight up and sees people looking over the railing from various floors above her. She wonders if any of them can see her, but she doesn't believe they can. She waves and nobody waves back. She looks up beyond the people to the smoky haze under the skylight. She imagines that something comes crashing through – space debris, maybe, or a meteorite. She wants it, closes her eyes and tries to will it, but nothing happens. She plays with the little silver medal hanging on a chain around her neck. Moe gave it to her. It's a medal with St. Jude on it, the patron saint of lost causes. Moe said there's a saint for lost objects, too, St. Anthony. A friend of his mother prayed to St. Anthony every day after her house was broken into and her VCR stolen. Eventually the police found the VCR and gave it back to her, and she was convinced St. Anthony had intervened. Moe thought it was funny, just like he thought it was funny there's a saint for lost causes. Carmen wonders if she should give the St. Jude medal to the woman who's crying in the lounge.

She sits up and watches the women come around again. Things have changed. She must have missed a couple of revolutions. For one thing, there are only two women now. The sad one is gone. And for another, two men are sitting at the table, one of them in a baseball uniform and the other wearing a fancy jacket and tie. They're both acting like they have big plans for the evening. The women are laughing and have apparently forgotten all about their friend and her problems. There are two rounds of drinks on the table. Carmen wishes she'd seen the circumstances of the third woman's exit, but she didn't, and now that the woman is gone Carmen's no longer interested in what's happening here. She knows all about it anyway. It's so predictable, even a baby like Daniel could figure it out.

She decides to put on a show, just for fun, for her own amusement. Still hidden by the plants, she takes off her jacket and T-shirt, turns them inside out, then puts them on again. She takes off her shoes and one sock and sticks them in her backpack, rolls up the legs of her jeans, digs around the roots of a fig tree for a handful of dirt and rubs it all over herself.

When she puts her hand into the soil for more dirt, she feels a hard object, like the handle of a hammer or an axe. Her hand closes around it and she tugs, freeing it from the dirt and roots. It's a bone. She stares at it. What kind of bone? A human bone, she imagines, a very old human bone. She feels as though she has something sacred in her hand and lies down again, hugging the bone to her chest. She thinks about ancient people, millions of them dead now, billions even, and the future, about astronauts and space stations, life in other galaxies. She thinks about the bone. What part of the body? Whose body? And how did it end up here, in this hotel, wrapped in the roots of a fig tree? Maybe the tree was imported and the bone came with it from some country near the equator where it's warm and fig trees grow naturally. She imagines the bone as a small dark person in a forest of exotic trees. She can't decide if it's terrible or miraculous that some part of that person travelled unwittingly so far from home, to such a strange place, a garden, but not even a real garden, to end up in her own warm hand.

Carmen sits up and digs in her backpack for a soft rayon scarf she knows is in there somewhere. She pulls the stolen shoe out and hangs it by its heel from one of the lower branches of the tree. Then she digs in her pack again and finds the scarf – red, with little silver threads running through the weave and silver fringes all around the edges. Her father and Becky gave it to her for Christmas, along with a pair of red gloves and some silver earrings. Carmen takes the medal Moe gave her from around her neck and lays it in the scarf, then she places the bone next to it. She remembers the peppermints, takes two of them out of her pocket and places them with the medal and the bone. She wraps the scarf and its contents into a bundle, carefully lays it under the tree, and then covers it with a sprinkling of soft dirt.

When the two women and their boisterous companions are close to Carmen again, she crawls out of the bushes on her hands and knees, shaking dirt from her hair and spitting it from her mouth.

"I've travelled here from another time," she says to them when she sees they're watching her. She intends it to be smart-alecky and belligerent, but as she says it she feels self-conscious and embarrassed. She stares at the two couples, if that's what they are now, and they stare back as the lounge turns them out of sight. Carmen ambles down the path, feeling, inexplicably, as though she really is from another time.

Dixie is relieved that Moe appears to be driving within the speed limit. She hopes he has a legal driver's licence and the presence of mind to know what to do if another deer jumps up out of the ditch. She tries to remember exactly how old he is and thinks, sixteen, maybe seventeen. He's driven a car before, that's obvious, but his mother doesn't own one, so how would he get a licence? Dixie just hopes, for his sake, that he makes it to Saskatoon without getting stopped by the police. She doesn't think she's prepared to lie for him, and the RCMP watch this stretch of highway like hawks.

"That's a nice-looking car in front of us," the man says. "I notice you've got your eye on it."

"I'm thinking about getting a new one," Dixie says. "The one I have is giving me no end of trouble." She realizes as she speaks that her headache is spreading down into the bones of her face, her jaw even. The Tylenol didn't do a thing.

She tries to carry on a conversation with the man even though her head feels terrible and she's thinking about Moe and what to do. She questions her own judgement. Maybe she's too lenient, too trusting. She's the one, after all, who left her keys on the table in front of Moe. But what's wrong with that? The alternative is to assume that every kid and every stranger is going to rob you blind or stab you in the back. But the little shit did steal her car. It's a fact. And now she's heading back to Saskatoon instead of home to a hot bath.

"If I myself were in the market for a car, I would look at the new domestic models," the man says. "I've never been much for the foreign cars. That's a Japanese make in front of us, I believe."

"Really?" Dixie says.

"Yes," the man says. "I believe it is. A Honda perhaps. They say you can drive those Japanese cars for years without a thing going wrong. But now, with the domestic cars getting better and the foreign cars getting so expensive, I think people will give our own makes another look. I think the end is near for the imports."

Dixie watches the interior light in the Acura come on for half a minute, then go off again. She imagines Moe looking at his watch, calculating how much longer until he's where he wants to be.

"I notice you didn't bring any luggage," the man says. "You must live in Saskatoon. Must have been south for just the day, I guess."

"That's right," Dixie says. She doesn't bother telling him that her toothbrush and her eye make-up and her appointment calendar are in a tapestry shoulder bag in the back seat of the car in front of them. She hasn't been thinking of these personal things, she's been thinking only of the car.

"Well," Dixie says, trying to sound casual, "how can you really tell the difference any more between the domestic cars and the imports? They make Toyotas in Canada. They make Chevs in Mexico."

"You've got a point," the man says. "But costs, tariffs, import taxes, that's how you tell the difference. That's the bottom line."

Dixie thinks, Moe stole my car, that's the bottom line. She wishes he'd taken a stranger's car. If he had, she wouldn't know, at least not yet, and she'd be home by now and probably in the bathtub drinking Scotch with a frozen Magic Bag on her head. The RCMP would be after Moe, and punishment would be determined by the system, not by her. Really, though, what she wishes is that Moe hadn't stolen any car. She's not hard enough to want him punished. For whatever reason, she just doesn't have it in her.

Carmen comes to a fork in the path. A sign tells her the swimming pool is in one direction and the English tearoom in the other. She decides to check out the tearoom. She doesn't like tea, but this seems to be an evening for trying things out. She stops at the next park bench and puts her shoes back on and turns her jacket right side out again. When she stands up she gives herself a good shake so most of the dirt falls off her clothes and onto the path.

The tearoom is situated in a sunken pit, surrounded by a circular stone wall. Plants hang over the top of the wall. Many of them are blooming and the flowers are various shades of pink and purple. The tables and chairs are white wicker. The tables have white linen cloths. Carmen doesn't like the look of this place at all, but has to admit it's the kind of place where you can't believe anything bad could happen to you. You could turn it into a watercolour painting and hang it in the children's ward of a hospital.

The tearoom is empty except for the waitress and an old couple with china teacups on the table in front of them, the kind Carmen's grandmother used to have but sold at a garage sale before she moved into the seniors' place.

Carmen chooses a table and sits down. As she does, dirt falls out of her hair and lands on the white tablecloth. She quickly brushes it off, but not before the waitress sees it.

"Excuse me," the waitress says, "but you'll have to leave." She has an English accent and is wearing a pink flowered dress with a little white apron over it.

"Why?" Carmen asks.

"Please don't make a scene," the waitress says. "The management reserves the right not to serve people."

"Are you the management?" Carmen asks. She deepens her voice, trying to sound older. Who'd have thought she'd be refused service in a tearoom? Maybe she should have tried the lounge.

"I am not the management, but I can very quickly get the management," the waitress says. "Now don't spoil the evening for these people. These are nice quiet people having their tea."

Carmen decides she really does want a cup of hot tea. And what was it her mother said goes with tea in an English tearoom? Scones. She wants a scone, with jam. She weighs her chances of winning an argument with this woman. She thinks polite is probably the only thing that will work.

"I'm sorry about the dirt," she says. "Maybe I can shake it off."

"Go and change your clothes and wash your hair and then come back," says the waitress. "We'll see about a nice cup of tea then." The woman's eyes say that she will never serve Carmen a cup of tea, even if she comes back with her skin scrubbed pink. Carmen notices that the old man has turned around in his chair and is listening to her exchange with the waitress. She decides she hates both of them, the waitress and the nosy old man.

"I have royal blood," she says. "I'll bet you don't turn away people with royal bloodlines just because they have a bit of dirt in their hair. If Prince Charles walked in you'd serve him, even though he's been bonking that Camilla woman. Talk about dirt."

"That does it," the waitress says. "I'm calling security." She turns and walks quickly toward a gate that appears to lead to the kitchen.

"Just a minute," the old man says. The waitress stops. In an instant the man is at Carmen's side and has her by the hair, lifting her from her seat and dragging her toward the stairs that lead back up to the entrance gate and the pathway. Carmen screams.

"I'll show you, young lady. I'll show you to be insolent," the man says.

"That's not necessary, sir," the waitress calls. "We are equipped to handle these things."

"Help me," Carmen screams to the waitress. She hears somebody saying, "Stop that. Stop that right now. She's just a girl." It's not the waitress. It must be the man's wife. The man pushes Carmen up the steps and against the gate, forcing it open, still holding her by the hair. She tries to kick at him, screaming, but she can't because she's in too much pain. He's pulling all her hair out. When he has her through the gate he lets her go, giving her a little shove down the path. Carmen holds her head, tries her hardest not to cry.

"Go home and learn a little respect," he shouts at her. "Didn't your parents teach you anything?"

"You old bastard," Carmen shouts. "You fucking old bastard." She runs down the path, away from the tearoom, but she's mixed up now about where exactly the path goes. She hears somebody calling after her.

"Are you all right, miss?" It's the waitress.

She ignores her; it's too late now for sympathy. Why didn't somebody step in when the man grabbed her, why did they just watch, the waitress and the wife, two stupid women watching him do his stupid fucking macho thing, like he was trying to prove his testosterone supply is still above the fill line? He could have really hurt her, broken something, her arm or even her neck when he twisted her head and shoved her through the gate. She hates women like them, all polite and scared to stand up to a stupid old man.

Carmen frantically searches for a signpost to tell her where the hotel lobby is. She needs to find a telephone that can connect her to the outside world and Moe. When she finally gets to the lobby, she can't wait to take the elevator up to their room. She needs to talk to Moe right now, right this second. She calls collect from a pay phone. It rings and rings and rings and he doesn't answer.

Moe knows that Dixie is in the car behind him. He spots her when the car pulls up as though it's going to pass, but then drops back again right away. He doesn't care that she's behind him, he'll deal with her later, give some reason for taking the car. At least she hasn't called the police, not yet anyway. He watches the car in the rearview mirror. It stays a steady distance behind him. He remembers that he told Dixie exactly where he was going. Dumb. But then again, maybe that will help his defence. He obviously didn't premeditate this crime.

The new Acura is a nice car. It has soft red upholstery and a glass sunroof, like a skylight. When he looks up he can see stars. He reaches for a disc in the dark, takes the first one his hand lands on and slips it into the CD player. Surprise me, he thinks, but then he isn't surprised because it's Garth Brooks or somebody like him and that's just the kind of music he would have guessed Dixie likes. When he reaches to pick up another disc, his hand lands on a hard plastic object. He flicks the interior light on to see what it is. A cell phone. He pushes the power button and dials the hotel number, which he has memorized because he dialed it so many times earlier in the evening, then he flips the interior light off again. The hotel operator answers and Moe asks for Carmen's room. The phone rings in the dark and no one answers. Too bad, Moe thinks. It would have been fun to say to Carmen, "Guess where I'm calling from?"

Carmen takes the elevator up to the fifth floor where their hotel room is, but she doesn't want to go inside. She doesn't want to see the double bed she'll have to share with her mother tonight, doesn't want to turn the television on, or look at herself and her dirty hair in the mirror. She stands in the hallway and looks down at the world below her. She glares at the tops of the pink umbrellas in the tearoom, picks out the one hiding the old man's table from her view. She looks up and thinks again of space debris coming through the skylight, part of a Russian satellite, only this time she pictures it smashing through the pink umbrella. She wishes she really were telekinetic so she could stare at the umbrella until it exploded in a ball of fire, like in a horror movie. She tries to make it explode but of course nothing happens.

She finds the spot where she lay hidden in the bushes next to the lounge. She was right: no one could see her from above. She picks out the dance floor with its twinkle lights. Now that it's later in the evening, there are a lot of dancers on the floor and several more people seated at the bar tables. Although she doesn't care, not one bit, Carmen wonders what the woman with the high heels did when she couldn't find her shoe.

Carmen sees the stream with its turquoise-blue bottom and follows it as it weaves around the umbrellas and the fig trees. She follows the stream to its source and sees that it begins and ends at the swimming pool, which is just now empty. It won't be empty for long, she thinks, not with the basketball players coming back for the night. The empty pool looks blue and inviting. She takes the elevator down, follows the path into the maze and finds the sign that says SWIMMING POOL. The path leads her through another white gate onto the pool deck.

There's still no one here, not even an attendant. Carmen takes off her socks and shoes and sits on the edge of the pool, dangling her legs in the water. One leg of her jeans is still rolled up, but the other isn't and she lets it get wet. Little particles of dirt float away from her. The water is cool. Her head hurts all over from the old man pulling her hair. She thinks she'll die if she can't talk to Moe. She could run away, she thinks, just head out and hitchhike home and go to all Moe's friends' houses, all the coffee shops where he hangs out, D. J.'s where he goes to play pool, searching everywhere until she finds him. But she can't do that. She would be afraid.

The water feels cool and she wants to be in it, all of her. She takes off her jacket and throws it on top of her shoes, then lowers herself into the pool. She pretends she's a seal and dives under the water. The cool water makes her head feel good.

When Moe gets to the hotel, he's relieved to see that Dixie is no longer behind him. In the city traffic he managed to lose her. He knows she'll be close, but that's all right, he just needs a few minutes to get into the hotel and then it should be easy to avoid her, until he can find Carmen. After that, he doesn't care what happens.

He parks carefully, steps out of the car and locks it, leaving Dixie's keys inside on the driver's seat. Maybe that's a mistake, he thinks, maybe it will just piss her off more, but he doesn't want the keys now that he's here; they make him feel like a car thief. He hopes Dixie has a second set in her purse. If she does, she can drive home and all she'll be out is a few hours of her time. What's a few hours? His need to see Carmen has got to be greater than her need to be home. He has to think of a way to convince her that he was desperate. He feels the nylon gloves in his pocket and wonders if he should have left them on the seat too. Then he thinks, no, he doesn't want to appear ungrateful.

When he gets inside the hotel he doesn't know how to begin looking for Carmen. He tries wandering around the courtyard, but it's hopeless, everything is hidden by the trees and flowers. He looks up and sees people peering down over the railing, sees that he can get an aerial view from up there. He takes the elevator to the third floor and when he looks down he sees Carmen in the pool, knows right away that it's her. He wants to call out, but then he thinks Dixie might be in the hotel by now. He laughs as he watches

Carmen, floating and diving with all her clothes on. He doesn't know a single other person who would do that.

When they reach the Saskatoon city limits, the man asks Dixie where she lives.

"Just drop me wherever it's convenient," she says. "I'll catch a cab."

"No need for that," the man says. "Just tell me where you want to go. I've got lots of time."

She tells him. He looks surprised.

"I'm meeting a friend from out of town," she says quickly. "I don't have time to go home first."

"I see," the man says.

He drives her to the hotel, passes by the Acura in the parking lot and pulls into the loading zone by the front doors. She thanks the man profusely, then realizes as he's pulling away that she left the bottle of Tylenol and the rosary beads on the seat next to him. She writes them off and goes looking for Moe.

When Moe gets down to the pool, Carmen's still paddling around. He takes off his jacket and boots and slips into the water. After all it's taken to get here, after all the urgency, he doesn't say a word to her, and she doesn't say anything to him. They just paddle around like two seals until Carmen hears the basketball players coming, shouting and laughing, shoving up against one another probably, trying to act like real basketball players, real men. Carmen swims to the spot where the water from the swimming pool spills over into the stream. She flops like a seal over the cement wall. Moe follows. Carmen knows they're visible from above as long as they're in the water, so she propels herself along quickly with her hands on the bottom. She imagines goldfish in the stream, flashing along ahead of her, darting out of her way. When she reaches a spot close to the revolving lounge, she crawls up out of the water and into the foliage, crawls to the spot where she left the red-and-silver scarf and its contents. She and Moe hide under the fig tree, among the palms and the hydrangeas, with mud on their hands and knees. She points to the high-heeled shoe hanging from a branch above them, and they both laugh. She says, "Pretend it's a thousand years from now." He nods. She brushes the dirt off the bundle and hands it to him. He unwraps it carefully and studies its contents. He picks up the St. Jude medal and says, "What should I do with this?" "Whatever you want," Carmen says. He puts it back around her neck. She takes the two peppermints and puts one in Moe's mouth and the other in her own. The dirt from her hands gets in her teeth. Carmen asks, "What do think we should do with the bone?" Moe looks at it for a long time, turns it over and over in his hands, then he stands up, steps out into the open and flings it as hard as he can, as high as he can, up toward the skylights.

Dixie looks over the railing from the third floor. She sees Carmen and Moe make their amphibious way along the stream and then crawl up on the bank and disappear into the plants. Briefly, Dixie feels as though she's watching something significant, the first life leaving the sea, perhaps. Then she tells herself, the significant thing is, there's no real harm done. Her car is in the parking lot, she's safe, Moe is safe. She decides she'll more or less forget about the stolen car. She'll book a room, have dinner and several glasses of wine, watch a movie in bed. She'll have to talk to Moe, of course, it would be irresponsible not to, although what she'll say, she hasn't got a clue. It's wrong to take things that don't belong to you, she can at least remind him of that.

She sees Moe stand up and throw the bone into the air. She doesn't know what it is, but it gleams like a piece of ivory. She watches, puzzled, until she loses it in the glare of the lights.

Carmen's mother sees Moe throw the bone, too. There's a direct line from where she's sitting poolside under a blue umbrella to where Moe is standing among the potted plants. She's not surprised to see him, she already knew he was here somewhere, knew from the jacket and the black boots next to Carmen's shoes on the pool deck. She watches and feels a sense of terror as the bone ascends.

Michelangelo

Dean Quigly wondered this: why was everyone he knew so inclined to turn a simple event – a corollary to ordinary living – into something momentous? Take parenthood. Its onset supposedly brought about vast changes, but he had an eight-month-old child and nothing profound had happened as a result of her birth. True, he had never seen the child. He had, though, been perfectly willing to accept his responsibility as a biological father. He had an arrangement with the child's mother, which had been arrived at amicably and with no grief to anyone.

And then there was home ownership. He was mystified that his purchase of real estate had caused so much excitement. In fact, there'd been nothing to it. He'd simply looked at a few houses, thought about it for a day or two, then called his agent and told her which one he wanted. So why all the fuss about such routine matters? Was there something wrong with him that he was immune? He didn't think so.

The new house, which Dean had comfortably settled into, was on a corner lot in an older part of the city. The area was definitely not upscale, but it wasn't exactly bohemian either. He had no idea who else lived on the block, with the exception of his next door neighbour. He'd have preferred not even knowing who lived next door but that was impossible. After all, he could see his neighbour over the fence and he had felt compelled to introduce himself when she moved in shortly after he did. She was about thirty-five (his own age), neither attractive nor unattractive, and the way she dressed on weekdays led him to believe she had some kind of office job. By his definition, she was a good neighbour: she left him alone. They backed their cars out of their garages at about the same time each morning and usually didn't bother waving. They had an unspoken agreement, one of mutual indifference.

One Saturday afternoon in June, the agreement came to an end. Dean was in a summer fog, basking on his deck like a cat, when he happened to look over his shoulder and there she was, profiled in a corner of her dining room window, her face ugly with anger, her lips silently shouting at someone he couldn't see. He quickly turned away. Anger in women made him uncomfortable. It frightened him far more than did anger in another man, which was predictable and familiar.

It occurred to him that he could have been mistaken about what he'd seen, so he chanced another look. There was no mistake. She was positively out of control with anger, shaking first one fist at someone, and then the other. He thought he saw a flash of silver. A knife? Or perhaps just her watch band, or a silver bracelet.

He tried to return to his blissful state on the sunny deck, but he couldn't. He was aware of his neighbour now and, although he found anger unattractive, he was strangely excited. She was close, just feet away from him. What he really wanted to do was turn his chair right around and watch her, let her anger excite him to the point of desire. But as soon as he thought of that, his own desire, he became disturbed and wished he hadn't seen anything at all. He went inside for a cold drink, carefully keeping his eyes away from her window, and got a grip on his imagination. She wasn't his type. It was an altered reality he'd experienced, half asleep in the sun, open to suggestion.

He was about to stir a pitcher of lemonade with an egg flipper when someone knocked on his back door. When he went to answer it, he saw that it was her. At first he was embarrassed, as though he'd had an erotic dream about her the night before and here she was, in the flesh. Then he had a terrible feeling that she was going to ask him to get involved in a domestic dispute.

"Hi," she said. "I hope I'm not disturbing you."

"No," he said. "I was just … well, doing nothing, really." He still had the egg flipper in his hand. He saw her looking at it and realized he was holding it as though he was standing at the ready with a weapon of some kind.

"Expecting unwelcome visitors, were you?" she said, looking at the egg flipper.

He tried to think of an explanation. Then he realized he didn't have to explain because she was smiling. She wasn't expecting an explanation.

How could she smile, he wondered, when just five minutes ago she'd been so angry? And why was she here? Did she want him to phone the police? If so, she was certainly taking her time.

"Look," she said, "I feel like an idiot, but there you go. I've gone and locked myself out. I was just about to go golfing, and what with trying to remember my clubs and my cap and my sunscreen, I left my keys on the kitchen counter. House, car, garage, you name it, they're all there."

"Oh," he said, surprised by the everyday nature of her predicament, trying to calculate whether or not there'd been time for all this since her outburst. "Well. Do you want me to call a locksmith for you?"

"Actually," she said, "I think I can get in the kitchen window if you just give me a boost. It's open a crack. Or I could go up a ladder if you have one."

"No," he said, his heart sinking because there didn't seem to be a way to avoid direct involvement. "No ladder. But I guess I can give you a boost." He put the egg flipper down on the counter and followed her out onto his deck.

"My name is Candace," she said. "But you probably remember that."

"Of course," he said, even though he didn't.

"And you're Doug."

He didn't correct her, even though his name wasn't Doug. He was glad she didn't really know his name; it didn't matter. He would give her a boost through her kitchen window, and then he would insist, through rudeness if need be, that they go back to more or less ignoring one another. He was already planning to turn her down if she asked if she could leave an extra key at his place. He would tell her he was never home and suggest she leave it with her neighbours on the other side.

"See," she said, when they reached the kitchen window. "I'm sure I can get in there." He looked up. It was open a crack, like she said, but it had to be at least eight feet off the ground. He would have to lift her to his shoulders for her to be able to crawl in.

"Don't worry," she said. "I'm agile. I won't break my neck."

It wasn't *her* neck he was worried about. He tried to guess how much she weighed, but he couldn't. She wasn't overweight by any means, but then again she was no waif.

"I don't know," he said. "That's a long way up."

"Let's try it," she said. "If I'm too heavy, I'll go round up a child from somewhere. You have a child, don't you?"

How did she know that? No one knew. Dean himself had known for only a short time. She must be mistaken, Dean thought, even though she wasn't really mistaken. He heard himself say, "I do. A very young child, though. She lives with her mother."

"I thought I'd seen one running around in the yard," she said.

"No," Dean said. "Impossible."

Candace kicked off her sandals, lifted one foot and placed her hands on the wall beneath the window. Dean squatted and hooked his hands together under her foot. She was wearing shorts and his face was right up against her bare white leg. He tried to judge its attractiveness as a leg, but he was too close to it. He had no perspective.

"Are you ready?" he asked.

"Anytime," she said.

He stood, trying to boost her with his legs rather than his back, thinking he was bound to pull something, when she scrambled up the wall like a monkey, pushed against the window and disappeared inside, head first.

"Thank you very much, Doug," she called. Her voice sounded as though it was far away, disappearing inside a tunnel.

She was out the back door again and pulling her golf bag toward the garage before he had a chance to move away from the window.

"I have to run," she said, waving to him. "Thanks a million."

He went back into his own house and finished mixing his lemonade. He wondered how the recipient of her anger, a man no doubt, had got out of her house so fast, and then he thought maybe the man was still inside and had refused to open the door. Dean decided he'd been lucky to get away from the situation so easily. All the more reason to have nothing to do with her.

But the lemonade pitcher had a curve to it that reminded him of her bare calf disappearing through the window. He absently ran his hand around the cool contour of the pitcher.

He couldn't stop thinking about her, his neighbour, even when he was with Lily at a dinner party that night. He kept seeing her face, contorted with anger. He tried to get his mind off her by concentrating on the conversation, but when someone passed the gourmet chocolates, he wondered if she was ever called Candy. He dreamily decided that's what he would call her, and then he was annoyed with himself for deciding to call her anything. He wished she hadn't told him her name.

He looked at Lily, who was stunning in a black velvet dress with tiny shoulder straps. Lily, with whom, it seemed, he had in the last six months become one half of a couple. When he'd been invited to Bob and Charlotte's dinner party, Bob had said, "We're having a few people over. We were hoping you and Lily could make it." You and Lily. Lily and Dean. The next step was cohabitation. It was inevitable, he supposed. It occurred to him that he should tell Lily about the child, but he preferred not to. It was just an arrangement anyway. He could hardly remember the child's mother, or even the one-night thing that had resulted in the child. He would make his payments, just like he did with the house. There was no reason for anyone, including Lily, to know his business dealings. He knew very little about hers.

Lily had her own successful interior design business. That's how Dean had met her, when she'd redone his company's office space.

He worked for a small multimedia company as a marketing consultant, or at least that's what it said on his business cards. Really, he was a salesman. The company had moved into an abandoned brick warehouse on the cheap side of the tracks, and they'd hired Lily to make them look successful, which she had done on a very small budget. Why she'd given Dean more than a cursory look, he had no idea, and neither had anyone else in the company. She had huge dark eyes and was tall and thin like a model. She had modelled, in fact, but had given it up as a demeaning profession for women. When Dean finally had the nerve to ask about her interest in him, she told him she'd been married for a short time to a tennis professional and that the marriage had been a big mistake.

"It's unlike me," she said, "to have made such an obviously wrong choice. I'm known for my good judgement. But then," she added, "he was very, very good-looking. I won't make that mistake again."

"So that's why you're with me," Dean said.

"Yes," Lily said, "and I'm not going to let you get away with any of that vain male pouting. You can't hope to compete with a professional athlete. It's unreasonable for any ordinary man to think he could."

"So I'm ordinary then," he said.

"Apart from the red hair, yes," she said. "But don't fret, ordinary is good. It's what I like about you. You remind me of a good piece of furniture. Comfortable and enduring, with its own charm."

Comfortable and enduring, he wasn't sure about. But she'd added charm. That was the thing about Lily. She knew just what to say. And he believed her, believed that she could find ordinariness attractive even though she herself was anything but ordinary. When he thought about it, he had the best of both worlds. He could be himself and still be envied by other men, because he had Lily. It was an ideal combination.

He did find it irritating that Lily kept a plaster replica of Michelangelo's David in her apartment living room. It was anatomically correct and enviably perfect, at least in the physical sense, and in what other way could you judge a statue such as David? It was life-sized, although life-sized was a reduction from the original.

Lily informed him that Michelangelo strove to create a giant in David, a heroic figure for the common man to look up to.

As if Michelangelo was ordinary, Dean thought. His name and work had survived for more than five hundred years. More than survived. Multiplied. After all, there was one of David's progeny in Lily's apartment, along with various other statues and curiosities, although most of them were at Lily's temporarily, on their way to one office building or another. The statue of David was apparently there to stay. Dean had asked Lily about it once, if it had any special meaning for her. He was a bit worried that it reminded her of the tennis pro, but she'd simply said, "I picked it up for a song when Regis Interiors went under." She'd pointed to a brightly painted plaster elephant in the corner. "That too. Isn't he fabulous?" Dean was still looking at David when he nodded agreement. Think charm, Dean told himself. David was perfect but he, Dean, was charming.

"I'm mad about candy," Dean heard Lily say. Charlotte, their hostess, was passing the chocolates around again. "But of course I don't dare." Lily puffed out her cheeks.

"What are you talking about?" Charlotte said. "You don't need to worry."

"I do," Lily said. "You wouldn't believe how I put on weight."

Dean was struck by Lily's insensitivity. She weighed all of a hundred and fifteen pounds and was complaining. Every other woman at the dinner party was wearing long sleeves, and for good reason. They must hate her, he thought.

"It all started when I hit thirty," Lily went on. "The very day of my birthday I woke up with two little dimples, one on each cheek. The next day there were two more. Panic city. That's when I vowed I'd never eat another chocolate."

"I'd like to see your idea of a dimple," Charlotte said. "I haven't worn a bathing suit for five years, since Vanessa was born."

"I'd like to see her idea of a dimple too," said Bob. Lily laughed, just a bit too loudly, Dean thought. He tried to remember how many glasses of wine he'd seen her drink. Quite a few. Everybody knew how many calories were in a glass of wine. He was sure all the women in the room were calculating her caloric intake, amused at her turning down a few chocolates.

"Anyway," said Lily, "I'm mad about chocolates. I dream about them."

"For Christ's sake, have one then," said Dean.

Everybody, including Lily, stared at him.

"Oh dear," said Charlotte. "I must have accidentally put some cranky bits in the sauce. Did anyone else get any?"

"Come on, Lily," Dean said. "Time to go."

"It's early," Lily said.

"What's the rush?" Bob asked. "The night's just getting started."

Dean said, "I've got to get up in the morning. An early appointment."

"On a Sunday?" Lily asked when they were in the car. "An early appointment on a Sunday?"

"I'm going golfing," Dean said, which was a lie. He hadn't been golfing since high school. He hated golf.

Lily was quiet all the way to her apartment and Dean started to feel like a jerk. He thought he was going to have to apologize, but when they pulled up in front of her building Lily said, "You're coming in, aren't you?" Dean followed her inside. Lily undressed him in the living room and he couldn't help but watch himself in the mirror that lined one whole wall. He was so white. His red hair was the only colour he possessed, and it served to make the rest of him look paler in contrast. Lily was white, too, but she was porcelain white, smooth and flawless. He was pasty, like the Pillsbury dough boy. Where was the charm now? he wondered. He couldn't see it anywhere in the mirror.

Lily seemed to have forgotten his bad behaviour. She led him to the bedroom and made love to him on her antique cherry-wood bed, which she'd refinished herself. Dean's mind wandered. He pictured himself golfing for some reason, but that didn't satisfy him so he changed it to hang-gliding. He soared over open fields, doing exceptionally well, until he crashed.

Lily said, "I think men are sluts."

"What?" Dean said.

"They call women sluts, but really it's men. Women are capable of sex when they're not interested. Men aren't supposed to be, I mean there's a certain physical requirement, but I find they're always ready and willing."

Dean didn't know what to say to that. Maybe she hadn't forgotten his behaviour after all. Maybe she didn't think he was charming any longer. After Lily fell asleep, he got up and dressed in the living room with the dim light of the street lamp coming through the window. He was in front of the mirror again and he studied his own body and thought about the strange reality that it had reproduced, just like David's had, although the method was somewhat different. Dean thought about his offspring, the child he had not seen and probably never would see. A nagging thought came back to him. What if the child wasn't his? He had simply taken the mother's word for it when she called him; the dates were bang on. He decided that, although he had no desire to see the woman again, he would have to bring up the matter of a paternity test. Paternity was the sort of thing you should make certain of before you committed yourself to anything long term, and child support payments were definitely long term. Eighteen years at the very least. But if the child was his, he wanted to do the right thing. Of course he did.

Dean shivered and realized he was cold. In the mirror, he watched himself covering his body with clothing, genitals and abdomen first, then ankles and calves, his chest, one leg and the other. It was so mechanical. It unnerved him. When he put his hand down on the arm of the couch to steady himself, he felt the soft black velvet of Lily's dress. He wondered if Lily always undressed in this room with the mirrors, with David watching. He wondered, what is she doing with me anyway? Why not a football player? A football player was the closest he could come, in modern times and this city, to David. He went home to his own bed feeling disconnected: he couldn't put together his physical self and the person he knew he was. What did people really see when they looked at him?

When he got to work on Monday his boss, Clifford, was waiting for him with an airline ticket to Vancouver.

"You mean today?" Dean said. "You want me to go today?"

"It's urgent," Clifford said. "We had a call from a distributor. It's a bite. We have to get on it. Yesterday, if you know what I mean. Shirley's going, too."

"Why don't you just send her?" Dean asked.

"You know why," Clifford said. "Shirley's got the content, but she can't close a deal. She convinces them we know what we're doing, then you do your sales thing. That's the routine."

Dean sighed, then left to get an overnight bag. When he and Shirley travelled together, Dean always tried to ditch her at the end of the day so he wouldn't have to have dinner with her. He suspected that she was attracted to him and he avoided situations in which she might be tempted to confess her feelings.

On this particular trip she came right out and asked him to dinner. They were in the hotel elevator and she said, "Would you have dinner with me tonight, Quigly? There's something I want to talk over with you."

If she'd said something vague like, "Are you doing anything special for dinner?" Dean might have lied or pled fatigue. Because she was so deliberate, he found himself unable to lie. He suggested they meet in the hotel restaurant, which was not great as far as food went, but offered ease-of-parting after they'd had the dreaded conversation.

It turned out she didn't have a crush on him, or at least that's not what she wanted to talk to him about. Her long-distance husband – how could Dean have not known she was married? – had found a job in the city and was relocating, and they were planning to buy a house.

"You bought a house recently," Shirley said. "What about neigh-bourhoods? That's what I can't decide. North, south, downtown, I don't know. They say location is everything. How did you pick your neighbourhood?"

Dean couldn't say. His real estate agent had shown him the house because it was in his price range. He hadn't thought for a minute to question the location. He had a car. He could live anywhere.

"The thing is," Shirley said, "now that we're able to live in the same city, we'll be thinking about children. Did you consider that when you bought your house? I know you're single, but when you buy a house you have to assume you'll be living there for a while. Take schools, for example. Did you think about schools in the neighbourhood? Whether they offer French immersion, for one thing, but also the kind of kids who go to the school. You hear so much about gangs these days."

Dean said, no, he hadn't considered any of that, schools or French immersion or gangs, but that got him thinking about the child again. He wondered about her mother and whether she was the type to choose French immersion. He knew very little about her other than her name (Madeline Dawson – he wrote it on the cheque every month). What did she do for a living? Did she have university education? If she'd told him, he couldn't remember. Anyway, French immersion or not was no concern of his. The arrangement was, no contact, and that was that.

"What about your neighbourhood?" Shirley asked. "Would you recommend it? There are a few listings that look interesting. And it has the advantage of being near the parks. Although I suppose there's the worry about old plumbing and wiring and that sort of thing."

"I don't know," Dean said. "I don't know anything. The nearest school – haven't got a clue. And I couldn't tell you whether the plumbing in my house is old or new. I know it has plumbing, but that's about it."

"You didn't have a contractor check the house?" Shirley asked. She sounded incredulous.

"No," Dean said.

"What about the basement? Weren't you worried about that?"

Dean shook his head.

"Oh my," Shirley said.

"What does that mean?" Dean asked. "Did I do something stupid? What?"

Shirley pulled a piece of paper out of her purse. It was a checklist she'd put together with twenty-six criteria for evaluating a house. She handed it to Dean, who looked at it, then handed it back.

"I guess I'm not that thorough," Dean said with a sinking feeling.

"Well, Quigly," Shirley said, "I'm sure your real estate agent would have told you if she thought there were problems."

Dean remembered that when he'd called his agent to tell her which house he wanted she'd suggested they look at the house again. "Just to make sure," she had said. "We didn't spend much time in it, did we?" She'd sounded cautious, unduly so he believed, but now he wondered if there'd been a reason, one that had to do with an item on Shirley's checklist.

"Should we get some wine?" Shirley asked. "Red or white?"

"I don't care," Dean said. "You order." He hadn't had any trouble with the house, but then there hadn't been any really bad weather since he'd moved in. What if there was a torrential rainstorm? It happened once in a while. But he was being ridiculous. If the house was a lemon, he'd know it by now. He decided he should try to be a little more helpful. Now that he knew Shirley was married, she didn't seem quite so disagreeable.

"Is there anything else you want to know about my neighbourhood?" he asked her. "Tell me about the houses you're looking at. Maybe I know them."

"That's okay," Shirley said. "I'm not looking at them very seriously. White, I think. Let's start with white."

"Where are they exactly?" Dean asked. "What block?"

"Never mind," Shirley said. "Maybe red. It's kind of cool in here. Must be the ocean air. I've been cold all day."

She obviously didn't want to talk about houses any more. Shirley ate quickly, or at least Dean thought she did, and then she excused herself.

"I'm off, Quigly," she said. "I told Philip I'd call him."

For some reason, Dean found himself saying go to hell in his head as she walked away, as though she had just dumped him. And why did she think she could call him Quigly? It was too familiar.

When he got home the next night after failing to make the deal (he blamed it on Shirley), he checked his basement. He didn't know what he was looking for, but he didn't see anything bad.

Dean was planning to phone the child's mother about the paternity test, but she beat him to the call. She phoned and asked if he'd like to meet his daughter. She had changed her mind, she said, about

Dean's contact. There were some things they should discuss, she said, if Dean was interested in having some kind of relationship with the child. Dean tried to take in this new development. He didn't know what to think. It was easier when all she wanted from him was money. But if the child was really his, how could he say no? He decided there was nothing to do but meet with Madeline, tell her he wanted to confirm that he was the father, and then go from there.

As soon as Dean laid eyes on the baby, he threw out the idea of the paternity test. She had flaming red hair and looked just like him. It was incredible, even he could see it. Madeline said the resemblance was the main reason she had changed her mind about contact.

"She looks so much like you, it seemed important," she said. "For her sake. I read that children separated from their birth parents often think about what they look like. It's the thing they're most curious about. And they experience certain anxieties when they don't know where they come from, especially in their teenage years. I thought I might as well save her that if I could."

Dean looked at the baby sitting in a highchair across the table from him. She'd been eating mashed sweet potato and had orangey mush all over her chin and cheeks. She smiled at him. He felt himself getting a little dizzy, as though he'd had too much to drink. The baby gurgled.

"When do they learn to talk?" he asked.

"Not for a while yet," Madeline said, "but sometimes she pretends to talk. It's really cute." The baby made another gurgling noise and spit out a string of sounds all starting with the letter *b*. "There are things we need to settle," Madeline said. "Obviously, we should start slowly – after all, I hardly know you – but when she's a little older, what kind of visitation do you think you'd like?"

"Visitation?" Dean said.

"Yes. I've been asking around. Every second weekend seems to be usual."

"You mean I'd take her? To my house?"

"I'd like to get a criminal record check first, if you don't mind. But eventually, yes, you could have her at your house. Of course she's too young to stay with you yet. But we could start with a few short visits on Sunday afternoons. Until she gets to know you."

"All right," Dean said. What else could he say? He had no idea what he would do with a baby, but he assumed Madeline would be there, at least at first.

"I want to be clear about something," Madeline said. "There's no need for you and me to have any kind of relationship. I want the baby to know her biological father, that's only fair, but the two of us – I have no interest, if you know what I mean. I hope we see eye to eye on that account."

"That's fine with me," Dean said. He meant it. He had no desire to get to know this woman, although he admired her level-headedness.

"We should go to a lawyer," Madeline said. "Get it all down in the legal sense. And I want to thank you for agreeing so readily to the support payments. Not all men would."

The baby began clamouring to get out of her highchair.

"Fine then," Madeline said. "I'll be in touch about the criminal record check, how we do that."

Dean nodded. "I told you I bought a house, didn't I?" he said.

"No," she said, "but that's good. I'm going to start saving for a house. With the baby, I think a house is better. The backyard and all that."

Dean agreed.

"What's your yard like?" she asked.

"Good," Dean said. "There's a lawn. And a deck."

"Is it fenced?" she asked.

"Not all the way around," Dean said.

"Oh well," she said, "you can get that done. It'll be a few years before she's ready for a yard anyway."

When Dean got home he realized he didn't know the baby's name. He hadn't asked. Madeline must have told him at some point. When she called to tell him about the birth, surely she'd told him the baby's name.

That Friday, he was barely home from work when he heard a knock at the back door. He considered not answering it because he was in a hurry. Charlotte and Bob had invited him and Lily over for drinks before the symphony, and Dean had to change, pick Lily up and get to their place before six-thirty. He did answer the door though, because it was the back door and that usually meant it was someone he knew. It was Candace.

"Hi," she said. "I just wanted to let you know I've had a break-in."

"You're kidding," Dean said. The memory of her anger had faded, but he was blushing anyway. "A break and enter, you mean? A robbery?"

"They jimmied the back door," she said. "Took my VCR. Microwave. CD player. Things like that."

"I'm sorry," Dean said. It was all he could think of to say.

"You weren't broken into then?" she asked.

"No," Dean said. "Everything's fine here."

"Oh," Candace said. "I was sort of hoping it was the whole block. It's creepy to think they might have been watching me, like they picked out me especially."

"Would you like to come in for a drink?" Dean heard himself ask, even though another voice was telling him to get rid of her quickly so he wouldn't be late picking up Lily.

"Might as well," she said, stepping into his kitchen. "I've got a carpenter over there replacing my door. I'm having a steel one installed. That's what the police suggested." Then she added, "It's a terrible feeling, knowing someone was in your house, going through your things. I keep wondering what they touched."

Dean said, "I can understand how upsetting it must be." His voice sounded like someone else's. It was too sympathetic. He poured her a Scotch over ice, then poured one for himself. They sat down at the table. Dean tried to decide what colour her hair was. He thought it was brown, mousy, but then he decided it was auburn.

"I've been thinking about getting a security system," he said, even though he hadn't considered it until that very moment. "Maybe if we went together, they'd give us a deal."

"Good idea," she said. "The police told me a security system is the only deterrent, really. Either that or a dog. They said it probably took them ten seconds to get into my house. Imagine that." She shivered.

"I'll check out the prices tomorrow," Dean said.

"Security systems, you mean?" she asked.

"Yes," Dean said.

They sipped at their drinks. Dean became aware of the clock ticking on the wall above the table.

"Look," he said, "I know this is sudden, but I have a ticket to the symphony tonight. I was just getting ready to go. They're doing Wagner. Would you like to come with me?"

She stared at him. Ten or fifteen seconds went by.

"Do you like classical music?" he asked.

"I'm not averse to it," she finally said. "I listen to it on the radio sometimes, but I wouldn't call myself a fan exactly."

"What do you say then?" Dean asked.

"I suppose," she said. "Should I change? I'm still wearing my work clothes."

Dean studied her dress. It was plain, with little generic flowers on it, the kind that could go absolutely unnoticed in almost any crowd. Lily would never wear such a dress. Still, there was something about it. It was quaint in a retro, sixties kind of way.

"I was going to change into a dark suit," he said, "but you look fine. We'll stop at some friends for drinks first. Is that all right?"

"I'll just go home and change my shoes," she said. "What time should I come back?"

"Right away," Dean said.

When she was gone, Dean phoned Lily. He told her he was sorry but he couldn't make it, he was ill.

"Will you go anyway?" he asked, trying to sound feverish. He knew Lily didn't like Wagner. He anticipated her answer.

"No," Lily said. "I don't care for Wagner anyway. It doesn't matter. Take care of yourself."

"I promise," he said. "I'm already in bed with the heating pad."

"Don't forget about dinner on Sunday," Lily said. "I'll cook something special for you. Something French with a nice sauce. If you're well enough, that is."

"I'll be better by Sunday," Dean said. "I'm sure of it."

After he hung up, he quickly changed and went back to the kitchen to wait for Candace. It seemed like hours before she was at the door again. She'd changed into a brown dress with what looked like deflated wings hanging limply down her sides. It was some kind of gauzy cotton material.

"Is this all right?" she asked. "I decided I should dress up a little."

Dean said it was fine, but he knew she would look underdressed next to Charlotte. She wasn't wearing any make-up.

"I don't suppose it matters," Candace said. "I've seen those ads on TV. You know the ones: 'Look who's going to the symphony.' They show guys in cowboy hats and jeans filing into the Arts Centre."

"It's true," Dean said, although the only time he had seen cowboy hats at the symphony was when they did the Pops concert with Emmylou Harris, and then people in the audience had booed and shouted things like, "We came to hear country" when she sang "How High the Moon" and "Mr. Sandman."

"I guess we'd better get going," Dean said, putting his ticket in his breast pocket. He was thinking they could buy Candace a ticket when they got there, and then she could sit beside him, in Lily's empty seat. He wondered how Bob and Charlotte would react. He felt as though he was doing something dangerous, like hang-gliding.

They rang the doorbell and Charlotte answered. Dean knew right away that something was wrong.

"Oh my," said Charlotte, looking at Candace.

"What?" said Dean. "What's the matter?"

"Lily is here," said Charlotte. "And haven't you made a speedy recovery?"

"Lily?" Dean asked dumbly.

"Yes," Charlotte said. "You remember Lily, don't you? I had the impression you knew each other rather well."

Candace recovered quickly. "You know, Doug," she said as he stood with his mouth open, trying to decide what to do, "I've just remembered something. My mother is coming into town tonight. I can't believe I forgot." Dean thought he heard a catch in her voice, as though she was trying to stop herself from laughing. She backed away from the door. "Would you mind calling me a cab? I'll just wait outside. I'm really sorry, but I have to run."

"Oh dear," said Charlotte.

Candace backed down the front step and around the corner of the house. Dean thought he heard a hoot, then stifled laughter.

"You might as well come in and call the poor woman a cab," said Charlotte. "Discretion shall be my middle name."

Dean went to the kitchen, where a teenaged girl was sitting at the table reading notes in a school binder. Vanessa's babysitter, Dean thought.

"Did she call you Doug?" Charlotte asked.

"I don't think so," Dean said. "Why would she call me Doug?"

Charlotte looked at him, then left the room.

The babysitter was paying no attention to him, so he ordered a cab in a low voice. After he'd hung up, he looked at the girl again. He felt like he had to say something, because obviously she'd overheard his conversation with Charlotte, and then his mysterious call to the cab company.

"Studying, eh?" he said. She looked up at him, but didn't say anything. He walked over to the table. He thought he saw a trace of a smile cross her face.

"So what do they teach kids in school these days?" he asked. He looked down at her book and saw a black line drawing of an unrolled condom.

"Test tomorrow," she said. "Sixteen steps. If you miss one, you get zero. Pass or fail, nothing in between."

"Sixteen steps?" Dean managed to choke out.

"Yeah," she said. "Sixteen steps to putting on a condom." She looked at him. Definitely the trace of a smile. "You do know the sixteen steps, don't you?"

"Yeah, sure," Dean said. He was thinking, sixteen steps? Then he thought, they study this in school? And that led him to, Christ, he was a dinosaur and he was only thirty-five. The girl said, "They have these wooden demonstrator things at school. If I had one, I could show you."

Dean could see she was enjoying herself. "That's okay," he said, heading for the living room. "I think I know … well anyway, good luck on the test." For the second time in fifteen minutes he thought he heard sniggering at his expense. He was still thinking, sixteen steps?

Lily was seated on the couch in yet another black dress, this one satiny and strapless. Five-year-old Vanessa was sitting beside her in a long flannelette nightgown, rubbing the fabric and looking up at Lily adoringly. Lily had one arm behind Vanessa's back. He tried to imagine Vanessa as a baby with mushy sweet potato all over her face. Would his child turn into a little girl like Vanessa – a real girl, as they say? Or would she play hockey and give the boys a run for their money? That depended on her mother, he supposed. He didn't imagine he would have much influence, one way or the other.

Dean bent over and gave Lily a peck on the cheek before sitting down in a wing-back chair.

"Surprised to see me?" he asked.

"Rather," she said.

"I'm feeling much better," he said. "I tried to call you back but you'd already left. I thought you might be here."

"I decided I wanted to go after all. I'd rather listen to Wagner than sit at home by myself."

"Isn't Lily good with Vanessa?" Charlotte said. "I do hope you're planning to have children some day, Lily. You'd be a wonderful mother. Wouldn't she, Dean?"

Dean glared at Charlotte. He was beginning to hate her, even though she had just done him an enormous favour.

Lily said, "Vanessa, tell Dean about Daddy's new car."

"Daddy got a new car," Vanessa said. "It's just his and it has his name on it."

"His name?" Dean asked.

Charlotte said, "Bob bought himself a new Miata and he's afraid I'm going to make off with it. So he got a personalized plate that says BOB'S."

"How clever," said Dean.

Bob was looking at him. "Well?" Bob said.

"Well what?" Dean asked.

"Don't you want to see it?"

Dean didn't really, but he pretended he did. They looked at the car, and then they all went to the symphony in Dean's car because Bob's wasn't big enough for four people.

All during the concert Dean tried to think his way through the sixteen steps. He could only count four, and one of those was "tear open the package." After the concert, Charlotte and Bob suggested going out to eat.

"We might as well take advantage of the sitter," Charlotte said. "It's getting harder and harder to find a good one."

Dean said that he felt a relapse coming on and thought maybe he should call it a night. He drove Lily to her apartment.

"Is something wrong?" Lily asked on the way.

"Just this flu or whatever it is," Dean said.

"I mean something other than your physical health," Lily said.

Dean was consumed by guilt. He went in with her to prove there was nothing wrong, but this time there didn't seem to be anything she could do to bring him to life.

"I give up," Lily said. "I guess you're not the slut I thought you were."

They were standing naked in front of the bedroom window. The moonlight glinted off Lily's white skin, making her look like polished marble.

"You know who we fall in love with?" Lily asked. "We fall in love with someone who allows us to be in love with ourselves. People are completely narcissistic, at least healthy people are. An unhealthy person will fall in love with someone who treats them like a dog."

Dean puzzled over why she was telling him this. He didn't think for a minute she was making casual conversation. She had her hand on his thigh, her fingers brushing lightly over his skin. He could feel the brush of her fingernails, which were long and manicured, and no sooner had he become aware of the sensation, the threat, when he felt a perfect fingernail dig into his thigh. He yelped and jumped back, beyond her reach, crashing into the footboard of the cherry bed.

"What the hell did you do that for?" he asked, rubbing what he was sure was going to turn into a bruise.

Lily brushed her hands together as though she were ridding them of carpet dust. She went to the bathroom and closed the door. Dean heard her turn on the bathtub tap.

"That hurt, you know," he said through the closed door. There was no answer. He tried the door, but it was locked. The tap ran until he thought for sure the bathtub must be overflowing. He didn't know what to do. This wasn't like Lily. Finally he heard her turn off the water. He knocked on the door, but she ignored him.

Dean found himself sitting alone and naked in a chair in the dim light of Lily's living room. He was sitting right next to David. He could see the two of them in the mirrored wall – David hard and perfect, Dean pliant and far too soft. He looked away from the mirror, away from himself. He reached over to touch David's plaster flesh and felt a tiny spot where the paint had bubbled. He picked it off. Then he picked a bit of plaster away from the spot and before he knew it he had picked a hole the size of a peach pit in David's thigh. He stared at what he'd done. He could still feel Lily's finger-nail, and the impending bruise. He wrote Lily a note saying that he thought it best they stop seeing one another, and taped it to her fridge.

The next day, he saw his neighbour in the alley. They were both putting bags of trash in the dumpster.

"Well," she said. "I guess I should thank you for the lovely evening." Her tone of voice gave away nothing. He couldn't tell if she was angry or laughing at him, whether she thought him a rogue to be castigated or a complete imbecile that deserved pity. He wasn't sure which of the two he preferred.

"I'm sorry," he said.

"Never mind," she said. "You have problems, that's clear."

"Yes," he said, "I have problems. True enough."

On Sunday at about noon Lily phoned to ask him if he had a bottle of wine he could bring for dinner. He was surprised but relieved to hear from her. At the same time, he was frightened, as though there was no logic to anything, as though things were happening all on their own, in no particular order.

"Red would be best, if you have it," she said. "Or white. It doesn't really matter. I meant go to the liquor store yesterday, but it completely slipped my mind. I don't know what I was thinking. I've decided not to do the French, by the way. I feel like Indonesian. Will that be all right?"

Dean tried to find his voice.

"Dean?" Lily said. "Are you there?"

"Yes," he said. "I'm here."

"You are coming, aren't you?" she asked.

Dean tried to think. Perhaps she hadn't seen the note. But she couldn't have missed it. Then he thought, of course, Lily was being gracious. She was saving him embarrassment, handing him forgiveness without mentioning his misdemeanour. He said, "I'll be there."

"Good," Lily said. "Come early. Let's spend the afternoon together."

"How early?" Dean asked.

"Why not right away?" said Lily.

"Right away," said Dean. "That's good. Right away."

"Don't forget the wine," Lily said and hung up.

Dean was just looking through his wine supply when Candace called from next door and asked him if he golfed. He didn't tell her he hated golf. He knew he should, but instead he told her he was rusty because he hadn't had time for golf lately. He said he'd been thinking he should make a point of getting out on the course more often.

"My partner just cancelled," she said. "I'm dying to get out for a few hours. It's such a great day. I know you'll probably make me regret this, but what do you say?"

He tried to calculate whether or not he could go golfing and still get to Lily's at a time that could be loosely interpreted as "right away." Candace misinterpreted his silence.

"Hey," she said. "This is not a date, if that's what you're thinking. I'm desperate." Then she said, "I know you've got a lady friend. I believe her name is Lily."

"She's not exactly a lady friend," Dean said. "She's more like ... well, an associate. And yes, nine holes, I think I have time for that."

"Great," said Candace. "Do you have clubs?"

"No," Dean said. "I used to, but I loaned them to a friend and he never brought them back."

"Some friend," Candace said.

"He's left the country," Dean said. "I don't imagine I'll see my clubs again."

Candace said she had a set for him. They were beauties. When he commented on them, she said, "I used to go out with a golf pro." She didn't explain why she still had his clubs.

There were big questions on Dean's mind as he hacked his way around the golf course. He kept wondering, how could he so easily slip into this deception? And to what end? He was not attracted to Candace. Definitely not. And as for her interest in him, it was hardly flattering. She couldn't even remember his name.

As Dean finally sank his ball into the cup on the fifth hole, he thought about his willingness to risk losing Lily, to come so close to the edge of impropriety, to behave so badly. Was he afraid of Lily? Perhaps he was.

A foursome caught up to them as they were teeing off on the sixth hole. One of the men was limping and Dean wondered about the tenacity of golfers. As they got closer, he heard someone call his name. It was Bob.

"Well, what do you know?" Bob said. "Dean on a golf course. Has hell frozen over or what?"

There were introductions all around. Candace shook hands with the four men and then whispered to Dean, "I thought your name was Doug." Dean noticed that Bob kept looking at Candace, as though he were memorizing her features so he could describe her to Charlotte. Dean suggested that Bob and his partners play through, but Bob said no, they were moving slowly because one of the men, Rick, had a sprained ankle. Dean knew he couldn't stay on the course with Bob dogging him, so he said he wasn't feeling well and asked Candace if she minded if they packed it in. Then Rick said that he'd had enough and that Candace could take his spot.

"I thought I could keep up," Rick said to Dean as they were walking to the parking lot. "Bob suggested we rent a cart, but I said no, let's walk, I'm back to normal. Guess I'm not."

"What did you do to it?" Dean asked.

"Broke a bone in my foot jumping out of an airplane," Rick said. "Oh well. Could happen to anybody, eh? No sense complaining."

"I guess not," Dean said. He was thinking, people really jump out of airplanes, they really do it. Then he started thinking that Bob was golfing with Candace, and he was pretty sure Charlotte would have told Bob about Candace, and Bob was probably grilling her at that very moment, trying to figure out what was what.

When Dean got to Lily's apartment he tried to explain. "When you said right away, I thought you meant three-ish. Earlier than dinnertime. I'm sorry. Really, I am."

"And the wine?" Lily asked.

"The wine," he said. "Well, I picked out a bottle and set it by the back door. I don't know how I forgot it. It was sitting there staring me in the face."

Lily, who was looking like a young Audrey Hepburn in a sleeveless black dress, turned on her heels and shut herself in the bedroom. After a minute, Dean thought he heard the sound of the bathtub water running again. He sat down next to David and picked another hole with his fingernail, this time in the small of David's back. He waited for Lily to get out of the bath, but she was clearly not planning to emerge as long as Dean was still in her apartment.

A few days later, when Dean got home from work, he found David in his backyard. He had been placed under the lot's only tree, a sprawling crabapple that needed trimming. Lily had drawn big circles with felt marker around the holes in David's thigh and lower back. The circles reminded Dean of a television program he had seen on plastic surgery. The surgeon had drawn on the bodies with a marker, and Dean had thought it seemed primitive, that surely there was a more professional way of charting the path for the incisions to come.

Dean tried to call Lily but he got her voice mail and a greeting saying, "Leave your number and I'll call you back. If it's Dean, fuck you." Dean thought that was careless of her, considering she was a businesswoman and might be getting work-related calls. It was uncharacteristic. She was usually such a perfectionist and very careful not to say anything unprofessional. He began to worry that she would lose customers, so he left a message saying, "You can change your greeting; I won't call anymore until you tell me to."

He checked the next day to see if she'd changed it but she hadn't.

A few nights later, after he'd had more Scotch than he was used to drinking, he checked again. The greeting still hadn't been changed and there were now a lot of beeps. Dean decided Lily must have gone away on a holiday. He decided to do her a favour and change her greeting before she ruined her interior decorating business; he still had keys to her apartment. When he got there he found everything gone. And he couldn't change her greeting because he didn't know her password. He tried to guess a few times, but he got nowhere so he gave up and went home to bed.

It was late on a Sunday morning, hot and humid. Rain was forecast. Two weeks had passed since Dean had heard from Lily. He pulled his lawn chair over next to David and sat under the tree, moodily picking at the hole in David's back. That's where he was when Madeline came around the side of the house, baby in arms, a huge diaper bag over her shoulder.

Dean jumped to his feet.

"Thank God you're here," Madeline said. "I tried calling but I guess you were outside. I've got a real emergency on my hands. I need a sitter for a few hours and I can't find one. I've tried all my friends, but no one's around. So I thought of you."

"You want me to take her?" Dean asked. "To babysit?"

"Just for a couple of hours. I know we haven't worked out any formal arrangement – I still want to do that – but I'll get fired if I can't get into the office and straighten out this mess. It's too complicated to explain but I really am desperate."

She *looked* desperate. "Okay," Dean said, "if it's not for too long."

"I'm sure you'll do fine," Madeline said. "She's a really good baby. I just changed her so she should be all right for a while. There's a bottle and a jar of peaches in the diaper bag, and my work number on a slip of paper. Two hours. I promise. Remember, they're into everything at this age."

The baby smiled at Dean. Madeline handed her over and dropped the diaper bag on the lawn. Dean knew he was holding the baby awkwardly. He'd never held a baby before. He couldn't believe he would be alone with this child for the next few hours. He knew nothing about babies. He didn't believe he could keep one alive any better than he'd been able to keep a goldfish alive when he'd tried that once or twice. She was reaching for his glasses. She seemed big to him, bigger than a baby should be.

"I'm sorry to do this to you," Madeline said. "Really I am." She kissed the baby and left.

Dean put the baby down on the lawn. She looked up at him and then headed off, crawling toward the deck. She obviously didn't like the prickly feel of the grass on her bare knees, and tried to crawl on her hands and feet, with her bum in the air. Dean would have thought it was funny if he weren't in shock. The baby finally gave up, sat down in the grass, and looked at Dean again. What now? he wondered. She'd probably cry and what would he do then? He had no idea.

He saw Candace come out into her yard. She had her purse over her shoulder and her keys in her hand.

"Help," Dean said.

She stopped. "What?" she said.

"I've got my daughter here. I don't know what to do."

She walked to the fence and looked over. "Oh my God," she said. "What's wrong?"

"Nothing," Candace said, "only she looks exactly like you. It's weird. I've never seen a baby that looked so much like its parent. Most babies look – you know – round. Not like anyone."

"Do you think she's too big?" Dean asked.

"What do you mean? You mean fat? All babies are fat."

"Not that," Dean said. "She just looks … big. Oversized. Look at her head."

"Don't be ridiculous," Candace said. "Babies' proportions are different from adults'. They have to grow into their heads. Surely you know that."

"This is the first time I've been alone with her," Dean said. "How about coming over for a cup of coffee or something?"

"I'm just on my way out," Candace said.

"I'm begging," Dean said. "I'm scared shitless."

Candace studied the baby and then said, "Fifteen minutes. I've got things to do."

Dean picked up the baby. When Candace came through the gate he gladly handed his child over and went into the house to make a pot of coffee. When he felt sufficiently shored up to go back outside, he found Candace sitting on the deck, bouncing the appreciative baby on her knee and making funny noises. Dean retrieved the diaper bag and his lawn chair from under the tree and sat down, tremendously grateful for Candace's presence. Because they were on the deck, near her dining room window, Dean was reminded of the time when he had seen her shouting at someone he couldn't see. He had never asked who and what had made her so angry.

"Do you remember that day you were locked out and I helped you crawl through the window?"

"Yes," she said. She stopped bouncing and waited. "And?"

It seemed pointless to ask. The answer, no matter what it was, would be just as useless to him now as his previous concept of paternity, the one that allowed him to write a cheque every month and remain, happily, at a distance. Still, he was curious.

"You were shouting at someone," Dean said. "I saw you through the window."

"Really?" Candace said. "I don't think so."

"But I saw you," Dean said. "Either that or I'm completely crazy."

Candace thought for a minute. "Was it a Saturday?" she asked.

"Yes," Dean said.

"Opera," Candace said. "The Saturday opera on the radio. I like all the melodrama, even though I know nothing about the music. I was probably singing along and hamming it up. It's all I can think of. I don't remember shouting at anyone."

"An opera ham," Dean said. "That is very weird."

"You get to do weird things when you live alone," Candace said. "You don't expect your neighbour to be watching through the window."

"Sorry," Dean said.

The baby grabbed at Candace's earrings and managed to get a grip on one of the gold hoops.

"She's cute," Candace said, prying the tiny hand away. "What's her name?"

Dean was silent.

"What?" Candace asked.

"I don't know her name," Dean said.

Candace looked confounded. "You don't know your own child's name?" she said. "How is that possible?"

"Like I said, this is the first time I've been alone with her. I've only seen her once before."

"Look in the diaper bag," Candace said. "Maybe there's something in there with her name on it."

Dean rummaged in the diaper bag. Nothing. Just diapers, a bottle and the jar of peaches, the piece of paper containing Madeline's phone number at work. And a little sweater, pale yellow with black Scottie dogs on it. It looked hand knit, Candace said.

The baby wanted down. She had her eye on a clay pot with some kind of blooming flower in it. Candace lowered her to the deck and she headed for the flower. Dean worried about slivers, and then he began to worry that Candace would soon leave.

"Do you want lunch?" he said to Candace. "I could whip something up."

"No," Candace said. "I have too much to do. Like I said, fifteen minutes."

Fifteen minutes had already passed, but Dean didn't bother to point that out.

They drank their coffee while the baby played in the flowerpot. It turned out she wasn't after the bloom, she was interested in the dirt. She put some in her mouth and then spat it out again. She made them both laugh, the way she looked with dirt and saliva running down her chin.

Two hours later the rain began to fall. Madeline still hadn't returned and Candace left in spite of Dean's attempts to convince her to stay. He dolefully watched her run to her garage through the drizzle, which was quickly turning into a downpour. He carried the baby inside and they stood in the dining room window and watched the rain splash off the smooth surface of David. Dean thought the statue would likely be a pile of wet plaster by morning, thanks to the holes.

The baby noticed little rivulets running down the windowpane and tried to grab at them through the glass. She kept trying, over and over again, as one disappeared and then a new one started. She looked up at Dean.

"Oooh," she said. It wasn't a question exactly, but Dean knew she was puzzled and he felt some responsibility to try to explain why the water droplets joined together and ran down the glass the way they did.

"It's like this," he said, then he realized he couldn't remember, or perhaps he just didn't know and never had.

The baby appeared to be studying him now, with the same intensity she had given the raindrops a few moments before. He knew her interest in him was motivated by a general curiosity and nothing more. After all, she couldn't possibly see their physical resemblance. He wondered if she would eventually grow to like him and supposed that he would have to earn her regard, which was a frightening prospect. Or perhaps – and this was even more frightening – she would go on trust, simply because he was her father.

"Oooh," she said again, looking at him as though expecting an answer. She continued to stare, her mouth open in a tiny *o*, her hand wavering just inches from his cheek.

A Reckless Moon

I was on my way to my brother Terry's place, which is a seven- or eight-hour drive north of where I live. One of my travelling companions was a dog. The other was a man named Finch who'd heard from someone I knew that I was driving up to Spiritwood and had called me to ask if he could catch a ride. Something about a funeral, something about his son dropping him off and then going on to a sale in the southeast, could I pick him up at the Shell station north of the city? At first, I was uneasy about driving to Spiritwood with Finch, a man I didn't know from Adam, but then I thought it might be an adventure, and that I might learn something new about men like him, who buy and sell horses for a living.

The dog, a German shepherd, I had acquired unexpectedly on my way out of the city when he'd run into the traffic and almost got hit, first by me in the northbound lane, and then by a minivan going south. He made it across, but I turned left at the next intersection anyway and drove back to where I thought he'd be. When I found him, I opened the passenger door of the truck and he jumped in without giving it a second thought. He was wearing a collar but it had no tags on it. I thought about Finch waiting for me at the service station, and then the stop to pick up a trailer, and I decided there was no time to drop the dog at the Humane Society. He would have to come along. I called him Jack, I don't know why. He didn't seem to mind.

"So you're looking for a horse," Finch said to me once we'd picked up the trailer and were on our way. The dog was panting happily on the bench seat behind us.

Finch, I should say, was a man with a reputation. I'd been told he could pay two or three thousand dollars for a horse in the morning and have it sold for twice that by the end of the day. I'd been warned about him, although it was not said that he was a crook. You just had to know what you were doing when you dealt with him.

I told him I'd just put my old Arab gelding down. There were details, but I didn't want to go into them. Finch nodded. He didn't need the details.

"So what are you looking for in a horse?" he asked.

"Smart, but not too smart," I said. "A little bit lazy would be all right, as long as he's not too lazy. Good feet, but that goes without saying." I thought I was telling him too much. It sounded like I was shopping, and Finch was not the sort of man a person like me should buy a horse from.

I went on anyway; we had to talk about something, at least for a while. Maybe we could get this out of the way, I thought, and then we could travel comfortably enough, either talking or not, whatever seemed right. "The Arab was smart as a whip and scared of his own shadow," I said. "I've had enough of that."

Finch laughed. He had an appealing laugh. He was a good-looking man, older than me by ten or so years, in his mid-fifties probably, and he liked women; I could tell. I felt pleased that I'd made him laugh. Most of us are suckers for men like Finch, men who like women, even when we know better. Or maybe *because* we know better.

"So, what do you know about this horse you're going to look at?" he asked.

"Five-year-old quarter horse mare," I said. "The sale catalogue is in the glove compartment if you want to have a look at it."

My brother Terry had bought the mare without consulting me, and then sent me the catalogue with a Post-it Note on page seven that said, "Is she what you're looking for?" The sale had been a couple of weeks back, the annual sale of a reputable quarter horse breeder. I was sure that Finch would know the man. He retrieved the catalogue and flipped through it without saying anything.

I told Finch the page number. When he found it he nodded in a manner that could not be interpreted as an opinion one way or the other.

"I recognize a few of the names," I said. "But I don't know much about bloodlines."

"What kind of money are you looking at?" he asked.

I said I didn't know. I told him that my brother and I had not yet talked money, and that I was sure there'd be a catch. I'd find out that Terry had bought the horse for himself or Phyllis and she hadn't worked out because of some problem. She'd turn out to be unsound, or she'd have a nasty or unpredictable disposition.

I told Finch, "I imagine I'll be hauling an empty trailer home. I don't even really know why I'm going."

"Long way to go for nothing," Finch said.

It *was* a long way to go for nothing. "Well," I said, "there's more to it than that."

"I guess there always is," Finch said. "If it doesn't work out, maybe I'll take the horse off your brother's hands." I was sure he would, for the right price.

We drove along the single lane highway heading north, past the mid-summer fields and through the towns that dotted the prairie landscape more and more infrequently. It was a hot day, the kind that spawns thunderstorms later in the afternoon. There'd been a bad one in Alberta the night before. A tornado had wiped out a holiday campground, throwing trailers and people into each other and a nearby lake. I wondered if there was any word on the extent of the damage, and I turned on the radio, which I normally kept tuned to a country station just so I wouldn't have to hear any news, at least not news that went beyond football scores and local crimes such as 7-Eleven robberies. There were terrible things going on in the world and though I was no proponent of the "Don't worry, be happy" way of thinking, some things are just too big to be understood. "Why try?" was more my style.

I switched the radio to CBC and immediately heard an RCMP spokesperson giving details about the tornado. We learned there had been deaths. He gave out a phone number you could call if you had friends or relatives that might have been in the campground. Then the announcer cut to various on-the-spot reports in which eye witnesses used words like "devastating" and "catastrophic." The newscast began to sound like those all-too-familiar disaster reports on American television.

Finch thought we should just turn off the radio, but I wanted to keep listening in case there was a change in the weather. He told the old joke about Saskatchewan being a place where you could watch your dog run away for days, and said if there was a change in the sky, we'd surely see it. I left the radio on anyway, and when they got to the weather report the announcer told us that the forecast for later in the day was not good. He said the conditions were right for tornadoes, like the one in Alberta, and he proceeded to give the disaster details all over again. He used the word "devastating" twice.

Just then, Jack started to whine and turn circles on the seat behind us.

"Either he has to go to the bathroom or he's tired of us and wants to go home," I said to Finch. I'd already told him about how I ended up with the dog.

"Pull over," Finch said. He'd thrown a gear bag in the back when I picked him up at the gas station. He rummaged around in it and pulled out a lead shank, the rough kind, probably homemade, not store-bought like the one I used, which was soft on the hands.

"Come on, Jack," he said. "Let's take a walk."

The two of them relieved themselves in the ditch, their backs to the passing traffic on Highway 6. Someone honked on the way by. Finch waved his hat.

"I could grow to like this dog," he said when they got back in the truck. Jack immediately curled up on the seat again, happy now and content to travel with us, a pair of complete strangers.

"Maybe you should take him," I said. "His owners obviously don't deserve him."

I imagined Finch going home with the horse and the dog, both of which seemed in some way like my responsibility.

I turned off the radio and we drove in silence for a while until Finch said, "You live in the city then."

"Unfortunately," I said. "There's a whole legion of us, you know, women of a certain age, stuck in the city, with horses instead of men for partners."

I'd thought I was making a joke, but it sounded bitter and possibly even pathetic, so I added, "I swear to God it's only temporary."

"Which part?" Finch asked. "The women without men part or the stuck in the city part?"

"Both, I guess."

"What do you mean by a certain age?" he asked.

Because Finch had asked the question in a serious way, I felt compelled to answer. It was tricky, though. I said, "Too old to contend but not old enough to be wise."

"I see," he said. "Well, you sound pretty wise to me."

It seemed like a compliment. The truck cab felt suddenly smaller.

"Some young sociology student could have a lot of fun with us," I said. "Women with horses, I mean. Or is it anthropology?"

"Don't ask me," said Finch. "I don't have a clue about any of that. Horses is about all I know. Horsology, if there's a such a thing."

"There could be," I said. Then I asked, "What have you got for a horse?" I'd been wondering what kind of horse a man like Finch would have.

"I have lots of horses," Finch said.

"Your own, I mean. The one you ride."

"They're all for sale," he said.

It was disappointing. I imagined him owning, say, a champion of some kind, a world-class reining horse, one that he'd come across in his dealings as a horse trader. When he didn't say anything else, I asked, "So whose funeral are you going to?"

"I'm not sure yet," he said – a mysterious thing to say – and he was not forthcoming beyond that. I thought I'd probably assumed too much familiarity and resolved to be quiet, but then Finch asked me where I was from and I told him the name of the town nearest where my father had farmed, and it turned out he had worked one summer as a hired hand for a man my family had known. We said something about small world and Saskatchewan being smaller yet, and I told Finch that I had not liked this man, who was famous for his short temper and impatience.

"How was it, working for him?" I asked.

"He fired me," Finch said.

"That's not much of a surprise," I said. "He fired almost everyone who ever worked for him."

"I hated him for it," Finch said.

"Why'd he fire you?"

"Let's just say I was young."

"That doesn't sound like a very good reason," I said.

"It was reason enough," Finch said. "But that didn't keep me from lying awake at night thinking of ways to get even. Good thing I never carried out any of the plans I came up with or they'd have locked me away for sure."

"He's dead now," I said. "So you can stop worrying about it."

"I'm not worried," Finch said. "I was never worried."

I said, "Anyway, I think we should all be forgiven for being young. It's a disease we can't help." It didn't sound like me talking. It sounded like some idiot on afternoon television.

"Well," Finch said, "you can't really forgive yourself, can you? They say you can, but you need to be forgiven by someone else for it to really work. That only makes sense if you ask me. Of course, no one's asking."

He turned away and pulled his hat down over his eyes. Then he went to sleep. The dog was asleep too. I could hear his deep breathing behind me. He whined in his sleep once in a while, the way dogs do.

I began to see clouds building to the west of us. The news from Alberta made the changing sky seem ominous, even though storms can be a daily occurrence during the hot part of the summer. I watched for funnel clouds, although I didn't really know what one would look like. It was a bit like watching for UFOs when you're driving alone at night.

Ahead, the sky was still blue. There was a sharp line between the two skies, the dark one building to the west and the one to the north where we were going. I kept thinking we should be moving past the line of clouds but they stayed right with us. I thought of waking Finch to point out this peculiarity, but decided that would be a presumptuous act, one that assumed something between us. People who know each other – a husband and wife, or a parent and child – say, "Would you look at this?" and then watch together, as though through the same eyes. Strangers keep their thoughts to themselves and watch things in a parallel kind of way. Each has its advantages.

An hour later I decided to pull off at a local picnic ground. The dog, I figured, would need water, and I wanted to stretch my legs. When I slowed down Finch and Jack woke up.

"Where are we?" Finch wanted to know.

"Spalding," I said. "We've still got a long ways to go. It'll be dark by the time we get there."

The picnic grounds were really just a grassy field with a pit toilet, a tap for water and a few picnic tables placed under scrubby poplars. The trees and the tables were crawling with ants. I got a bucket from the empty trailer and filled it with water for Jack. We kept him on the lead so he couldn't decide to head down the highway in the direction of home.

There was another vehicle parked in the picnic ground, a big black car with South Dakota plates, pulling a small camper trailer that had MURPHYS' SHOW DOGS painted on the side in bright red. A man and a woman (they might have been the same age as Finch, I thought) were having lunch at one of the tables. They were dressed in matching white western shirts with bright red diamonds all over them. They had a can of Raid and every once in a while the woman – Mrs. Murphy, I supposed – would spray the table to clear it of ants. Finch wandered over and struck up a conversation. He had Jack with him.

"What kind of dogs have you got?" he asked. I could hear well enough.

"Shelties," Mr. Murphy said.

"High-strung, I hear," Finch said.

"Full of energy," said Mrs. Murphy. "Good, though, when you put them to work. People think high-strung dogs are stupid, but that's not right. You have to channel the energy, give it an outlet, just like people. People get into all kinds of trouble when they're not busy."

"You're right there," Finch said. Jack was straining on the lead, trying to sniff the tires of the Murphys' trailer. I listened for dog sounds coming from inside the trailer but couldn't hear any. "So where are you folks headed?" Finch asked.

"Prince Albert," said Mr. Murphy. "The fair's on next week. We do a show at the grandstand."

"Would you and your wife like a Coke?" asked Mrs. Murphy. "We've got plenty. There was a sale at Safeway in Regina. Buy two cases and get one free."

"Honey," Finch called to me, "you want to have a Coke with these people? They've invited us."

I joined them, amused at Finch's little joke, which did not seem in the least self-conscious. The smell of Raid was overpowering. Mrs. Murphy went inside the trailer and brought out two cans of Coke. They were ice cold, which I quickly appreciated. It was getting muggy.

"Don't like the look of those clouds," Mr. Murphy said. "I think we'll pull out soon and try to get ahead of them. We wouldn't want to be caught like those poor people in Alberta last night."

I agreed.

They asked us where we were going and Finch told them.

"Business or pleasure?" Mr. Murphy asked and Finch said, "Both." I was curious about that, how pleasure and the funeral might fit together.

"How many dogs have you got?" I asked Mrs. Murphy.

"Eight adults and five puppies," she said. "The puppies are two weeks old. They're cute as can be. Do you want to see them?"

I said I did. Jack wanted to follow us into the trailer but Finch held him back.

The trailer was small. The Murphys had customized it so the dogs' cages fit in two layers along one wall. The dogs wagged their tails like crazy when we entered the trailer, and made strange whispered barking sounds as though they all had laryngitis. The bitch with the new litter was in a big cardboard box by the Murphys' bed, the five puppies against her soft belly, scrambling over one another in their efforts to latch onto a teat.

"I'd offer you a puppy if they were old enough," said Mrs. Murphy. "As you can imagine, we don't have much need for five more dogs. We'll keep a couple if they work out, but the others will have to go. They're not all suited for the act."

I looked again at the line of dogs in their cages, all wagging their tails and making the strange sounds.

"How come they're so quiet?" I asked.

"Oh my dear," said Mrs. Murphy, "we have them debarked. You can't live in campgrounds all summer and have eight barking dogs in your trailer. You can imagine how that would go over."

She got a Tupperware container of dog treats from the counter and gave each dog one through the wire door of its cage.

I asked, "So you mean they can't bark, not at all?"

"They can still make sounds," Mrs. Murphy said, laughing. "But they're not very effective, are they?" She looked at me then. "It might sound cruel," she said, "but it's not. Like I said, you can't have barking dogs when you do what we do. You can imagine the racket."

"I'm not judging," I said. "Anyway, thanks for the Coke. I guess we should hit the road too."

I took one last look at the almost-silent dogs. I was thinking about my Arab gelding, how he'd been before I put him down, not making a sound even as he thrashed in the stall at the clinic, trying to kick the pain from his gut.

Outside, Finch and Mr. Murphy were looking at the sky in the west. It looked the same. The clouds were hanging there like a huge black quilt. They didn't look like they were moving at all, but they had to be or we'd have left them behind two hours ago.

When we got back in the truck neither of us mentioned Finch's little joke, referring to me as his wife. I wanted to let him know I thought it was funny, because I did, but at the same time I was uncertain about drawing attention to it now that it was over. As we pulled back onto the highway I wondered what Finch was thinking about. I glanced at him periodically as we drove along, and it began to bother me that I was admiring him. I chided myself. We'd be where we were going in another four or five hours. I'd look at the horse Terry had picked out. Finch would go to the funeral, if there really was one, and then do whatever he had in mind for business and pleasure. Finch's trips probably always included business and pleasure, and I knew I would be wise to avoid any involvement in either. Still, I was aware of his presence in that familiar, heightened way, and I began to wish I was travelling on my own. Let's just say there's something in between contending and wise, a confusing mixture of hope and caution. It's the hardest part of not being young anymore.

We were no longer travelling in what could strictly be called prairie. Between Spalding and Melfort, the land is more wooded. The bush changes from scrub to consequential stands of birch and poplar, the kind that have to be bulldozed and burned to create arable land.

"This doesn't look like such bad country," I said to Finch, remembering my father's opinion, which I thought about each time I made the drive to Terry and Phyllis' place. "My father had a fit when Terry decided he wanted to live up here instead of taking over the family farm. I would have done it – taken over from my father, I mean – but that wasn't in the cards."

"Why not?" Finch asked.

"Terry was the son, with a capital *S*," I said. "No capital *D* on daughter."

"I get it," Finch said.

"Yeah," I said. "That's about it. Nothing more to be said."

We were close to Melfort by this time and when we got there we decided to stop for a bite to eat. There was a pizza place on the road through town and we sat at a booth and ordered individual pizzas. I ordered a beer and couldn't help but notice when Finch didn't. The bar counter was situated close to our booth and we were both amused by the bartender's wife, who sat on a high stool with a Coke and watched over her husband's every move. We knew they were married because one of the waitresses made a joke, something about the bartender being handsome, and the woman on the stool said to her, "You'd better watch it, his wife is sitting here." Finch asked me if I thought the bartender was handsome and I said, "Not especially." We wondered if his wife sat there the whole time he was at work, and tried to imagine what circumstances led to her watchfulness. I was certain the reason was his infidelity. Finch leaned more toward a scenario that involved jealousy without cause.

When we were on the road again, the weather took a turn for the worse. I could see two funnel clouds, there was no mistaking them. They were cone-shaped, long and narrow, and hung down menacingly from the solid blanket of dark cloud. They were both moving north, one of them straight ahead of us, and the other behind. We were driving west by this time, having turned off Highway 6 at Melfort, so we were right between the clouds. If we kept driving, we'd be going into the path of the one that was ahead of us.

"What should I do?" I asked Finch.

He thought we should pull over and keep an eye on things, so I pulled onto the shoulder and turned off the truck motor. Several other cars did the same. Soon there were twenty or thirty cars and trucks sitting on the shoulders in both directions. We all got out to watch. The funnel clouds were moving fast, but they were well above the rolling hills that surrounded us.

"What's the plan," I asked Finch, "if one of those clouds touches down and heads straight for us?"

"Beats me," said Finch.

The whole quilt was moving north now at a tremendous speed and it started to rain. We got back in the truck. We tried to keep an eye on the funnels but then the rain started falling so hard we couldn't see what was happening. I thought the funnel ahead of us was touching down but I couldn't be sure. It was raining so hard we could barely hear. Jack was on the floor, shaking, obviously terrified.

The sirens were the first sign that something had happened up ahead. Several police cars passed us, probably coming from the detachment in Melfort. When the rain let up, we moved ahead in a slow line with everyone else, not sure what we might find. A few miles up the road we came to a road block. I could see a semi-trailer overturned across the road and something was spilling out onto the pavement. The police were warning everyone away.

Finch told me to go back to Melfort, he'd stay in case they needed help. I backed the trailer onto an approach and was about to turn around when I saw Mrs. Murphy coming down the highway with her dogs on leashes. I waited for her. We put the dogs in the empty horse trailer and then headed for Melfort. Finch said he would tell Mr. Murphy she was with me.

I had counted seven dogs as we were loading them in the trailer. The bitch and her puppies were not there. Mrs. Murphy's shirt was soaked from the rain and her black eye make-up was smeared. The only thing I asked was if Mr. Murphy was all right and she said he was. She looked stunned and I wondered if I should be worried about her. She was older than I'd thought. I wondered where I should wait for Finch. It was eight o'clock by this time and who knew how long they'd be? Several more police cars met us on the highway, and a couple of ambulances. There was a steady stream of cars and trucks heading west, curiosity seekers, I thought, or maybe just people wanting to help.

When we got to Melfort I decided to get a motel room so Mrs. Murphy could be comfortable. At first I'd suggested that we wait in a restaurant, but she didn't want to leave the dogs. There was a motel on the highway where Finch would be sure to see the truck and trailer and I got a room for thirty-five dollars, which I thought I could afford to waste. Mrs. Murphy took the dogs inside. Jack had growled when he saw them coming down the highway so I left him in the truck cab. After all, I didn't know him. He was a German shepherd and could make short work of the Shelties if he chose to.

When the rain slowed to a drizzle I walked across the parking lot to the coffee shop. It was full of women. I assumed the men had all gone down the road to the scene of the disaster, if that's what it was. I still didn't know for sure. Mrs. Murphy hadn't said much, other than that their trailer had jackknifed into the ditch when the wind hit. The radio was on in the coffee shop but so far there hadn't been any news. I thought maybe I should call Terry and tell him we were all right, in case he heard anything, so I got my cell phone from the truck and called from the parking lot.

Terry hadn't heard anything about a tornado near Melfort. I told him that I was travelling with a man named Finch, a horse buyer, and that I was at a motel and Finch was down the highway where the tornado had struck. I was waiting for Finch, I said.

"You're waiting for Finch?" Terry asked. "Melvin Finch from Belle Plaine?"

"I didn't know his name was Melvin, but I guess that's him," I said.

"In a motel in Melfort?"

"It's not how it sounds," I said. "There's an old lady with me, and a bunch of Sheltie show dogs. They have some kind of act. I'm sharing the room with her."

"Not the Murphys," Terry said.

"Yes," I said. I couldn't believe that he'd heard of them.

"There was an article in the P.A. paper," he said. "They're coming to the fair. Wait'll I tell the girls." That's what he called Sarah and Phyllis, the girls.

"Anyway," I said, "I just wanted to let you know we're all right. I don't know when we'll show up. Late tonight or sometime tomorrow. Finch said he was going to a funeral, but I'm not sure it's one that involves an actual death."

"I don't know about any funeral," Terry said, "but then lots of people die without me knowing."

I knew I couldn't talk long because my phone card was about to run out of time, but I suddenly thought to ask Terry how much he paid for the horse. It was a question I should have asked before I started out. Terry was silent on the other end of the line.

"What?" I asked. "Why aren't you answering? It's a straight-forward enough question."

"I suppose Finch told you to ask that," he said.

"No," I said. "Finch could care less. I want to know. Maybe I could have saved myself a trip if I'd asked that when you first called."

"Didn't you see the note on the sale catalogue?" Terry asked.

"Yeah," I said. "So?"

"So, just what the note said."

"The note said almost nothing, Terry. You bought this horse. Is she what I'm looking for? I assume I can buy her from you if I like her. Isn't that the idea?" Then something clicked. "You're expecting me to buy this horse sight unseen, aren't you? I should have thought of that. I knew there'd be some kind of catch."

"For Christ sake," Terry said. "Not buy her. Have. You can *have* her. I bought you a horse. She's yours."

It was still spitting rain and I walked over closer to the motel so I wouldn't get so wet.

"You bought me a horse."

"Yes. That's simple enough, isn't it?"

"Why did you do that, Terry?" I asked.

"What do you mean?"

"Why did you buy me a horse?"

"I don't know," he said. "What does it matter?"

"It matters," I said. "What if I don't like her? Then I'm an ungrateful bitch. I want some choice. I don't want you making decisions for me. Anyway, what do you know about horses? I can do a better job finding my own horse."

"Go to hell," Terry said, and hung up.

There were some plastic lawn chairs on a narrow strip of grass in front of the motel and I sat in one of them. It was wet. My hair was wet and I could feel droplets running down the back of my neck. A man pulled into the motel parking lot with news from up the road. Several people came out of the motel office and stood by his open window as he told them what was going on. The tornado hadn't done as much damage as it might have if the area had been more populated. A couple of people were hurt but no one had been killed, at least not that anyone knew. Three or four cars were overturned on the highway and a farm yard had been levelled. Someone's camper trailer was overturned in the ditch – the Murphys', I assumed. The biggest problem was the semi-trailer, which was leaking some kind of hazardous chemical. The highway was closed while the RCMP and highways department tried to figure out what to do and how to clean it up.

Once the man had conveyed the news, he backed the truck out of the parking lot and drove across the road to the restaurant. The people went back inside the motel office. The woman who had rented me the room saw me sitting in the rain and asked if I wanted to come inside, but I said no.

Slowly, the clouds passed and the sky mellowed and turned pink. Mrs. Murphy came from the motel room with three of the dogs and a Hula Hoop, and she had the dogs jump back and forth through the hoop. Several young girls gathered on the lot to watch. I wasn't sure where they'd come from. One little girl clapped each time a dog jumped through the hoop and the others told her to stop. The tallest girl said the clapping would bother the dogs. She said it as though she knew what she was talking about, and the other girls agreed as though they also knew. I walked over close to where the dogs were jumping and clapped. The little girl who'd been chastised stared at me, a frightened look on her face. "It's okay," I said. "They like it. They're show dogs." She looked to the tall girl for direction. The tall girl gave me a look that was far too disdainful for her age.

Mrs. Murphy gave the three dogs a signal and they all immediately sat and looked at her.

"Do any of you girls have questions?" Mrs. Murphy asked.

"You have the buttons on your shirt done up wrong," the tall girl said.

It was true. Mrs. Murphy had probably taken off her clothes to dry them out after the rain, and had mismatched the buttons and holes when she got dressed again. One side of her shirt was longer than the other.

"That wasn't a question," Mrs. Murphy said. "It was a comment, and a very rude one at that."

"I don't care," the girl said, turning to leave. She headed down a back alley behind the motel. The others followed her.

"I guess they have gangs in Melfort," I said.

"I used to be a school teacher," Mrs. Murphy said. "Girls are the worst. Give me a class full of boys any day." She hung the Hula Hoop over one arm, then held her arms out in front of her in a circle and all three dogs jumped up. She carried them that way back into the motel room.

I got Jack out of the truck and sat in the lawn chair, keeping hold of the lead so he wouldn't run off. Finch and Mr. Murphy showed up a couple of hours later, having hitched a ride back to town because the Murphys' car needed a tow. They had the Sheltie bitch with them, and two of the puppies. The others had been killed when the trailer overturned. They were too small to survive being tossed about.

Finch asked what I wanted to do. We could probably find a way to go around, he said, or we could wait a few hours until they had the highway open again. I said we might as well try to find a grid road that would take us around the roadblock but first we should find some dog food for Jack, so we walked to a service station that had a confectionery. I felt badly about the puppies, and I could tell Finch did too. Before we left, we said goodbye to the Murphys. We agreed to keep in touch, but didn't exchange addresses. I wondered if Finch had told Mr. Murphy that we weren't married and that we'd known each other less than a day, but then I thought it probably hadn't come up.

By the time we could see Prince Albert ahead I was tired. I asked Finch if he wanted to drive for a while and he fessed up and said he'd recently lost his driver's licence for being drunk. That explained why I was driving him to Spiritwood.

"I don't know how I'm going to keep doing what I do," Finch said. "My own fault though, isn't it?"

I remembered that Finch had a son, the one who'd dropped him at the gas station where we'd arranged to meet.

"What about your son?" I asked. "Can he do the driving?"

"For now," Finch said, "but I hate to depend on him. How long is he going to do what I say without getting sick of it and telling me to go to hell? Besides, he has his own talents. He's going to want his own life. That's just the way it is."

"You could hire someone," I said.

"Yeah," he said. "I could do that, but I don't want to. I'm damn mad at myself."

I thought about how Finch was different from my own father, who'd expected Terry to do the same thing that he'd done, live the same life, no questions asked. And then I thought about how Terry, in the end, was like our father, and was just as hard to get along with even though he'd gone his own way.

I told Finch about Terry then, beginning with how I had no memories of feeling anything but annoyed by him, with one exception. When he was eleven years old and I was sixteen he had meningitis and almost died, and at the worst of it I did worry that he might die and wished, even prayed, that he wouldn't. This was in southern Saskatchewan on a farm that now belongs to a neighbour. He bought it when my father got sick and it became clear once and for all that Terry wanted nothing to do with the place.

Why my father continued to pin his hopes on Terry for so many years is a mystery to me. Terry had never willingly assumed the role of my father's hired hand, and did as little as he could manage. He was not good with machinery, and he used every breakdown as an excuse to quit for the day. He showed slightly more interest in the cattle, but could not be relied on to be there when he was needed. He took the term "summer holidays" to heart. He had pretty good grades at school, though, and my father agreed to pay for a university education with the caveat that Terry study agriculture. When Terry quit midway through his second year, my father assumed that he had gotten it out of his system and would now be happy to join him on the farm. But Terry went north instead and worked in a uranium mine, and while he was there he met Phyllis, a woman from Big River.

Phyllis was not immediately a hit with my parents. For one thing, she was Métis, a word my parents didn't even know how to pronounce. And for another, she had no interest in moving south. When she became pregnant with Sarah, my father concluded that it was a mistake caused by Phyllis' carelessness, and even questioned whether the baby was Terry's. For once, my mother took a stand against my father, possibly because she feared losing a grandchild.

Terry and Phyllis worked in the north for years and when Terry was thirty or so they bought the place at Spiritwood on the advice of someone they knew, who talked them into trying to raise buffalo, or I should say talked Terry into trying to raise buffalo. Phyllis was skeptical from the beginning. Terry ended up buying a young bull and three cows for a small fortune, and they immediately knocked the fence down and got loose. The bull was hit by a truck on the highway. The cows ran off into the bush. Hunters found the carcass of one of them that fall and the other two disappeared. I have hopes they're still out there, but the likelihood is slim.

The next year, Terry tried elk and didn't do any better with them. Chronic wasting disease hit the province and they all had to be put down. He bought a sawmill and tried to operate a small lumber business but he didn't make a dime at that, and the mill sat by the road with a hand-painted FOR SALE sign on it until finally someone from Alberta bought it.

Eventually, they did get their lives on track. Phyllis decided to go back to school and become a nurse. Terry got a job working seasonally for the municipality. They bought a herd of cattle, nothing exotic, Hereford Angus crosses just like my father had. They built a new house and bought a big warmblood horse for Sarah, who was twelve years old by this time and horse crazy, just like I've always been. Now they drive her to dressage shows all summer long. I don't visit often, because Terry and I can't be in the same room for longer than an hour without acting like children who can't, or perhaps refuse to, get along. It's a pain in the ass for everyone, I know.

Terry does appear to be happy and I can't begrudge him that. It seems he was right in his decision to turn down my father's offer of the farm. My father never really got over his disappointment but at least he quit harping. My mother is crazy about Sarah, and I'm sure she is thankful for Phyllis, who turned out to be sensible in all the ways Terry isn't. I don't know how they did it, how they got the money they needed to get straightened out, but I suppose their day jobs gave them leverage at the bank, and once you've got a solid start, things begin to pay off.

"The thing is," I said to Finch, who turned out to be an exceptionally good listener, "I have a day job, and I don't see a payoff anywhere in the near or distant future. But I'm not complaining."

"The hell you aren't," he said.

After I'd told Finch about Terry and my father, I started to feel badly about my phone conversation with Terry. When I stopped at a service station for a take-out coffee I decided to call him back. I stood outside, my coffee on the hood of the truck, and dialed. Sarah answered and when she called Terry, saying it was me, he wouldn't come to the phone. I could hear Sarah say, "Well, what am I supposed to tell her?" and then there was a long silence, and finally Phyllis came on the line.

"I'm not the one who should be talking to you," she said.

"I know that," I said. "But you know Terry. He's hot-headed."

"Must run in the family," Phyllis said.

"Okay," I said. "Point taken. But someone has to tell me what's going on. Why is Terry trying to give me a horse? It's not my birthday. I haven't made a dying wish. There's no reason for you to feel sorry for me, just because you two have managed to get it together and I'm still working as a telephone operator, not that I'm complaining."

"Just a minute," Phyllis said. She held the phone away, but I could hear her say, "Terry, for Christ sake come and talk to her. Just tell her and get it over with."

He still wouldn't come, and finally Phyllis told me that Terry bought the horse to ease his conscience. That's what she said, her exact words, to ease his conscience. When I asked what for, she said, "You must know. You must have guessed." I said I didn't have a clue what she was talking about.

Phyllis covered the receiver with her hand. I could still hear her talking to Terry but I couldn't make out what they were saying. I was worried my phone was going to die. Finally, Terry took the receiver.

"All right," he said, "I'm coming clean."

"Clean about what?" I asked. I knew he wasn't referring to all the disagreements we'd had over the years. No single disagreement was even important enough to remember. It was the accumulation that made our relationship what it was.

"This place," he said.

"What place?"

"Our place. Dad paid for it."

It took a minute for that to sink in. "Your place?" I said. "You mean your land?"

"He bought Mom the house in town," Terry said, "and he set up a trust for her, and then he bought me this place. He paid off the mortgage, and he bought the machinery and the cattle. He said if I insisted on farming here instead of on his place, I might as well do it right. He paid for all this."

I was having a hard time taking in what Terry was telling me. I didn't see how it could be possible.

"So how much money did he leave you?" I asked. I'd never thought about an inheritance. He hadn't left me anything, but I hadn't thought a lot about that because I assumed he hadn't left Terry anything either, and that whatever money had been in the estate had gone into the trust he'd set up for Mom.

"He didn't leave it to me," Terry said. "It was all taken care of before he died."

"How much?" I asked.

"You don't want to know," Terry said.

I tried not to think about what this meant.

"Did Mother know?" I asked.

"No," Terry said.

That was something, at least, although he could have been lying for all I knew.

"And now you've bought me a horse? To make up for it?"

"That's right," Terry said.

"Fuck you, Terry," I said. "Fuck you all to hell." And I would have hung up on him this time but my phone card ran out of minutes and I didn't have to.

When I got back into the truck I slammed the door and my coffee slid off the hood, onto the pavement. I ordered Finch to get the sale catalogue out of the glove compartment.

"Okay," I said. "I know that you know more about this horse than you let on. I want you to tell me everything you know. Everything."

Finch looked at me.

"I mean it," I said. "Or you can get out right now and walk to Spiritwood."

Jack had his paws on the back of my seat and was trying to reach his head around so he could lick my face. I pushed him away. "And you can take this dog with you, too. I don't know why I picked him up. What a stupid thing to do."

Finch still hadn't taken the sale catalogue out of the glove compartment.

"I mean it," I said.

"I don't need the catalogue," Finch said.

"Spit it out then," I said.

"Don't get your shirt in a knot," Finch said.

"It's already in a knot," I said, and then I started to cry. I wasn't crying because I felt sorry for myself. I was just so mad. It didn't last for long, and when I stopped, Finch told me about the horse. He'd been at the sale, a possibility that had crossed my mind earlier. There were a lot of people there, Finch said, just because of this horse, a pretty dappled grey who'd been bought in Montana earlier in the year. She was a great-granddaughter of the famous Doc Bar, he said, and another distinguished sire named Leo. She was out of a good mare, he explained, who was known to produce winning horses with exceptional temperaments. I said I'd seen Doc Bar's name in the catalogue but hadn't thought much of it, and that as far as I knew every second quarter horse went back to Doc Bar one way or another.

Finch ignored me. He said that a lot of people were at the sale to bid on the horse, or just to watch and see what would happen. Everyone knew before it started that she would fetch a good price, and that other horses would go high as well because of the mare. You could feel the excitement, Finch said, and the auctioneer held off to let it build. When the bidding started, the buyers went crazy. All the horses sold high, even the mediocre ones, and the mare, of course, was the high seller. A PMU farmer from Alberta was the last to bid against Terry, and when Terry finally outbid the man, complete strangers shook his hand. They wanted to talk to him and find out where he was from.

"Well, that's all just Terry's inexperience," I said. "He probably paid twice too much." I asked exactly how much he had paid.

"Ask me the selling price of any other horse in that catalogue and I'll tell you," Finch said, "but I'm not going to tell you what your brother paid for the mare. That's between the two of you."

"Just tell me if she's worth the price, whatever it was," I said.

He wouldn't tell me that either. I supposed he was holding out to see what was going to happen between Terry and me, and whether the horse would be for sale again by morning. I supposed he was doing his job, buying and selling horses at any time of the night or day.

I thought for a minute, and then I thanked Finch for telling me as much as he had, and he asked if he still had to walk to Spiritwood. I said no. We pulled back onto the highway, and in the hour-long drive between Prince Albert and Spiritwood I told him about me, and how I had tried to talk my father into letting me farm with him when Terry went north instead of going home. My father said the farm was Terry's birthright, and that he would come around. We quit speaking over it. I moved to the city, got a job as a telephone operator, married a teacher and divorced him two years later. I moved to the East Coast and then I moved to Vancouver Island. I took a massage therapy course but that didn't work out because I didn't like to touch people. And I talked too much. Too much talk, not enough touch didn't suit the patients. I moved home again and tried one more time to talk my father into some kind of arrangement where I would gradually take over the farm. I got nowhere and we quit speaking again. I went back to the city and married a fireman. We were married for ten years. I wanted a child. He didn't. We divorced. My father sold the farm to a neighbour when he found out he had inoperable lung cancer and bought my mother a house in town with the money, or at least that's what I'd thought. My mother asked me to bury my anger so that we could become a family again before he died. We were all present the day he stopped breathing, Terry and my mother and I. I forgave him. I went back to work for the phone company and bought a horse, the Arab gelding. I joined the legion of women I told Finch about. Now I thought about my father dying and the three of us in the room with him. If my mother had been in on the secret, she would have been thinking of Sarah. I couldn't hold that against her.

When I stopped talking, Finch said it sounded like I had fought with a lot of people in my life, men in particular, and what was that all about. "Your father," he said. "Your brother. Two husbands. I couldn't help but notice."

"I can't believe you just said that to me," I said. "I've known you for less than a day."

"Ah," he said, "but it wasn't a normal day. We've been through a lot together."

"What should I do?" I asked Finch.

"Beats me," he said.

"You can't just go out and buy a horse for someone without asking them. Especially not a good one. I remember the time my father bought new living room furniture without asking my mother what she wanted. He brought home this really expensive velvety stuff that she hated, and he didn't understand why he wasn't getting his brownie points. It's like that. It's about yourself, not the other person, when you do something like that."

"Who's it about when you turn down a gift?" Finch asked.

I glared at him. He must have seen the look on my face.

"Just asking," he said.

"Don't try to make out that I'm in the wrong here," I said.

"I wouldn't dream of it," he said. "I have no particular desire to hitchhike in the middle of the night."

When we got to Spiritwood an hour later, I asked Finch where he wanted me to drop him and he gave me directions. We pulled up in front of a little house off the main drag. The sky was perfectly clear and a full moon shone in the rear window. It was a reckless moon, I thought, shining as it was on the heels of a tornado.

"Maybe I'll catch a ride home with you, if you don't mind," Finch said.

I said that I didn't, but that I might not be staying, in fact probably wouldn't be. I hadn't decided yet.

"Do you really think you could drive all the way home again tonight?"

I said I didn't know, but I might do it anyway.

"I tell you what," Finch said. "Drop me off and go and do what you have to. If you decide to leave, come round and pick me up and we'll run like a pair of greyhounds."

I looked at him. I couldn't tell if he was serious, or what exactly he was suggesting. It could have been an invitation.

"What about the funeral?" I asked.

"It won't take much time to get that over with," he said, opening the passenger door.

Jack and I watched him walk up the sidewalk to the house carrying his gear bag. A light was on, as though someone was waiting for him. I hoped to get a glimpse of whoever it was but no one came to meet him and he let himself in without knocking.

Terry and Phyllis were waiting up. From down the road I could see the lights on in the house. I turned off my truck lights and pulled over to the side of the road, a quarter mile away from their yard. I decided I wanted to see the horse, this descendant of quarter horse royalty. I took Jack with me, hoping that he wouldn't bark to announce our arrival. When we got near the yard Phyllis and Terry's mutt barked, but I called him and he came wagging his tail. Once he and Jack had made friends I turned Jack loose, and we headed for the barn. I worried that Jack might chase Terry's cattle, but there was a young bull in one of the pens behind the barn and Jack paid him no mind, which made me think he was not a city dog at all and had maybe been left behind by accident.

In the moonlight I could see Sarah's towering horse, and in the pen next to him was a nice-looking quarter horse, grey in colour. This had to be the mare, as Terry had no horse of his own and worked his cattle with a four-wheel ATV. I let myself into the pen and the mare came to me. She had a keen and gentle face. It was too bad, I thought, that I couldn't have this horse. I wished I could think differently about Terry buying her for me, that I could see it as a family thing, which it was, but not in a way that made me feel happy or connected. I rubbed the mare's neck for a while. Then I sat on the fence and watched her pick through what was left of her hay ration. When I decided it was time to go, I told Jack to stay and he did. I knew Phyllis and Terry would keep him, or should I say Phyllis and Sarah, who were both completely soft on the subject of animals.

When I got back to town I drove by the house where I'd dropped Finch off. I was half-hoping that he'd be waiting for me, but at the same time I was relieved that the house was dark and Finch was nowhere in sight. I drove around the block just to make sure and then headed toward the highway and home.

I had not seen the last of Finch. He called me a few weeks later from his place at Belle Plaine and said, "I've got a horse you might want to look at." It crossed my mind that maybe he had done what he was reputed to be good at – played Terry like a violin and got the grey for a bargain price. But Terry's not a fool, and the horse Finch had for me was not the well-bred mare. He was a sorrel gelding with a lazy streak and a no-name pedigree, the combination of which kept him in my price range. He was nothing special, Finch said, but he was a good horse. He told me I could have him for the same price he'd paid, and if I didn't like him I could bring him back. It was a deal I could be happy with.

When I went to look at the horse, Finch told me that his son had been offered a job in Europe training cutting horses for a wealthy German. He showed me a picture of the German, who was wearing a cowboy hat, and we laughed at the idea of cowboys in Germany. Finch asked me if I would consider quitting my job and going to work for him, hauling horses to and from sales.

I thought about our trip to Spiritwood. It didn't take me long to conclude that the trip with Finch was one I had no particular desire to repeat. We'd covered the distance.

I wrote him a cheque and we loaded the sorrel gelding.

As I was getting in the truck cab, I said, "I wonder what Terry will do with the mare. Maybe he'll keep her. That would be a bigger waste than if I'd taken her."

"Maybe," Finch said, "but then again, she's just a horse."

It surprised me that he would say that, but of course it's true. All things considered, a horse is just a horse. That's probably the first thing you have to learn on your way to becoming a horse dealer.

Long Gone and Mister Lonely

1. KARMA

Shortly after ten o'clock on Saturday morning, just as Sheryl finished stripping the beds, the front door opened and Sean came in and confessed that he and Perry had spent the night in jail.

"It wasn't our fault, Hon," he said. "It was that bouncer at Lenny's. You know the one. He has it in for us. We weren't doing anything that you could call criminal."

"Umm," said Sheryl, standing in the hall with the dirty sheets in her arms. She already knew about the night in jail, but she didn't say so. Kate had made her promise not to. She wasn't quite sure what to say so she just stood there. She had a burn blister on the ball of her foot and it hurt.

"I guess I should have called," Sean said, mistaking her silence for anger.

"Never mind," Sheryl said. "You're home now."

"You're not mad then?" Sean said.

"No," Sheryl said. "I'm not mad." She headed for the basement stairs and threw the sheets down. The blister hurt when she walked on it.

"I'm hungover," Sean said. "I feel like shit."

Sheryl suddenly felt like laughing. She decided to follow the sheets to the basement so she wouldn't have to face Sean, at least not for a few minutes.

"They're not going to charge us, if that's what you're wondering," Sean called down the stairs. "I thought for sure we'd get hit with mischief. Perry and I spent most of the night talking about it, what our chances were for this and that. It's surprising how much you know about the law when push comes to shove. Anyway, we got off lucky."

Sheryl buried her face in the dirty sheets, which she'd picked off the bottom step, then she managed to say, "That's good." She dropped the sheets on the floor by the washing machine. When she climbed the stairs again, Sean was still standing in the hall.

"So you were in jail," she said, having regained her composure.

"That's right," Sean said. "I can't exactly say it was a good experience, but I think in the long run I'll be able to look back and see how it was meaningful. I never want to go through that again though. Once was enough."

Teddy came into the front hall and wrapped himself around Sheryl's leg. He was five years old, but small for his age, a funny little blond boy with thick glasses that he kept losing. His head was right at the level of her hand and she stroked his fine yellow hair.

"Hey kid," Sean said. "How's my kid? Did you wonder where I was?"

"Me and Mom went camping," said Teddy.

"I'm through with Lenny's," Sean said. "At least until that bouncer is gone. He's not the kind of guy you can take on. He's got too many friends and they're all built like brick shithouses." He looked down at Teddy. "You went camping?"

"Yeah," Teddy said. "Me and Mom."

"In the backyard," Sheryl said.

"Oh," said Sean, "I wondered." Then he said, "I don't care about Lenny's anyway. It's a dump. I'm tired of it."

"You look terrible," Sheryl said. His hair was greasy and his eyes were red and swollen.

"Yeah. I guess I'd better take a shower. Make me some scrambled eggs, will you? With cheese and onions. And toast, but don't put the toast on until I'm ready to eat, so it doesn't get cold."

"We stayed up all night," Teddy said.

"No kidding," Sean said. "Me too." He looked at Sheryl. "Mom stayed up all night?" She knew what he was thinking. Since she'd started teaching she hadn't made it past ten o'clock on a Friday night. Even in the movie theatre, she'd fall sound asleep. Sean teased her about it, but she knew it irritated him.

"Yeah," Teddy said, "we stayed awake all through the stars."

"I feel good," Sheryl said. It sounded lame, but she couldn't put into words how she really felt.

"I feel like hell," Sean said. "Physically, at least. Mentally, I'm not sure. I haven't figured it out yet." He went upstairs to the bathroom and turned on the shower. Sheryl remembered that all the towels were on the floor in the basement, dirty. She shouted up the stairs at him.

"What's that, Hon?" he shouted back, turning the water off.

"The towels are all dirty," she said. "I haven't done them yet."

"Christ," Sean said.

"Sorry," Sheryl said.

"I just spent the night in jail. I need a towel."

"Check the back of the door," Sheryl said. "I think I left one there."

She heard the shower again and hoped she hadn't used all the hot water in the washing machine. She leaned against the wall, slipped her foot out of her sandal and examined the burn. It didn't look bad, she decided. The blister was small and would heal on its own.

"So what's it like," Sheryl asked later, "being in jail?"

"I'll tell you one thing," Sean said, "they have no respect for you." He was eating the scrambled eggs Sheryl had made. "Did you use Velveeta cheese?" he asked.

"Yes," she said.

He took another bite. Sheryl could tell he was trying to figure out what was wrong with the eggs. "They don't let you ask questions in a dignified way," he said. "When you get arrested it's your right to ask questions. They treat you like someone who's there just to give them grief, as though you planned it."

"You were caught red-handed," Sheryl said. "You had the evidence in the back seat of the car, as I understand it."

"We never claimed to be innocent," Sean said. "But it was just a caper. They didn't have to throw us in jail. It's that bouncer. He has it in for us. I wish there was something I could do about him, but I don't see what. I'd like to get him fired but I think he's too well-connected."

"He's probably too good at his job," Sheryl said. "That would be the real reason."

"I don't see why you would say that," Sean said. "Perry and I won't be going back there. He's bad for business, the way I see it."

Teddy was playing on the floor under the table. He had his cars and trucks and was imagining roads in the linoleum pattern, a game he played often.

"Goddamn it," Sean said to Teddy. "Don't do that."

"Your foot is a big mountain," Teddy said.

"It's not a mountain," Sean said. "It's my frigging foot. Take your trucks out to the sandbox."

"The sandbox is all burned up," Teddy said.

"You should go to bed, Teddy," Sheryl said. "You were up all night, remember?"

"I'm not tired," Teddy said.

"Well, go out on the deck then. You shouldn't be listening to us talk about this anyway. Don't tell anybody Daddy was in jail."

"I'll kick your butt if you do," Sean said.

"Did you kill someone?" Teddy asked Sean as he came out from under the table with his trucks in a plastic tackle box.

"Jesus, no," Sean said. "What's wrong with him anyway?" he asked Sheryl. "He's always saying weird shit. And what's he talking about, the sandbox is all burned up? Jesus."

"Just go out to the deck, Teddy," Sheryl said. "I'll be out in a while. I'll bring some Kool-Aid."

Sean finished off the scrambled eggs and Sheryl poured him another cup of coffee.

"It feels good to be home," he said. "I think that night in jail was good for me. I appreciate things more. A hot shower. Scrambled eggs. I don't mind saying, you get scared when they put you in a cell and lock the door, even if you know they can't keep you there. Even if you know you haven't done anything of any consequence."

"I lied about the cheese," Sheryl said. "It wasn't Velveeta. I bought the store brand because it was cheaper. I didn't think you'd notice."

"Oh," Sean said.

"Is that all?" Sheryl asked. "Oh?"

"Well, I'm not going to have a fit, if that's what you mean," Sean said. He drained his coffee and then rocked back on his chair.

"Don't do that," Sheryl said. "It's hard on the chair legs."

Sean paid no attention. "Is the kid going to have a nap or what?" he asked.

"Probably not," Sheryl said. "You know him. Why?"

"I think I could do with a conjugal visit," Sean said.

"You can think all you want," Sheryl said, "but I'm in the middle of washing clothes and somebody has to get the groceries."

She took his plate to the sink and rinsed it. As she stood there, she lifted her sore foot. She wished Sean would take a nap. She wished they hadn't let him out of jail so soon.

"I'll tell you why I don't care about the cheese," Sean said. "It's pointless to get worked up about trivialities. The night in jail had an effect on me. Maybe it was like one of those near-death experiences. You come out of it and you can never look at life the same way again."

Sheryl turned and stared at him, her sore foot resting against the calf of her other leg. "What are you talking about?" she said.

"I don't know," Sean said. "Karma, I guess."

She took a glass pitcher from the cupboard and mixed up a package of grape Kool-Aid.

"You know," Sean said, "you've been acting strange ever since I came through the door. Before, you were almost smiling. But now there's another look. I don't know what it means."

Sheryl handed him the jug of Kool-Aid and a glass. "Take this to Teddy," she said. "And if he spills it, think karma."

"What's that supposed to mean?" Sean asked.

"Figure it out," Sheryl said.

2. THE KOENIG BROTHERS

It was Kate that Sean first liked the looks of, not Sheryl. The two girls were staying in a cabin a quarter mile up the hill from the lake. Sean drove the bread delivery truck then, and he passed them most mornings as they walked down to the beach in their bikinis. He told Sheryl that at the end of the day, after he'd finished making his deliveries, he would often go looking for them. First he walked up and down the beach, then he checked the café and the hotel bar, but they were never around. A few times he even peeked in the window of the cabin he thought was theirs, but they weren't home. It became a mystery to be solved, what the two girls did, who they did it with, where they went.

Early one Friday afternoon there was a fire at the bakery. It wasn't much but the sprinkler system cut in and made a mess and the boss told everyone to go home for the rest of the day. Sean drove out to the beach and parked his car across the street from the cabin, and at about four o'clock the two girls came walking up the hill. They walked right past his car without looking at him and went inside the cabin. Shortly after that they came out again wearing tight T-shirts and faded jeans and sandals, and they got in the old mustard-yellow Toyota that was parked in the drive. It took them a long time to get it started, but they finally did and then they headed for the highway. Sean followed their trail of blue smoke at a distance. He didn't think they'd noticed him, but of course they had.

In the Toyota Kate said, "That guy who drives the bread delivery truck is following us."

Sheryl wanted to turn around and look, but she didn't want to be obvious. Kate, who was driving, watched him in the rearview mirror.

"Are you sure he's following us?" Sheryl asked. "It might just be a coincidence."

"He was parked in front of the cabin," Kate said. "I hardly think it's a coincidence. It's pretty weird, if you ask me. I hope he's not a psycho."

"If it's the bread delivery guy, he's not bad-looking," Sheryl said. "I wonder which one of us he fancies."

"It better be you," Kate said. "I'm not interested in having any lost dogs follow me around."

"You don't think he's good-looking?" Sheryl asked.

"I didn't say that," Kate said, "but right now it's beside the point."

They turned off the highway and headed west toward Morgan. Kate reported that the car following them had driven on past the turnoff, but before long it was behind them again.

"A pea brain could do a better job of following us than that," she said.

Kate pulled over onto the shoulder and the car behind them went by in a cloud of grid-road dust. Then, minutes later, Kate and Sheryl passed it again, poorly camouflaged in a stand of trees by the road.

"I guess he is a pea brain," Sheryl said.

Kate honked the horn at him as they drove by.

Sheryl started to laugh. Then Kate got the giggles and could hardly drive. She had to slow down. By the time they pulled up in front of the Morgan Hotel they were both laughing so hard their sides hurt. They sat in front of the hotel for a few minutes, waiting for the other car to appear, but it was nowhere in sight.

Finally Kate looked at her watch. "Goddamn it," she said. "It's quarter after five. That idiot made us late for work."

"Good thing the boss is your uncle," Sheryl said.

Sean came into the bar with Perry about half an hour before last call. They were wearing baseball team jackets and caps, and were already three sheets to the wind. Sheryl was waiting tables and Kate was in the women's washroom cleaning up vomit. It was Sheryl's turn, but she'd talked Kate into doing it for her. "I'll do anything you ask," Sheryl had promised. "I'll kiss your feet if you want, just please, please don't make me clean up that vomit. I'll get sick, I swear it."

"Why would I want you to kiss my feet, for God's sake?" Kate said. But she'd agreed to clean up the mess, saying, "Just remember, you owe me."

Sean and Perry sat down at a table and when Sheryl went to wait on them Sean said, "Where's your partner in crime?"

"My partner in crime?" Sheryl said. "I don't know what you mean."

"The other one," Sean said. "The cute one."

Perry gave Sean a clip across the back of the head, knocking his ball cap off.

"Don't mind him," Perry said to Sheryl. "He's an asshole."

"Tell me something I don't already know," Sheryl said. "Now, what'll you have? Not that you need anything else, but it's my job to ask."

"Where'd you say your friend is?" Sean asked.

"I didn't say, but if you must know she's mopping up puke in the women's can."

"Oh," Sean said. "I wish you hadn't told me that."

"Bring us a couple of Buds," Perry said.

When Sheryl went back to the bar to order the beers, Kate came out of the washroom.

"Christ," she said, "I'd like to know who made that mess."

"Well, there's not a woman in the house right now except for you and me," Sheryl said, "and I don't think it was either of us." The bar was almost empty. There was a dance at the lake and a dance always cleared the place out early, except for the old men.

"Maybe it was one of the Koenig brothers," Kate said. "They wouldn't know the difference between the men's and the women's can." The Koenig brothers were playing pool. They were both over eighty and spent most of their pension cheques in the Morgan Hotel bar.

Sheryl pointed at Sean. "Look who's here," she said. "And guess who he's got his eye on. I'll give you a hint. It's not me."

"Great," said Kate. She looked at the two Budweisers on Sheryl's tray. "For them?" she asked. Sheryl nodded. Kate took the beers and said, "We'll see what he thinks of bitch-barmaid-from-hell."

The bartender, who was Kate's Uncle Steve and the owner of the hotel, heard her. He said, "I don't know where she learned to talk like that. Not from my side of the family."

"You have to talk like that, working in this place," Sheryl said. "No offence intended."

"None taken," Steve said. He came around to Sheryl's side of the bar and sat down on a stool.

"Christ almighty," he said. "My feet hurt."

"Mine too," Sheryl said. She sat on a stool next to Steve and they watched Kate deliver the beers. They couldn't hear what was being said.

"So how's the cabin working out?" Steve asked.

"Great," Sheryl said. The cabin was Steve's and he let Sheryl and Kate live there for nothing. They almost always worked the night shift, which meant they got to spend the day on the beach, as long as the sun was shining.

"How's the boyfriend?" Steve asked.

"He dumped me," Sheryl said. "For a girl who plays basketball."

"Is she tall?" Steve asked.

"I don't know," Sheryl said. "I've never seen her. Anyway, I don't care. He was nothing special."

Sheryl didn't think she should moan about her ex-boyfriend to Steve. She hadn't cared much about him, and Steve had an ex-wife that he apparently cared about a lot. He referred to her as Long-gone Lucy, even though her name wasn't Lucy, it was Marian.

"Well," said Steve, "I was going to say I was sorry he dumped you, but if he was nothing special I guess I won't bother. Maybe I should congratulate you instead."

"I don't know if I'd go that far," Sheryl said.

Steve looked at his watch and then turned his attention to the Koenig brothers, who were still playing pool. "It's about time for the Two Stooges to go at it," he said. "You can just about set your clock by them."

"They're late tonight," Sheryl said. The words were hardly out of her mouth when the Koenig brothers began waving their pool cues around and shouting at one another.

"Same damn thing every night," Steve said. "One of these nights someone's going to take it in the eye and I'll be the one who gets sued." He got up, shouting, "Yo, you old buggers cut that out before you hurt somebody."

Sheryl watched as he expertly manoeuvred his way between the waving pool cues. He managed to disarm the two brothers and steer them toward a table where several other old men were sitting. Sheryl heard him say, "Last call, boys." The spectre of last call usually made the Koenig brothers forget whatever it was they'd been arguing about.

The old men always ordered the same thing, draft beer, so Sheryl went behind the bar and filled a dozen glasses and took them to the table. She had to make two trips. By the time she got back for the second time Steve had the Koenig brothers shaking hands, first with each other, then with whoever they could reach without getting up. They wanted to shake Sheryl's hand, too, but she was sick of them so she left Steve to collect the tab.

She went back to the bar, put her tray down on the counter and kicked her sandals off. The soles of her feet were burning and she regretted not wearing her running shoes. She looked at Kate, who was now seated at the table with Perry and Sean. She appeared to be deep in conversation with Perry.

Steve came back to the bar with a handful of change and small bills. "It must be true, what they say about old people reverting to childhood," he said. "Look at them. This place is like a daycare centre, only they drink beer instead of Kool-Aid." Sheryl laughed. Then she pointed at Kate and said, "Look what's happening over there."

"So much for the bitchy barmaid or whatever it was she called herself," Steve said.

"They'll probably give her a huge tip," Sheryl said. "That would piss me off."

At twelve-thirty Steve kicked Perry and Sean and the old men out. Usually the bar stayed open until one, but it was so dead Steve decided there was no point. Sheryl and Kate were going to help him clean up, but he told them to leave.

"I'm going home," he said. "I'll clean up in the morning. You girls can still catch the dance. Go have some fun."

On the way to the car, Sheryl said, "Your uncle is a pretty cool guy." She was thinking about how hard it would be for Steve to find a replacement for Long-gone Lucy in a town the size of Morgan. "Why don't we go get him and take him to the dance with us?" she asked Kate.

"Don't be an idiot," Kate said. "He won't want to come with us."

"Why don't we ask him?" Sheryl said. "He can say no if he doesn't want to come."

"You ask him then," Kate said. "I'm not going to."

Sheryl went back into the bar. All the lights were out except for the ones over the pool table. Steve was about to rack up the balls.

"I thought you were going home," she said.

"This is home," he said. That was true, sort of. He lived in a suite in the back of the hotel.

"Why don't you come to the dance with Kate and me?" Sheryl said. "Maybe we can find you someone to dance with."

"What makes you think I need someone to dance with?" Steve said. There was a cool edge to his voice. Sheryl felt herself blush.

"Okay," she said. "I just thought … I don't know, you're here on your own."

"There's more to life than having someone to dance with," Steve said. But you're young and stupid. Don't take that personally. I was young and stupid, too."

"You're still young," she said, backing toward the door. "Anyway, never mind."

"Just a minute," Steve said. Sheryl stopped. "You work for me," he said. "That's all. Don't get any ideas."

Sheryl felt as though she was being rebuked by her father, or a favourite teacher. Then she figured out that Steve thought she was coming on to him. She knew she was beet red when she turned and hurried out the door.

"I told you he wouldn't want to come," Kate said as Sheryl got in the car. "He's too old to go to dances at the lake."

"It didn't hurt to ask," Sheryl said. She was glad it was dark so Kate couldn't see her red face. She felt completely humiliated and didn't know how she'd face Steve when she came to work on Monday.

Kate tried to start the car. It wouldn't turn over.

"Maybe it's just flooded," Sheryl said.

They sat there for a few minutes, then Kate tried again. The car still wouldn't start.

"Great," Kate said. "Now I'm going to have to go and ask Steve to drive us back to the lake."

"No," Sheryl said. "We can't ask him to do that. He's tired. He said he was really tired."

"Well, if we're going to ask him, we should do it now," Kate said, "not half an hour from now when he's in his pyjamas."

"I don't imagine he wears pyjamas," Sheryl said. "I can't see it."

"You know what I mean."

"We can't ask him to drive us," Sheryl said. "He's pretty good to us already. It would be taking advantage of him." She was afraid Steve might think they'd engineered the car breaking down. He might think it was a ploy.

"Well, what are we going to do then?" Kate wanted to know. "Hitchhike? Like someone trustworthy is going to come along at this time of night."

Sheryl was trying to think of a solution that didn't involve Steve, when Sean and Perry came driving up the street.

They angle-parked next to Kate and Sheryl, on Kate's side. Perry rolled down his window and said, "Anything we can do for you ladies?"

"Yeah," Kate said, "you can give us a ride to the lake. This God-damned car won't start."

Perry got in the back seat and Kate climbed in next to him. Sheryl got in the front with Sean.

"So this is your car," Sheryl said to him, conversationally.

"You noticed," Sean said. He was obviously sulking. Sheryl supposed that was because *she* was sitting beside him instead of Kate. She was tempted to tell him to go fuck himself and take her chances hitchhiking, but she quickly decided that would be excessively dramatic. Instead, she said, "You drive the bread delivery truck."

"Tell me something I don't already know," Sean said.

"I guess that's touché," Sheryl said, and gave up.

Kate talked all the way to the lake. She told Perry how she and Sheryl had taken the job at her uncle's bar so they could live at the beach for the summer and save money living for free in Steve's cabin. They were both going to university, she said, to get their teaching certificates, because teachers worked only ten months of the year and earned a pretty good salary. It wasn't just for the salary though. They both liked kids, they wouldn't do it if they didn't, how could you? In fact, she told Perry, she liked kids so much she was planning to major in handicapped kids. They were challenging to work with, she said, but if you had the talent for it, that's what you should do, not everyone's cut out for it. By the time they got to the lake road, Sheryl wanted to scream at Kate to shut the hell up.

Sheryl was hoping they wouldn't get stuck for the rest of the night with Sean and Perry, but when they reached the townsite, Sean drove straight to the cabin without mentioning the dance. Sheryl wanted to put him on the spot and ask him how he knew where they lived, but she didn't bother. At this point, it seemed like too much trouble. She opened the passenger door to get out and Perry said, "How about we drive over and see if the dance is still going?"

Kate said, "I'm up for that. How about you, Sheryl?"

Sheryl said she was too tired.

"Great," said Kate. "Well, I guess I won't go either then."

"You can go," Sheryl said.

"I'm not going without you," Kate said. "Come on. Just for an hour. The band will still be playing."

Perry said, "Come on, Sheryl. Just for an hour."

Sheryl was about to say no with conviction when Kate said, "Remember, Sheryl, you owe me. Earlier tonight? You said you'd do anything, all I had to do was ask. Well, this is it. I'm asking."

Perry tapped Sean on the shoulder and said, "She should come with us, don't you think, Sean?"

Sean said nothing.

Sheryl thought, *What a prick*. Still, it was true that she owed Kate for cleaning up the vomit, so she went to the dance. Sean disappeared as soon as they got inside the door, and Kate and Perry headed for the dance floor. No one showed any interest in Sheryl, who sat at a table and nursed a beer. It was like she was invisible. She hated being there and kept going over and over her conversation with Steve. After what seemed like hours, Sean showed up and sat down at the table with her.

"So what's your name anyway?" he asked her.

"Sheryl," she answered. "Miss Sheryl to you."

"Well, Miss Sheryl," he said, "do you want to dance or what?"

"I suppose," she said. "I don't seem to have anything better to do at the moment."

They danced, and by the time he took her home, she knew that she had grown on him. She felt just a bit triumphant, and also relieved, because she'd thought of a way to deal with Steve on Monday. She'd be able to slip into the conversation that she'd found a new boyfriend to replace the one who had left her for the basketball player.

3. BLACK WATER

One warm spring day Sheryl took her grade two class to the country. She wanted the children to see the farmers at work in the fields. She took Teddy, who was three at the time, along on the school bus, and the girls played with him and pretended he was a doll. They loved the way he looked with his thick glasses and his long yellow hair. One little girl braided his hair and tied the braid with a pink elastic. Teddy loved the braid. He wouldn't let Sheryl take it out at bedtime that night. In the morning he took it out himself and was mystified that his straight hair had gone curly.

The school bus delivered Sheryl's class to a farm and then went back to the city. The farmer's wife toured the grade twos around the yard and took them through the barn to show them the animals. She'd kept the animals in, she told the children, so they could get a better look at them. There were cows with new calves, and horses and even a goat, but what really caught the children's interest was a cardboard box placed in the manger of an empty stall. The box held a pair of baby raccoons. The woman explained to the children that her husband had found them when he was working one of the fields. The mother raccoon was nowhere to be seen, so the farmer had brought the babies home. He'd carried them in his cap; that's how tiny they'd been. The woman showed the children how the babies were fed, with a bottle. She told them that at first they'd had to feed them with an eye dropper.

One little boy asked, "What will happen to the raccoons when they're grown up?"

"Well," the woman said, "grown-up raccoons are a bit of a problem on a farm. We're not sure what to do with them."

"Couldn't they live in a cage?" the boy asked.

"Maybe that's what we'll do," the woman said. "We'll build a nice cage so children from the city can see raccoons when they visit the farm."

Sheryl had a picture of the farmer and his wife gassing the raccoons with the exhaust from the pick-up truck. That's what she remembered her father doing with unwanted litters of kittens. He'd put them in a gunny sack and tie the opening around the truck's exhaust pipe.

"They just go to sleep," her father used to tell her, before she was old enough to know better. "When they wake up they're in heaven."

After the class had finished touring the barn and chicken coop and the other outbuildings, the woman suggested to Sheryl that she take the children just west of the farmyard.

"My husband is seeding," the woman said. "The children can watch and when he gets to this side of the field he'll stop and explain how the machinery works."

"Would he mind?" Sheryl asked.

"Oh no," the woman said. "He enjoys the children."

The woman also told Sheryl that they might be able to find a duck's nest if they looked in the grass along the edge of the field. There was an irrigation ditch, she said, and sometimes water birds nested there.

"An irrigation ditch?" Sheryl asked, alarms going off in her head. "Is it safe? I wouldn't want anyone to fall in."

"Wait till you see how much water is in it," the woman laughed. "I don't think you have to worry."

They set out, Sheryl and Teddy, seventeen grade two students and a couple of volunteer mothers who intimidated Sheryl but, still, she was glad to have them along. The farmer was on the far side of the field when they got there, so Sheryl suggested that the children look for birds' nests in the grass while they waited for him to come around. She had the children look in pairs, and the little girl who had braided Teddy's hair on the bus took him for her partner.

They had no sooner got the children off searching the edge of the field and the grass along the ditch when Teddy's partner began to scream. At the same time, one of the mothers discovered a nest and shouted for everyone to come and see. Sheryl wasn't sure where to direct her attention, but she quickly realized the screaming girl was frantic and that her screaming had something to do with Teddy.

Sheryl raced over to the girl and discovered that Teddy was down in the shallow irrigation ditch, standing in mucky black water. It was up over the tops of his running shoes. He had a puzzled look on his face, but it was because of the girl's screaming and not because his feet were muddy and wet. In fact, he liked the ditch and didn't want to come out. Sheryl tried to coax him out so she wouldn't have to go in after him, but he shook his head and then, grinning devilishly, sat down in the water. The girl kept crying, "Oh teacher, I'm sorry, I'm sorry," and finally Sheryl decided to leave Teddy where he was for the time being. She put her arms around the girl and comforted her. "Hush now. Never mind, Teddy likes the water."

"But he might drown," the girl said, still crying.

"He won't drown," Sheryl said. "There isn't enough water in the ditch to drown."

"You can drown in an inch of water," the girl sobbed. "That's why you never leave a baby in the bath."

"That's true," Sheryl said. "And I can tell you'll make a very good babysitter when you're a little older. But Teddy won't drown in the ditch. We're right here to see that he doesn't."

Sheryl remembered then that one of the mothers had found something, and when she looked she saw the woman with a crowd of children gathered around her.

"I think they've found a nest over there," Sheryl said to the girl, pointing at the group of children. "Maybe it has eggs in it. Go and see."

The girl stopped crying and said, "How will you get Teddy out of the ditch?"

"You leave that to me," Sheryl said. "Go on. Hurry now."

The girl ran over to the circle of children.

So far, the two mothers and the other children were oblivious to the fact that Teddy was in the water, and Sheryl decided she would try to keep it that way. She figured she'd have to bribe Teddy out of the ditch. The mothers would probably not approve of the grade two teacher using bribery, but Sheryl was willing to try just about anything so she wouldn't have to take her shoes and socks off and wade into the muck.

Sheryl said, "Teddy, please get out of that ditch. You'll catch a cold if you stay there." Luckily, she had a change of overalls for him in her backpack. He still had accidents once in a while.

Teddy shook his head and began slapping his hands down against the surface of the water, the way he did in the bathtub at home.

"Don't do that," Sheryl said. "You'll get covered in mud."

She immediately realized her mistake. Covered in mud sounded fine to him.

She was searching her bag for treats that she could bribe him with when she noticed the farmer coming toward them on his tractor. He had been going in a circle around the perimeter of the field, but now he was coming across the field, travelling erratically and leaving a bizarre zigzag trail in the black earth.

Something was wrong. This was not how farmers seeded their fields. It crossed Sheryl's mind that maybe the farmer was doing something odd and amusing for the benefit of the city children, but then she quickly realized how ridiculous that was.

Sheryl called to the mothers, pointing at the tractor. Then she turned back to Teddy, who was still splashing in the ditch. She was beginning to get angry. She was also beginning to wonder what the mothers would think of her as a teacher if they got the idea she couldn't control her own child. Sheryl could just imagine this story of Teddy's bad behaviour circulating among the members of the school's parent advisory group. She could think of nothing in her bag that would suffice as a bribe.

"Teddy," she said, "get out of that water right now. I'm losing my patience."

Teddy deliberately splashed her.

"That's it," she said. "Next time we go on a field trip like this you can't come. You'll have to stay home with the babysitter." She immediately felt guilty for saying that. It was mean. It was also an idle threat, which she tried not to use.

Just then the farmer's wife came running. She had noticed the tractor's unusual course. She was shouting as she came across the yard, and when she got close enough, Sheryl realized she was saying, "He's having a seizure."

The children watched the woman approach, and when they realized she was shouting about the farmer they all looked out across the field. They rearranged themselves so they could see better and soon they were lined up, watching, as though they were at a parade.

The farmer's wife ran past them and into the field, toward the tractor. Sheryl began to think maybe they should get the children away – it appeared that something terrible was about to happen – but she was transfixed. She watched the woman approach the tractor, managing to stay out of its unpredictable path, and then run along beside it, still shouting. Sheryl prayed that the woman wouldn't try to climb onto the tractor, as to do so she would have to step into the path of the seed drill the tractor was pulling. What if she fell? She would be run over. Sheryl found herself holding her breath. Her heart was pounding.

The tractor was getting close enough that it became imperative to get the children out of the way. The two mothers realized this, too, and began herding them up, pushing them toward the farmyard. Sheryl could see the farmer slumped over the steering wheel. His path had straightened, and he was now heading for the spot where she was standing and straight for Teddy, who was still sitting in the ditch splashing mud all over himself.

Sheryl jumped down the bank and into the ditch, losing her footing on the soft bottom and falling forward onto her knees. Teddy thought it was funny, Sheryl struggling to get to her feet, grabbing him and leaping out of the ditch, dripping black silty water.

The tractor was very close. Sheryl ran for the farmyard, but when she felt they were out of harm's way she had to stop and see what would happen. With Teddy in her arms, she watched the tractor go nose down and sideways into the ditch. The seed drill jacked up and the hitch broke, tearing the hydraulic hoses. Fluids spewed out onto the ground and the tractor tipped awkwardly, becoming wedged in the ditch, half on its side. The motor continued to roar and the tractor's huge rear tires chewed into the soft earth until the farmer's wife managed to climb inside the cab and turn off the ignition.

She was shouting again and waving at Sheryl. Sheryl put Teddy down and went closer so she could hear what the woman was saying.

"Call an ambulance!" the woman shouted. "Go to the house and call an ambulance."

Sheryl picked up Teddy again and ran to the house, but then she sent one of the mothers inside to make the phone call because she was covered in mud.

"Is it bad?" the other mother wanted to know. She was holding a large spotted egg in her hand.

"I don't know," said Sheryl. "I don't think the tractor could have gone over on him. He's still inside the cab, as far as I could see. I think it must have been a seizure, like she said. Or maybe he had a heart attack."

"One of us should try to help her," the mother said. "Do you know CPR?"

Sheryl shook her head.

The mother said, "I'll go. You have yourself and the little boy to get cleaned up." She handed Sheryl the egg, then went into the house. She came back with a couple of blankets and hurried across the yard toward the ditch.

The egg was still warm. The children were all standing quietly, subdued by the turn of events. Sheryl said to them, "Does anyone know what kind of egg this is?" No one did. She said, "We should try to keep it warm, shouldn't we? How could we keep it warm?"

A little boy said, "Your hands will keep it warm until we get back to school. Then we can put it under a light bulb."

"That's a good idea," Sheryl said. She wondered why the woman had removed the egg from the nest in the first place; she would talk to the children about that the next day when the mothers weren't there.

Teddy said, "I'm cold."

"You shouldn't have gone in the water," Sheryl said. She herself was uncomfortable in her wet jeans. She was thankful it was a warm day. She said to Teddy, "Never mind. I have dry clothes for you in my bag."

Teddy wouldn't change in front of the other children so Sheryl took him behind the house.

"Take those wet pants off," she commanded, putting the egg down in the grass and digging around in her backpack for the dry overalls.

Teddy sat down and took off his shoes and socks. They were covered in mud. When he took off his overalls, Sheryl discovered a leech stuck to the side of his leg. She was horrified, but Teddy was fascinated. He pulled at it, but his fingers couldn't hang on to its slippery body.

"It's brown jelly," he said.

Sheryl thought she was going to be sick. She couldn't bring herself to touch it. She found a stick in the grass and tried to scrape it off, but it stuck like glue.

"Salt," she said to Teddy. "We need some salt. They fall off when you put salt on them."

"Don't want it off," said Teddy.

"Teddy," Sheryl said, "don't try my patience any more. You'll get sick if we leave it on. You'll get some terrible disease."

She pulled Teddy's dry overalls on and rolled up one pant leg so the leech was still visible. Then she put the wet clothes, including Teddy's shoes and socks, in the plastic grocery bag she'd brought for just such a purpose. *What a disaster of a day*, she thought.

Sheryl sent the remaining mother into the house for a salt shaker, while Teddy showed off the leech to the children. They all watched, fascinated, as it shrivelled up under a sprinkling of salt and then fell off. They were poking at it with a stick when they heard the ambulance coming. Sheryl ran to direct it to where the tractor was.

The attendants drove as far as they could through the farmyard, then got out and carried a stretcher the rest of the way on foot. Moments later, they returned with the farmer on the stretcher. He was motionless. They put him in the back of the ambulance, his wife got in too and they sped away. It was all over in what seemed like an instant.

The mother who had taken the blankets to the farmer came walking back slowly. She had the blankets with her. She folded them carefully and took them into the house. When she came out again she said to Sheryl, "I don't think he's going to make it. It didn't look good." She said it quietly, so the children couldn't hear.

The farmer's wife had promised them cookies and a drink as part of the visit, but neither Sheryl nor the mothers felt comfortable helping themselves in her house, so they went to the barn to see the baby raccoons again while they were waiting for the school bus to collect them. Teddy, who was still in his bare feet, wanted to go in the barn with the other children so Sheryl put his muddy shoes on him. She didn't feel like arguing.

Finally, the school bus showed up. On the way back to the city one of the children asked where the egg was. Sheryl was embarrassed to admit that she'd laid it in the grass and left it there. The mother who'd collected it in the first place seemed to have forgotten she'd given it to Sheryl, so Sheryl didn't bother explaining. The mother kept saying, "I wonder what could have happened to it." Sheryl felt a little bad about the egg, but she was pretty sure it would have rotted under a light bulb in the classroom anyway.

Over the next few weeks, Sheryl became obsessed with the obituaries in the paper. When several weeks had gone by and she hadn't seen the farmer listed, she decided to call his wife. The woman thanked Sheryl for calling and apologized for leaving without giving the children their cookies.

"Don't worry about that," Sheryl said. "How is your husband doing?"

"He had a pretty bad concussion," the woman said, "but he seems to be all right. He's epileptic, you know. I've been thinking for years that he should quit farming and this clinched it. We're going to try and sell."

"What will you do?" Sheryl asked. She was thinking about her own father, and how he didn't know how to do anything but farm.

"I don't know," the woman answered. "I just know he can't go on. All that machinery is too dangerous."

"I'm glad he's recovered," Sheryl said. "We were all pretty worried."

"I'm sorry the children had to be here," the woman said. "I've thought about that many times in the last few weeks. But these things happen. Life is never simple, is it?"

"No," Sheryl said, "life is not simple. It certainly is not."

She hung up the phone then, surprised that she'd been able to agree so quickly and with such certainty that life is not simple.

4. PIG'S HEART

It was Friday night. Sean and Perry were out playing pool. Kate had phoned earlier to ask if Sheryl was interested in going to a movie, but Sheryl said she was too tired. She didn't know how Kate could manage to have so much energy after spending the week with her class of emotionally disturbed children, several of whom had serious behaviour problems and hit one another and threw temper tantrums. Sheryl had a class of perfectly normal grade twos and she was so tired at the end of the week she could hardly drag herself upstairs to the bedroom. On Friday night, she and Teddy usually fell asleep on the couch with the TV on. She was glad that Sean went out with Perry on Friday nights. It meant she didn't have to entertain him.

The phone rang at midnight and Sheryl woke just as Teddy picked up the receiver. He listened for a minute and then said, "She's sleeping."

"No, I'm not," Sheryl said. "Who is it?"

"It's Kate," Teddy said. "She says to wake you up."

"You don't have to wake me up," Sheryl said. "I'm already awake." She crawled off the couch and went to the phone.

"Guess what," Kate said.

"I can't imagine," Sheryl said, trying not to sound sleepy.

"They're in jail."

"Who's in jail?"

"Perry and Sean. I'm not supposed to tell you, so when Sean gets out or calls you or whatever, you have to pretend you don't know. Perry called me because he didn't want me to worry when he didn't come home, but Sean's afraid to call you. He knows you'll be really pissed. He told Perry to make me promise I wouldn't call you."

"Did you promise?" Sheryl asked.

"Of course, but you don't think I was going to let you worry all night, do you? What kind of friend would I be then?"

"I doubt if I would have noticed he wasn't here," Sheryl said. "At least not until morning. But anyway, thanks." Then she asked, "What are they doing in jail?"

"It's too stupid," Kate said. "They were at Lenny's, and Perry left ahead of Sean and was waiting for him in the car. Sean comes running out carrying a bar stool and shoves it in the back seat, and they take off and immediately get pulled over by the cops, and now they're in jail. I can't believe what a pair of idiots they are."

It sounded like it was Sean's fault. Sheryl asked if Perry wanted to kill Sean for getting him thrown in jail.

"I don't think so," Kate said. "I think he's getting off on pretending to be an innocent victim of police harassment."

"Did Perry say when they're going to let them out?" Sheryl asked.

"No," Kate said. "It won't be tonight though. I guess I'll go down there in the morning and see what's up. Maybe I'll get to 'post bail.' That'll be a new experience. Anyway, I thought you'd like to know."

"You're not going down now?"

"No way," Kate said. "I hope they're in the drunk tank with someone really disgusting. Besides, I'm in my bathrobe. I was just on my way upstairs to have a bubble bath."

"I guess I'd better go put Teddy to bed," Sheryl said. "We were sleeping on the couch. Thanks for phoning." It was true that she would have worried if she'd woken up in the morning and Sean wasn't there. She probably would have thought he was in an accident.

She hung up the phone. "Daddy's in jail," she said to Teddy. After she said it, she thought maybe she shouldn't have. She wasn't sure why she told him.

"For how long?" he asked.

"I don't know," Sheryl said.

"For a long time, probably," Teddy said.

Sheryl looked at him. "Why do you think he'll have to stay there a long time?" she asked.

"That's just what I think," Teddy said. "We should do something special, like when Nanna died."

"It wasn't Nanna," Sheryl said. "I keep telling you, Nanna didn't die. It was Nanna's sister, Aunt Dorothy, who died. Nanna still lives in Calgary."

Six months ago, Sean's Aunt Dorothy had died and his mother asked him to go with her to the funeral in Edmonton. Sheryl couldn't bear the thought of being trapped in a car and then in some relative's house in Edmonton with Sean and his mother, so she and Teddy had stayed home alone and gone to the museum and McDonald's for supper.

Sheryl wondered why Teddy kept getting mixed up about who had died. She'd told him half a dozen times it wasn't Nanna. She supposed the problem was that Teddy didn't know Aunt Dorothy so he filled in the blank with someone he knew. She hoped he wouldn't think Nanna was a ghost next time her saw her.

"Let's go camping," Teddy said.

"Camping?" Sheryl said. Where had he heard about camping? They didn't even own a tent.

"In the backyard," Teddy said. "Like the neighbours."

"Oh," Sheryl said. "Marcie and Joelle, you mean."

"Yeah," said Teddy. "Camping like Marcie and Joelle."

One night the previous summer Sheryl and Teddy had looked out his bedroom window and seen the two teenaged girls next door in the backyard with their father. They had a fire going in the barbecue and were roasting marshmallows.

"What are they doing?" Teddy had wanted to know when he saw the fire.

"I guess they're pretending they're camping," Sheryl had said.

"Who's that man?" Teddy asked.

"That's their father," Sheryl said. She wondered if she was going to have to go into an explanation of divorce. "He doesn't live there, you know."

"I know," said Teddy. "You don't have to tell me that."

"Oh," said Sheryl. "How did you know?"

"Marcie," Teddy said. Marcie babysat Teddy sometimes.

Sheryl and Teddy had watched the neighbours for a while, from the window. The father and his two daughters were sitting around the barbecue in lawn chairs, talking quietly and roasting their marshmallows. The scene was surprising to Sheryl, the father so relaxed in the mother's yard. She'd wondered, briefly, if there was some kind of reconciliation in progress. Then she remembered that the mother was away on a golf holiday.

"Can we go camping?" Teddy asked again.

Sheryl thought about it. There was a bit of firewood in the garage. She could probably light a small fire in the barbecue, roast some marshmallows and then send Teddy to bed.

"Get your jacket," she said. "It will be cool outside until we get the fire going."

The wood in the garage was too big for the barbecue and Sheryl couldn't find the axe. She tried to get Teddy to give up on the idea, but he was like a dog with a bone.

"Look some more for the axe," he said.

"I've looked everywhere," Sheryl said. "Daddy must have loaned it to someone. It's probably at Kate and Perry's house."

She looked up at the sky, which was sprinkled with stars, like a clear night sky in the country.

"We could have a campfire in the sandbox," Teddy said.

"I don't think so," Sheryl said. "Someone might call the fire department."

"No one would," Teddy said. He went into the garage and began carrying out blocks of wood and loading them into the sandbox.

"It won't start without kindling," Sheryl said. "We need the axe to make kindling."

Teddy ignored her and went back for more. He carried out all the wood there was. Sheryl decided the only thing she could do was try to light the fire and then Teddy would see it wasn't going to work and they could go to bed. She sent him into the house for newspaper, and he came back with some small pieces of wood from the fireplace. Not enough, Sheryl thought as she built a fire – paper first, then kindling, then the smallest logs in the shape of a teepee. She let Teddy hold a match to the newspaper.

To Sheryl's amazement, the fire caught. It flared up into a regular campfire, and she began to worry that someone would indeed call the fire department. She got the garden hose from the garage for safety's sake. Teddy thought they should put all the logs in at once, but Sheryl convinced him they should burn just one at a time.

Sheryl kept listening for a fire truck but none appeared, and she eventually quit worrying and began to imagine that she and Teddy really were camping under the stars somewhere. She tried to get him to help her find the Big Dipper but he was too busy poking sticks from the caragana hedge into the flames and then watching them smoke. After a while, he ran out of sticks and went into a kind of trance staring at the fire, which was now burning over a bed of red-hot embers. She asked him if he wanted to roast marshmallows and he shook his head, so they just sat side by side on lawn chairs, both of them mesmerized by the fire. It was four in the morning when the last log burned down to coals.

"I guess it's bedtime," Sheryl said, but Teddy wouldn't go in. She sighed and wondered why she had such a hard time being firm with him. Then she thought he wasn't being unreasonable, he was just taking pleasure in a simple thing, and what was wrong with that? She went into the house for a couple of sleeping bags and convinced Teddy to crawl into one of them.

She thought he'd gone to sleep. She was staring at the coals, trying to figure out why fire so enticed people, when she remembered a TV program she'd recently seen about a group of new-age Californians who went around the country doing workshops on firewalking. She'd been amused by the queue of spacey-looking people who, one by one, hot-footed it across the bed of coals. They moved so quickly that their feet hardly touched ground. It was no wonder they didn't get burned.

To prove a point, she stood up, kicked off her sandals and put her right foot in the fire, thinking she would hop across as quickly as the people in the TV show. But Teddy screamed just then and distracted her, and she burned her foot. She wanted to scream herself, because of the pain, but now she was aware of what Teddy had seen, and how bad it must have looked to him, his mother walking into the fire. She sat down on his sleeping bag and put her arms around him. She could feel his little heart pounding in his chest. She knew she should be running cold water from the hose over her foot, but she didn't want to frighten Teddy, so she pretended she hadn't hurt herself.

"Shhh," she said, trying not to think about her foot. "I'm all right. I was just making sure the coals were out before I went to sleep. They weren't though. Pretty dumb, eh? Boy, your old heart is just a-pounding away in there." She took his hand and placed it on his chest. "Feel that," she said.

His beating heart reminded him of something. "We had science fair today," he said.

"You're kidding," Sheryl said. "You should have told me. We could have done a project."

"Just the big kids," Teddy said.

"Oh," Sheryl said. "That's right, I forgot." It was the same in her school. "So you went to look then," she said. "You got to see the big kids' projects."

"There was a heart," Teddy said. "A pig's heart, and it was still beating."

"It couldn't have been," Sheryl said.

"It was," Teddy said. "I saw it."

"It couldn't have been beating if it wasn't in the pig," Sheryl said. "Was it still in the pig?" She was thinking maybe there was a real pig hooked up to a monitor.

"It was in a pie plate," Teddy said.

"Oh," Sheryl said. "Well, it couldn't have been beating then. Maybe someone jiggled the table and you saw the heart move."

"No," Teddy said. "It was beating."

Sheryl said, "What kind of teacher have you got anyway? Didn't she explain to you that a heart can't beat unless the pig is alive?"

"It was dead," Teddy said. "But it was still beating."

Sheryl gave up. Teddy often said things that worried her, but right now she didn't feel like dealing with it. There were so many things to worry about and now there was something else, because he had just seen his mother stick her foot in a fire. How could she explain that? She didn't even try, beyond what she had already said, and they simply sat together until the coals were dead and the stars disappeared. When it was light, Sheryl was struck by how odd everything looked, especially the blackened sandbox. There was a plastic dump truck, now half-melted, that neither of them had noticed in the dark. She didn't mention it.

"Are you tired?" she asked.

"No," Teddy said. Sheryl was wide awake too. They went to McDonald's for breakfast. Sheryl tried to walk without limping so Teddy wouldn't know she'd burned her foot, but eventually she had to tell him that it hurt.

5. FIRE

Sean was on the phone all the next afternoon talking to Perry, going over and over what had happened the night before. He'd just get off the phone when he'd remember some other detail and call Perry back again. Finally Sheryl got sick of it and grabbed the receiver and told Perry to put Kate on the phone.

"Do you guys want to come over for a barbecue?" she asked. "You might as well, if all they're going to do is talk about this on the phone."

Kate agreed. Sheryl went for groceries and picked up beer on the way home. When Kate and Perry showed up at the door at six-thirty, half an hour early, Kate brought up the jail incident right away. Sheryl wished she hadn't. She'd been hoping she and Kate could talk about something else.

"So has this jail thing brought about some kind of spiritual awakening in Sean?" Kate asked. "I'm half expecting Perry to get up and go to church tomorrow, join some born-again movement."

Sheryl got Kate and Perry each a beer from the fridge and then took them out to the back deck. When the barbecue coals were ready, she put Sean in charge of cooking the chicken breasts. Fat from the chicken dripped onto the coals and periodically burst into flames, which Sean sprayed with a plant mister. Teddy wanted to spray the flames, so Sean gave the mister to him, but then Teddy sprayed the barbecue so often it looked like the coals were going to go out.

"Jesus Christ," Sean said, grabbing the mister out of Teddy's hands. "Give me that thing. You're not the fire brigade, for Christ sake." It looked for a minute like Teddy was going to cry, but then Perry pulled him over onto his knee and started to tickle him.

"I can't figure out how he's still awake," Sheryl said. "He was up all night."

"So what did you think when old Sean didn't come home last night?" Perry asked Sheryl.

"I don't know," Sheryl said. "I can't really say."

"Well, did you think he might be in jail? I'll bet it never occurred to you he might be in jail."

"She probably thought I was in an accident," Sean said. "That's the first thing a woman will think of. An accident. She probably called all the hospitals. Jesus. It's embarrassing. 'Hello. Would you mind checking your comatose accident victims in case one of them is my husband?' I wonder how often the hospitals get that call."

Kate snorted. "More likely they get, 'Would you mind checking your comatose accident victims, I'm hoping one of them is my husband,'" she said.

"Very funny," Sean said. "Ha ha."

"What would your first thought be if I didn't come home?" Sheryl said to Sean.

"That's easy," Sean said. "I'd think you were with another man." Then he said, "Well, did you call the hospitals?"

A beeping sound came from inside the house. "That'll be the microwave," Sheryl said. "The potatoes are ready. How are the chicken breasts?"

"They'd be ready if the kid hadn't given them a frigging shower," Sean said.

"Well check," Sheryl said. "They look done to me."

"They're not done," Sean said.

Kate reached over and picked up the long-handled fork. "I'm starving," she said. "I could just about eat these things raw." She poked the fork into one of the chicken breasts. "This one's done," she said.

"Good," said Sheryl to Kate. She handed her a platter. "Put the chicken on this, will you?"

"Who's the cook here anyway?" Sean wanted to know.

Teddy was still on Perry's knee. "Daddy was in jail," he said.

"I know," said Perry. "I was with him."

"You're not supposed to talk about that," Sean said. "Mommy told you not to tell anyone."

"For Christ sake, Sean," Perry said. "It's not like I didn't already know. Leave the little bugger alone."

"Go play in the sandbox," Sean said.

"Can't," said Teddy. "It's burned up."

Sean looked over at the sandbox, which was littered with ashes and blackened bits of wood. "What happened to it?" Sean asked Teddy.

"I told you," Teddy said. "We went camping."

Teddy climbed off Perry's knee and went over to the barbecue. Kate had taken the chicken from the grill and the coals were glowing red. Teddy stood staring at them.

Sheryl was on her way into the house to take the potatoes out of the microwave, but she stopped when she noticed Teddy staring at the coals.

"Be careful with the barbecue, Teddy," Sheryl said.

Sean got up out of his chair and walked over to the sandbox. "What the hell were you doing?" he wanted to know. He picked up the melted dump truck. "Did you do this?" he asked Teddy. Teddy shook his head. "Well, who did then? I suppose you're going to tell me Mommy did it."

Teddy looked at Sean, then deliberately lowered his hand toward the grill.

Kate, who was closest to Teddy, pulled his hand away, then Sheryl swooped him up into her arms. She balanced him on one hip and took the plate of chicken from Kate. "Come and get it," she said. She was shaking, but she didn't let on.

"I've had just about enough of that kid tonight," Sean said.

"Let's go in the house and get some potatoes and salad," Sheryl said to Teddy. "Do you want some chicken?"

"I don't want anything," Teddy said. "I'm not hungry."

"Okay then," Sheryl said, "it's bedtime. You're dead on your feet."

Sheryl lead the way to the kitchen, where she had the dishes and the food laid out on the counter. She set the platter of chicken down and took the potatoes from the microwave. "I'll be back in a few minutes," she said. "Don't wait for me. Help yourself to more beer in the fridge." She carried Teddy upstairs, got him into his pyjamas and tucked him into bed. She found his blue stuffed dog and tucked it under the sheets next to him, then sat on the edge of the bed.

"You could have burned yourself," she said to Teddy. "Remember what happened to my foot." Teddy wanted to see the blister again, so Sheryl showed it to him.

"I can't tell you a story tonight," she said, brushing Teddy's blond hair off his forehead. "We have company. I have to visit with the company."

"Are they staying long?" Teddy asked.

"Not long," Sheryl said.

"When is Daddy going back to jail?" Teddy asked.

"I'm not sure," Sheryl said. "Soon, though." She kissed Teddy on the nose. When she stood to leave she saw Sean standing in the doorway.

"What's going on?" he asked.

"Nothing much," Sheryl said. She turned out Teddy's light.

"Why did you tell him I'd be going back to jail?"

"Good night, Teddy," Sheryl said and started down the stairs.

"I don't understand you," Sean said, following behind her. "Why did you tell Teddy that? You'll give him the wrong idea."

"I'm not worried," Sheryl said.

"Were you worried when I didn't come home last night?" Sean said.

"Not really," Sheryl said.

"Even though you thought I was in an accident?"

"I didn't think you were in an accident," Sheryl said. "Where did you get that idea?"

Sean pushed ahead of Sheryl. He spread his arms and blocked her way on the landing at the foot of the stairs.

"What are you doing?" he said. "Just what game are you playing here?"

Sheryl started humming, nothing in particular at first, but then an old song popped into her head, something about Mister Lonely, so she hummed that. Not like a sad ballad though. She kept it upbeat.

"The chicken's not done, you know," Sean said. "And the coals are out, because of all the water the little pissant sprayed on them. We're going to get sick from eating raw chicken."

Perry came from the kitchen and saw Sean blocking Sheryl's way. "What's going on?" Perry wanted to know.

Sheryl stopped humming. Sean let his arms drop to his sides.

"Nothing's going on," Sean said. "I just don't feel wanted around here. I was missing and no one noticed."

"We noticed," Sheryl said.

"Your whining is really starting to get to me," Perry said to Sean. "Last night was enough to last me a lifetime."

"What do you mean by that?" Sean wanted to know. "You mean, I was whining last night? Fuck you. I wasn't whining."

Sheryl stepped past Sean and Perry.

"She wants me to eat raw chicken," Sean said. "She doesn't love me anymore."

"That's true," Sheryl said. Then she went to the kitchen and filled her plate.

Moving Pictures

Gerri had the photographs – the Polaroids of Greg and Nina – tucked away in a candy box with Nina's letter, mailed from a small town just south of the Canadian border. Greg had given them to her as a kind of peace offering when he returned from his failed attempt to find the woman who had expressed her love for him so powerfully in that inspired message. Whenever Gerri saw Greg now, especially if he was with his French professor wife or his teenaged son, she found it hard to believe that years ago, when he and Gerri were living together, he brought home a girl he'd just met and asked Gerri if it was all right if they got married. Greg and the girl, that is. Greg eventually accepted that his proposition was part of a mad plan rather than a love affair, but he still believed Gerri had been a co-conspirator, which was not the case.

The day Greg brought Nina home, Gerri had been in the kitchen watching the former tenant of their house, a middle-aged spinster named Miss Kershaw, position herself behind a rusty old station wagon belonging to the family next door. The station wagon no longer ran and was parked in the alley with all of its tires flat. Miss Kershaw believed that the family had stolen her cat, and she was obviously planning to snatch the cat back should the opportunity arise. Gerri, who believed the neighbours probably *had* stolen the cat, was trying to decide if she should have pity and invite the poor woman into the house so she could spy in comfort, when Greg walked in the front door with Nina. She was young – seventeen, eighteen, Gerri couldn't really tell – and she immediately sat on the couch and ate a whole mango, expertly working her way through it with the spoon attachment on her Swiss Army knife. It was a warm day in April and she was wearing old cut-off shorts and a sweatshirt. Juice dripped down her chin and she wiped it off with her sleeve.

"A mango," Gerri said, trying to make conversation. "I've never been able to figure out how you eat them."

"It's from the fruit market on Broad Street," Nina said. "Do you go there?"

"Never," Gerri said. She knew the fruit market was there but she couldn't imagine why the fruit would be better than the fruit in the produce section at Safeway. When you lived in the middle of the prairie, all fruit was shipped from somewhere else. She imagined the market would have the same fruit, but it would be more expensive.

"Nina needs a favour," Greg said to Gerri. "Let me explain."

"Explain away," Gerri said. She was watching Nina, who was working on the mango.

Greg said, "I know what you're going to say."

"Go ahead," Gerri said. "I'm listening."

"She's from Tacoma, Washington," Greg said. "She's being deported. There's no way she can get out of it, but she can get back in if she's coming to get married. I was thinking, I could marry her. I don't really believe in marriage anyway – *we* don't, we're agreed on that, right – so what does it matter?"

Nina finished the mango and wiped her face on the sleeve of her sweatshirt again. She sat on the couch with her hand open, as though she was waiting for someone to come and collect the remains of the mango, the peelings and the huge pit.

"Would you mind leaving us alone for a few minutes?" Gerri said to Nina. She was remembering a story about someone who married a Central American girl so she could get into Canada more quickly and be with her boyfriend, a legitimate refuge. It had been complicated, and involved at least one trip to El Salvador. Gerri didn't even know if the story was true, but Greg loved the idea of such conspiracies.

Nina got up from the couch and went outside. Gerri could see her sit down on the front step. She could just see her head through the glass panel in the door.

"This is unbelievably stupid," Gerri said to Greg. "How long have you known her?"

"I don't know her at all," Greg said. "But she's been staying at Martin and Sandy's." Martin was a good friend of Greg's. They worked for the same courier company. "Sandy met her at a party. Martin says she left home a year ago because of her father. He's a general or something high up in the air force and he has a really nasty temper. Nina hates the U.S. and all that military shit. She wants to be a Canadian. We should help her out. Come on, Gerr. What do you say?"

"I'm not saying anything. You make your own decision. I think it's idiotic, and I won't lie if anyone from Immigration asks me questions."

"We'll worry about that later," Greg said. "For now, all I have to do is take her to the bus tonight. That's in case someone from Immigration is there to see her off. Then we'll write letters to each other and keep them. For proof. That's the plan anyway." He paused. "So it's okay with you?"

"Of course not," Gerri said. "But do what you want. You will anyway."

Greg went outside and sat beside Nina on the step. Gerri could see them through the glass. She could see Nina nodding her head in response to whatever Greg told her. Later, Greg went over to Martin's to pick up Nina's duffle bag, and then he decided they should have a farewell party for the sake of authenticity. He cooked a big pot of spaghetti sauce and invited several friends over, including Martin and Sandy and their baby, who were the only ones who actually knew Nina, and even they didn't know her very well. It was an eclectic mix of guests, the common denominator being availability. There were a few people Gerri had never met before, friends of Greg's from one pool hall or another.

As people were beginning to arrive, Gerri heard a knock at the back door. It was Miss Kershaw, looking forlorn, wondering if Gerri ever caught a glimpse of the pilfered orange cat. Gerri had to tell her no, and she found herself inviting Miss Kershaw to join the party. If it was going to be a party for strays, there might as well be another one. She knew the woman lived alone and it was clear she was lost without the cat, whose name was Amanda.

"Oh, I couldn't," Miss Kershaw said.

"Of course you can," Gerri said. She convinced her by telling her she could keep watch for the cat out the kitchen window.

Gerri introduced her to the others as the person who had lived in their house before them. She felt a little funny introducing her as Miss Kershaw, but that was the only name she knew, and Miss Kershaw didn't offer a first name. She asked if the party was in aid of something special, a birthday perhaps, and Greg took great pleasure in explaining that he and Nina were engaged and that Nina was returning to the U.S. to renew her visa. Miss Kershaw didn't bat an eye, even though she knew Gerri and Greg lived together in the house. She congratulated Greg and Nina and then retired to the kitchen and positioned herself in the window to watch for the cat.

The atmosphere was festive, as though the party guests had all known Nina for years and she was leaving on an exciting expedition. Someone went to the Dairy Queen for an ice cream cake with BON VOYAGE written on it in lime green. Someone else took Polaroid photographs, several of Greg and Nina with their arms around each other, for the immigration officials. Gerri saw an improvised drama taking shape with Greg and Nina as the stars. She found it hard to believe that everyone so readily embraced this plan, which was ludicrous and destined to fail, but even *she* eventually got into the celebration and took a photograph of Nina sitting on Greg's knee, feeding him a mouthful of cake, this time with the fork attachment on her knife. Later in the evening, Greg took Nina downtown to the bus depot. As they left the house, the party moved out to the front yard and everyone hugged Nina goodbye and gave her the thumbs up. Then Greg and Nina left on Greg's motorcycle, Nina perched on the back wearing Gerri's helmet, her bag balanced in front of Greg. The rest of the party followed in cars, all but Gerri and Miss Kershaw.

By this time it was dark and Miss Kershaw had hopes that the neighbours would let the cat out for a night time ramble, but Gerri said she didn't think they would, they kept the house locked up like Fort Knox at night because of the unsavoury types who were apparently "after them." Miss Kershaw shook her head and said that was the reason she'd decided to move, the neighbourhood had gone downhill. She said she supposed she'd best call it a night and begged Gerri to phone her if she saw the cat outside. Gerri promised she would, although she wasn't sure she'd be able to keep the promise because the neighbours had three little boys who were no doubt attached to the cat, no matter how it had been acquired.

When Greg got home an hour later he told Gerri he'd kissed Nina goodbye. They'd put on a really good act, he said. Everyone waiting in line at the bus felt sorry for them. He showed Gerri another Polaroid. Gerri had to admit it was convincing.

"You know you'll never see her again," Gerri said.

"Don't you believe her story?" Greg asked.

"I have no reason to either believe or disbelieve it," Gerri said. "But that's not the point. No immigration official with half a brain would believe you'd known each other longer than a day."

"Well, no harm in trying," Greg said. Gerri didn't bother pointing out that this sort of fraud was probably against the law and there might, in fact, be some harm should they get found out. Greg said, "As far as Nina goes, I believe her."

Gerri didn't want to be bothered thinking about it anymore, at least not tonight. She decided to get a start on the mess from the party and was emptying ashtrays into the fireplace when there was a knock at the door. It was the three neighbour boys, on one of their regular missions. It was surprising they hadn't been over sooner, sent by their mother to find out what was happening at the party.

"What does your mom need now?" Gerri asked the oldest boy.

"A cigarette," he said. "She says you have to give her one."

Gerri would have told them to forget it but Greg, who was putting on his jacket to go out, stepped in front of her. He handed over the remains of a pack and said, "Tell your mom she owes me twenty bucks for this." He winked at the boys. The oldest grabbed the pack and the three of them ran home before Gerri could intervene.

Greg gave Gerri a peck on the cheek. "Stop worrying," he said. "I don't take wooden nickels."

Gerri heard the motorcycle start up and roar down the street. The neighbours, whom she referred to in conversation as the weird neighbours, were no doubt watching Greg leave. They were always watching, given as they were to attacks of paranoia, especially at night. You could usually see the lit end of a cigarette in one window or another.

Without really thinking, Gerri gathered the half dozen Polaroids that were lying around and propped them on the fireplace mantle. She played with the order for the imaginary immigration official. Should the kiss come last? It had in the camera, but because the whole thing was fabricated, she could create whatever order she wanted. If she put the kiss first, it would look like Nina was arriving rather than leaving. And the cake could be a wedding cake; you couldn't read the BON VOYAGE in the picture. What an absurd thing to be thinking about. That's when Gerri got the tin candy box and put the photos in it. There would, she believed, be no need for them, whatever order they were in. As she closed the lid, she wondered what she would have thought had she happened across the photos without knowing the story.

The weird neighbours – Kurt and Nancy – claimed to be movie people from California. Claiming to work in the movie business was not in itself so outrageous. There was, in fact, a burgeoning film industry in the city – mini-series and action movies with one minor star brought in from Hollywood. But this was not the movie business Kurt and Nancy professed to be a part of. *They* were on a first-name basis with people like Steven Spielberg, who apparently had given Kurt his first big break. "Check the credits in the first *Star Wars* movie," Nancy once said to Gerri. "Kurt's name is there. His first principal role. Just check sometime." Gerri didn't bother to tell her that Steven Spielberg hadn't made the *Star Wars* movies.

The threat to Kurt and Nancy – the one that had inspired them to add several padlocks to the front and back doors of the house – was gangsters from Hollywood. Not black or Latino gangsters – they only killed each other, Kurt said. The gangsters who were after Kurt and Nancy were real, the old-fashioned kind, the mob. Something to do with a movie deal. Kurt had been cast in an action thriller, but then he backed out – couldn't say why, extenuating circumstances, let's just leave it at that – and had cost the producer a lot of money. Now the producer had hired the mob to track him down and make him pay. Gerri figured the deluded Kurt had himself confused with someone else. The story was right out of a supermarket tabloid.

Gerri and Greg lived in an old two-storey house close to the city's core. The landlord also owned the houses on either side, one of which was rented to Kurt and Nancy. An old couple, the Duncans, lived in the third house. They'd been there for years and had once owned the house, but had sold it to the present owner and stayed on as renters. Gerri supposed they would not be there for long, as she had seen an ambulance out front several times. According to Mr. Coots, who collected the rent, the old lady had serious heart problems and consequently suffered from panic attacks whenever she felt short of breath.

The neighbourhood was known as a transition neighbourhood, which meant it was being rezoned from residential to commercial because of its proximity to downtown. As each old house sold (at a great profit for its owner, thanks to the rezoning) it was torn down and replaced by an office building. Half the houses on the block were already gone, and the remaining ones were falling into disrepair because no owners wanted to invest money in them. They were all waiting for the right offer, and then it was the wrecking ball. The houses that were left were rented cheaply to people who wouldn't complain about the lack of upkeep. They all lived under the threat of eviction because the houses could be sold at any time. The owner of Greg and Gerri's house was sitting on a gold mine, with the three lots adjoining one another.

Mr. Coots was not the owner. He was a real estate agent who acted on the owner's behalf. He never called his employer by name, but rather called him "The Owner." He spoke it with a certain amount of reverence, as though he was referring to someone really important. Mr. Coots collected the rent personally on the first day of every month, and he managed to get inside and get a good look at the properties when he did so. Gerri had tried to discourage him at first, believing the right to privacy should keep the landlord in the front hall, but Mr. Coots was not to be discouraged and he ignored hints. Gerri eventually gave up. He wasn't that bad, as far as landlords went. He was a small man, made smaller by a deforming curvature of the spine, and he walked with a cane, bent forward in what must have been an uncomfortable position. She thought he was lonely, although she had no evidence to support that other than his insistence on collecting the rent himself, which Gerri took to mean he had time on his hands.

It was apparent that Mr. Coots expected Gerri to provide him with any news on the goings on at Kurt and Nancy's. Gerri knew he was on a fishing expedition one particular rent day when he mentioned the recently installed locks.

"I know the neighbourhood isn't that good," he said, "but really, there are more locks than necessary." Gerri didn't think there was any point in telling him about the Hollywood gangsters. It was a ridiculous story, too ridiculous to repeat, even to someone who loved gossip.

"They're probably just a little paranoid," Gerri said about the locks. "Maybe because of the kids. There aren't many kids in this neighbourhood." It sounded as though she was defending the neighbours, but really she just felt sorry for the boys. They were going to school now; maybe they'd make it through the year without their transient parents dragging them off again.

"I believe they have a cat," Mr. Coots said. "I noticed two small dishes on the floor in the kitchen. The owner has a rule about pets.

He made an exception for Miss Kershaw, but only because she lived alone and was known to be a responsible tenant."

"They do have a cat," Gerri said carefully, without telling him it was the same cat. "Mary Poppins, I think they call her." When Gerri had made an attempt at explaining to Nancy that Miss Kershaw was convinced the cat was hers, Nancy had become defensive and insisted they got the cat from the Humane Society. "Phone them up," Nancy had said. "Phone them up and ask, you'll see." Gerri hadn't phoned them up. She didn't want to get that involved.

"I hope you'll overlook the cat," Gerri said to Mr. Coots. "The kids are crazy about her."

"Hmm," Mr. Coots said, rubbing his thin hands together.

"Any offers on the houses?" Gerri asked.

"Oh, the owner isn't interested in selling," Mr. Coots said, which was an amusing claim, to say the least. "I suppose I could overlook the cat," he said. "But I'm very suspicious about the other, all the locks. I'm afraid they're doing something illegal. Like growing marijuana. They could have one of those hydroponic operations."

"Oh, I don't think so," Gerri said. "I've never noticed much coming and going. Besides, I don't think they're the type." What she meant was, she didn't think they were that ambitious or capable.

"In the movie business," Mr. Coots said.

"So they say," said Gerri. She began inching toward the door, trying to give the message that she had to go out, even though she didn't. For once, he got it.

"I wonder if they're going to be in that movie about the famous Indian chief," Mr. Coots said as he was leaving. "I hear they'll be filming soon out in the valley."

"Big Bear, you mean," Gerri said. "Maybe I'll mention it to them, "in case they haven't heard. Maybe they can get work as extras or something."

"If they were really in the movie business, they'd already know about it," Mr. Coots said.

Gerri watched from the front porch as he made his way to Kurt and Nancy's and knocked. There was no answer. He looked at Gerri and shook his head.

Gerri did mention the movie to Nancy a few days later. She just wanted to know what Nancy would say. When she saw her sunning herself in a lounger in the backyard, her out-of-shape body stuffed into an orange bikini, Gerri carried her coffee over. Nancy didn't invite her to sit down even though there was a plastic deck chair next to the lounger.

"I hear they're making a movie out in the valley," Gerri said. "I wondered if you and Kurt knew anything about it."

Nancy swung her legs over the side of the lounger and sat up, trying not very successfully to keep herself inside the bikini.

"What kind of a movie?" Nancy asked, fiddling with her cleavage.

"I don't know," Gerri said. "Full-length feature, I think. About Big Bear."

"Who the hell is Big Bear?" Nancy asked.

"A famous Indian chief," Gerri said.

"A western then?" Nancy asked.

"More of a historical drama, I think," Gerri said. "I wondered if you and Kurt were working on it."

"I don't know what we pay our agent for," Nancy said. "As far as I can tell, he drinks coffee for fifty bucks an hour. Not our Hollywood agent. *He* works for a living, and I mean works. You have to in Hollywood or you're out on your ass and pumping gas. Our agent here, I mean. But this is a two-bit movie town all around."

"I don't know anything about that," Gerri said. "I just thought I'd mention it."

"That's what the yo-yo downtown is paid for," Nancy said. "Wait till I tell Kurt. He won't stand for it. Fifty bucks an hour for sitting on your keister. Kurt won't stand for that."

"Anyway," Gerri said, "I'd best get going." As she left, Nancy was rearranging herself on the lounger, pulling down her bikini straps for a better tan, apparently planning to tell Kurt about the movie later rather than sooner. Gerri was pretty sure Kurt was in the house doing nothing more than sitting on his keister.

The morning after Greg's motorcycle accident (the morning after Greg put Nina on the bus) Gerri arrived home from the hospital exhausted from a night of waiting – for doctors, for answers, and then for Greg's parents, whom she had not met before. The house was still pretty much a mess from Nina's bogus going away party, but Gerri was too exhausted to deal with it. She climbed the stairs and crawled into bed with her clothes on, hoping to catch a few hours' sleep before she went back to the hospital. She didn't bother to take her boots off. She just lay down on the bed and pulled a quilt up over herself. She had no sooner closed her eyes when she heard a knock. Martin, she thought, or some other friend of Greg's who had somehow heard what happened. Bad news travelled fast.

She got up and went to the door. It was the three neighbour boys again, standing as usual on the steps in descending order from oldest to youngest. Their faces stared at her through the glass.

She was tempted to ignore them but they'd already seen her. She wondered what it would be now – sugar, Cheerios, a screwdriver – it could be anything. She opened the door.

"We want to know why there was a cop at your house," the oldest boy said. He spoke defiantly. "My mom says you have to tell."

"I'm tired," Gerri said. "Go home."

"You have to tell," the boy said. "My mom says you have to."

"It's none of your mom's business who comes to my door," Gerri said. "You can tell your mom I said that. I'm going to bed now."

She closed the door on the boys and went back upstairs. She could hear them knocking, pounding on the glass, but they finally gave up and went home. She remembered that when she'd left for the hospital at four in the morning, Kurt and Nancy had been watching through their front window.

As soon as Gerri lay down on the bed the phone rang. She knew it was Nancy – this was the pattern – but she had to answer it anyway. It might be someone from the hospital.

"Hello," she said.

"Why wouldn't you answer my boys?" Nancy said. "They're just little boys. You don't need to treat them like dirt."

"I don't treat them like dirt," Gerri said.

"Everybody loves the movies," Nancy said, "but when they find out you're in the movie business they treat you like dirt. Unless you're a big star, but let me tell you, those big stars are all smoke and mirrors. They're all cosmetic surgery and airbrushed photographs. I know. I've seen them up close."

"Look Nancy," Gerri said, "I'm not going to be bossed around by you, and I want the boys to know that."

"You've got something to hide, don't you? That's why you won't say, about the cop."

"I've got nothing to hide," Gerri said. "And if you must know, I think it's wrong that you send those boys to make your demands for you. You should be ashamed of yourself."

There was a silence that Gerri recognized as the transition from belligerence to self-pity. Whining would come next, about all the bad luck that had befallen her and Kurt. Sometimes Nancy blamed everything on Kurt, although Gerri soon learned that no one else was allowed to express an opinion on that topic. Gerri decided it would be best to end the conversation before Nancy got rolling. "Look," she said, "if you must know, Greg was in an accident. That's why the police came to the door. It had nothing to do with you or Kurt. So I have to get off the phone, in case the hospital calls."

"An accident?" Nancy said. "What kind of accident?"

"Someone sideswiped him on his motorcycle. He's in the hospital."

"An accident," Nancy said. "I wonder. Well how is he, anyway? Pretty banged up?"

"He's in a coma," Gerri said.

"Wow. Wait until Kurt hears about this."

"Did you hear what I said?"

"An accident. Ha. I'll just bet."

"For Christ sake, Nancy. I said he's in a coma."

Gerri heard one of the boys say something in the background, and then Nancy shouted, "What'd you go bothering her for anyway? I told you not to. Don't you go bothering her again, you hear me?"

Gerri said, "You people are unbelievable."

"I'd re-evaluate that accident business," Nancy said.

Gerri hung up.

She couldn't sleep. She wanted to call the hospital, but then again she didn't. They hadn't called her, so that was good. If she phoned, she might hear something bad. She went downstairs and cleaned up the mess from the party. As she did, she ran through the details of the previous evening, the whole cockamamie Nina thing, and then Greg's departure after the boys came for cigarettes. She could still hear the motorcycle. Later, a police officer at the front door told Gerri that Greg had been taken to the trauma centre. A head injury, an emergency room doctor told Gerri when she finally got to talk to him. If it weren't for the helmet, he'd be dead.

"How serious?" she asked the doctor.

"All head injuries are serious," the doctor said. "He's in a coma. For now that's a good thing."

He said something else about not knowing what's ahead, and how unpredictable head injuries are, but after Gerri heard the word coma her own brain pretty much stopped working.

She called Greg's parents then, in Saskatoon. They drove down immediately and took over from Gerri as the next of kin. The doctors didn't talk to her anymore, they talked to Greg's parents. Gerri kept trying to get in on the conversations and the updates on Greg's condition, but it was clear they didn't want to include her. She was afraid they were talking about brain death, but when she cornered a doctor and came right out and asked, he said no, tests did not indicate that, she should remain optimistic. That's when she decided to go home.

Over the next few days Greg's mother positioned herself by Greg's bed and made it nearly impossible for Gerri to get close to him. Gerri tried to be understanding – this was Greg's mother, he was her child – but she couldn't understand why Greg's mother was shutting her out, treating her as though she didn't exist, or like the whole thing was her fault. A week after the accident Gerri went to the hospital and found out that Greg's parents had had him flown to Saskatoon by air ambulance. They hadn't even called to tell her.

How could things change so quickly? She was in the house alone now. Greg had been completely reclaimed by his parents. She called them every day and they gave her a brief, polite update – no change. Whenever she suggested that she drive to Saskatoon the message was clear; they didn't want her to come. She wondered what they knew about her. Maybe they didn't understand. Maybe they thought she was just a friend. Every night she planned to drive to Saskatoon the next day, but in the morning she changed her mind. She was afraid of Greg's parents, and of what she might learn when she got there.

A few days after the accident a letter from Nina had arrived but Gerri hadn't been able to bring herself to open it. For ten days it sat on the table, until one morning, after she'd reversed another of her own decisions to drive to Saskatoon, her eye landed on it and she finally decided to read it. Surprisingly, the letter made her cry. She pictured Nina, just a few kilometres north of the American border, writing the letter at about the same time Greg was being rushed to the hospital. Gerri wished she'd written it herself, it was so intimate and such an expression of love. The letter was a metaphor for loss; it didn't matter that it was fiction. She read it again, aloud, and listened to her own voice giving life to the words.

> Dear Greg. I am scrawling this on the bus, forgive the messy writing. I'm still in Canada, but not for long. I wish you were here with me. There is a young couple a few seats ahead of me and they are making me miss you more than I already do. They have their arms wrapped around one another and you can tell they're off on an adventure. I heard one of them say something about Mexico. Is it possible they are travelling all the way to Mexico by bus? Well, I guess if you are in love. I could travel all the way to Mexico if you were here too. I wish you were. How long do you think it will be before we see each other again? You could come to visit me. I guess it depends where I end up. Back home in Tacoma, I imagine. Unless my father is so awful I have to head for the East Coast, as far away as I can get. My parents' address is above, and I'll send a new one if I have to leave. I'm hoping I can stand to live at home because I can save more money that way, and as you know I want to save lots of money so I can come back and we can get married. (Pause.) I just took a little mirror out of my purse so I could describe to you exactly how I look right now. My eyes are sad. They're a funny colour, in between green and brown.

Have you ever noticed that? My jaw is too square. Do you think the mole on my left cheek is sexy? I've never understood why they're called beauty marks. I think maybe it's because they're associated with whores. I ache for you. My nipples are hard for you, I can see them through my shirt. I wish you could touch me … The closer we get to the border the more awful I feel. The couple in front of me are practically making out. I bet they will, when it's dark and the lights are out. I'll really miss you then. I miss you now. I'm crying. See. This is a teardrop on the page. We just passed a sign that said, "U.S. border, 5 kilometres." I'm almost gone. Love, love, love, Nina.

Gerri folded the letter and put it in the candy box along with the Polaroids from the party. As she did so, she caught her own reflection in the mirror above the fireplace mantle. Her eyes too were a colour somewhere between green and brown. Were they sad? She couldn't tell. Did she feel sad? She must, because the letter had made her cry. She carried the candy box upstairs and put it in Greg's sock drawer.

The news was always the same when she phoned Greg's parents. No change. And then she found out from Martin that Greg was, in fact, out of the coma and his parents were lying to her. It was unbelievable.

"Are you sure?" she asked Martin.

"I saw him," Martin said. "I was in Saskatoon and I stopped by the hospital and there he was, sitting up in bed."

"He hasn't called me," Gerri said. "Why wouldn't he call me?"

"I don't know," Martin said. "He's pretty confused. Apparently a lot of his memory is gone. The doctors say he has to build it back. That's common with head injuries. I'm not sure he knew who I was, not at first anyway. You could see he was really working to put things together."

"He didn't know you?" Gerri said. "You're his best friend."

"Yeah," Martin said. "Pretty heavy, eh? So maybe that's why he hasn't called."

Gerri took that in. Then she said, "But his parents know about me."

"I wouldn't count on them. His mother was sitting in the corner knitting the whole time I was there. Some blanket thing that was the size of a football field. And his father stood in the corner with his arms folded like he was some kind of security guard."

"What should I do?" Gerri asked.

"I don't know," Martin said. "Go see him, I guess, and then take it from there."

She took some familiar objects with her, some things Greg was especially fond of. Not the letter from Nina, of course, although it did cross her mind to take one of the Polaroids, since the party for Nina was the last thing that had happened before the accident. Instead, she took Greg's favourite old denim shirt and a pair of cowboy boots he'd bought a few years ago on a trip with Martin to the motorcycle museum in Sturgis, South Dakota. She also took a photo album, and she made sure the album contained several photographs of her and Greg together.

It wasn't that he didn't remember her, he said her name right away when she entered the room. But conversation seemed to have left him. The ability to put words together, and to connect the past and present. He would start to speak and then quit mid-sentence because there was some part of the thought he couldn't complete, or some memory he needed that wasn't there for him. Gerri wasn't sure, after a terrible fifteen minutes of start and stop sentences, whether Greg knew where he remembered her from. He seemed frustrated by his inability to communicate, and then he quit trying and withdrew. His mother was there, still knitting the huge blanket or whatever it was supposed to be. Gerri thought the colours were incredibly ugly – orange and green and purple. It was hard to believe someone could have such bad taste. Without looking up from her knitting, she told Gerri she thought it best if she left, Greg was getting tired.

"It just plays him right out," she said, "trying to talk. Talking is such a struggle, as you can see."

"But isn't that good?" Gerri asked. "Won't it help him remember, eventually?"

"It just plays him right out," Greg's mother repeated, obviously choosing not to make eye contact with Gerri.

Gerri had thought she and Greg might look through the photo album together, but she realized that Greg wasn't up to that yet. It would require too much of him. It might even be embarrassing, because she knew more than he did. Did he remember the nature of their relationship? She wasn't sure he did, although he had squeezed her hand when she took his. She decided against even taking the photo album out of her bag. She did leave him the shirt and the boots, though. He was staring at them when she stood to leave.

"Maybe I should take some time off work," she said. "I could stay in Saskatoon and visit every day."

Greg was silent, still staring at the boots.

"Do you have any idea how long you'll be in the hospital?" she asked.

His mother answered for him. "We don't know, dear. It'll be a while yet. And when he gets out, I'm sure he'll want to come home."

At first Gerri thought home meant home in Regina, with her, but then she realized Greg's mother meant home in Saskatoon. She wanted to have a tantrum, tell Greg's mother she had a claim; they were, after all, like man and wife. She was capable of looking after Greg, and he was more likely to get his memory back with her. But then she looked at Greg and saw the state he was in, staring at the cowboy boots, and it frightened her. He was so far away. She decided to leave it for now, to give him a bit more time before she took a stand and insisted that he come with her, to his adult home, the place of recent memory.

A week later, in the middle of the night, she heard voices in the yard. She thought it might be Kurt and Nancy or the boys, but then she heard two men talking. She heard someone calling her name. She went to the window that overlooked the front step and saw Martin and Greg. She hurried down the stairs and to the door, filled with relief that Greg was all right and free of his parents' clutches, for that's how she'd come to think, that he was in captivity and his mother was the jailer.

She opened the door. Greg looked disoriented and didn't say anything. She noticed he was wearing the shirt and boots she'd left at the hospital. He was carrying the ugly orange blanket his mother had been knitting.

"I busted him out," said Martin.

Greg saw Gerri looking at the blanket.

"She made it for me," Greg said. "I thought I'd better take it."

"Are you okay?" Gerri asked Greg.

"I'm okay," he said. He was looking toward Kurt and Nancy's house. The curtains were pulled back, just a bit, and Gerri could imagine the pair of them staring out like cats into the darkness. "Who are those people?" Greg asked. "They're watching us."

"Those are our delightful neighbours," Gerri said.

"I don't remember them," Greg said.

"Lucky you."

They stepped into the house. Greg entered uneasily, like a stranger. Gerri thought the house would be a window to his memory, that he would check everything, touch things, but he didn't seem that interested. When he saw the couch he sat down and lay his head back, closed his eyes.

"Is he okay?" Gerri asked Martin, worried now.

"He's got this headache. He's had it ever since the accident. I've got his medication." Martin took a prescription bottle out of his pocket and gave it to Gerri. "It's okay, really," Martin said. "The doctor said he could come home. It was his mother who wanted to keep him in the hospital."

"I couldn't stand it another day," Greg said, his eyes still closed. "I phoned Martin to come and get me." Gerri thought he sounded like himself again, although exhausted.

Gerri sat down beside Greg and picked up his hand.

"I'm really glad to have you home," she said. She kissed his fingers. After Martin left, they went upstairs to bed. Greg carried the blanket his mother had knit. He stood in the middle of the bedroom with it, not knowing what to do, so Gerri took it from him and put it in the closet. She wanted to touch Greg, gather him to her, but she was afraid to. She thought of his body as broken, even though there were few physical traces of the accident.

"I'm so tired," Greg said. "I feel like I'm only half alive."

"How much do you remember now?" Gerri asked.

"Bits and pieces," Greg said. "I know I love you. I know we've made love in this bed. But I can't remember any one particular time. I just can't."

"Well," Gerri said, "if you put it that way, I can't say that I remember the particular times. Maybe you're expecting too much of yourself. Maybe you think you should remember details that no one remembers."

"That could be," Greg said. "But if it's true, it's just one more loss. I don't know how things are supposed to be. I've got no perspective."

"It'll come back," Gerri said. "Give it time."

"They say a year or more. That's what they told me."

"There you go," Gerri said. "Don't expect so much of yourself."

"My mother saw a clean slate," Greg said. "She thought she could raise me all over again and turn me into someone different." He laughed, and then stopped, surprised by something.

"What?" Gerri wanted to know.

"That's the first time I've laughed since the accident."

Gerri and Greg were not the only ones with troubles. Miss Kershaw showed up regularly wanting to know if Gerri had any news of the cat, and it turned out that Mrs. Duncan next door had Alzheimer's. Mr. Coots told Gerri that she had put a dozen eggs in the washing machine with the clothes, instead of laundry detergent. And she'd started hiding things around the house, like cutlery, so that whenever Mr. Duncan wanted a sandwich he had to go searching for a knife. Plant pots were among her favourite hiding places for things. Gerri knew it wasn't funny, but then again it was. Funny in the way of bizarre juxtapositions. Eggs in the washing machine. Cutlery in the plant pots. The good thing, Mr. Coots said, was that Mrs. Duncan had stopped having panic attacks, but she became disoriented sometimes, which was a big concern. She'd gone missing twice now and Mr. Duncan had found her hiding in the garage both times. He'd installed locks, Mr. Coots reported, to keep her in. Gerri wished the other neighbours, Kurt and Nancy, had done the neighbourhood such a favour and locked themselves in instead of the gangsters out. Since Greg's return from the hospital, they'd become a concern rather than an annoyance.

Gerri was furious with Nancy when she heard that she'd got Greg to fix a broken window instead of fixing it herself, or getting Kurt to. Gerri was at work at the time, and Greg told her about it later. Apparently Nancy had sent the oldest boy over, who'd told Greg, "My mom says you have to. My mom says to check if you have a piece of glass we can have, so we don't have to go buy one."

Greg had obediently gone to the basement to check. There was an old window that didn't seem to belong anywhere, so he took it. Nancy's broken pane was in the kitchen over the sink and it was small enough that he was able to cut a square the right size.

"You mean you went over there and fixed their window?" Gerri said, incredulous. "Christ Greg, you're going to be at their beck and call from now on. Don't you know that?"

"I just did them a little favour," he said.

"That's not like you," Gerri said.

"Why not?" Greg wanted to know.

Gerri didn't know how to explain. She didn't really know what the difference was. She just knew that the old Greg, who had done a lot of favours for people, would not have gone over and fixed the window just because Nancy told him to.

"If I'd been home I would have stopped you," Gerri said. "They're maniacs. Don't you remember all that weird stuff about the gangsters?"

"It could be true," Greg said. "You never know. I don't think it is, but you can't be certain."

"It isn't true," Gerri said. "I'm quite certain." She suddenly thought of the cat. "Did you see Miss Kershaw's cat while you were there?"

"I don't think there was a cat, no," Greg said. He was silent for a minute, and then he said, "Nancy says Kurt's probably going to need a ride out to Fort Qu'Appelle tomorrow."

"Why does he have to go to Fort Qu'Appelle?" Gerri asked, not that she was planning to drive Kurt anywhere, and Greg hadn't driven since the accident.

"He phoned from downtown and he got some kind of work on that movie about Big Bear. Nancy figures he got a really good part."

Gerri didn't believe it for a minute. Nancy probably had some other reason for going to Fort Qu'Appelle, like to spend the day in the bar drinking.

Just then she noticed Nancy easing her way through the flower bed between their two houses. Gerri had planted petunias and wished that Nancy would go around. Gerri didn't want her in the house so she stepped outside before Nancy could get up the step and knock.

"Did Greg tell you about Kurt?" Nancy asked. "He got work in that movie about the famous Indian."

"What kind of work?" Gerri asked.

"He doesn't know yet," Nancy said. "He phoned from the Travelodge. That's where they were doing auditions. It'll be one of the principals for sure. Kurt said they just about shit their pants when they got a look at his cv."

"Well good," Gerri said. "That's good. Only you know I can't drive him out to Fort Qu'Appelle."

"Why not?"

"Nancy. I have a job. I can't just get in the car and drive out to the valley."

"What about Greg?"

"He's busy," Gerri said. "Besides, he still gets those headaches."

"I don't know what we're supposed to do then," Nancy said. "That piece of junk in the backyard isn't going anywhere."

"I don't know either," Gerri said.

"Great," said Nancy. "Just great." She turned and walked through the flower bed again, this time not making any attempt to miss the petunias. The boys were sitting on the step watching, and Nancy stomped past them into the house.

"Mom says we might be able to go with them to the movie shoot," said the youngest. "They might need kids."

"What about school?" Gerri asked.

"They have teachers on the set," said the oldest boy.

"Maybe in Hollywood," Gerri said. "You boys should go to school and get a good education. Then you can do anything you want when you grow up."

A taxi pulled up in front of the house and Kurt got out. He saw Gerri and said, "It's a joke. A stand-in, is all. It's a fucking insult."

Nancy heard him and came back outside. "A stand-in?" she said. "Are they out of their minds?"

"What's a stand-in?" Gerri asked.

"You're a double for one of the principals," Nancy said. "Same colouring and all that. They use you to set the lighting. Mostly you stand around and wait."

"In this two-bit town," Kurt said. "As if anyone here has a stinking clue about making movies."

Kurt pulled a pack of cigarettes out of his pocket and lit one.

"Maybe it's better," Nancy said.

"How's that?" Kurt asked.

"Your name won't appear anywhere."

"That's great, Nancy," Kurt said. "That's just what I want, for my name not to appear anywhere. That's what all actors want."

"Think about it," Nancy said.

Kurt did, and then he said, "Oh. I see what you mean."

"Not the gangsters," Gerri said. "You don't mean that."

"Good thinking, Nancy," Kurt said. "You're a smart old gal."

Nancy beamed.

Gerri said, "I would've thought someone on the run for his life would be using a phony name."

"Yeah," Kurt said, "I am. But a phony name won't protect you for long. Word gets around. They catch up to you."

"So you can see why he needs a ride out there," Nancy said. "When, Hon? When do they need you?"

"Tomorrow morning," Kurt said. "Eight o'clock sharp. That's good. I like that. Sign of professionalism."

"I thought it was a two-bit movie town," Gerri said.

Greg, who had been standing in the open doorway, said, "I'll drive you. I'm not doing anything."

"Greg," Gerri said, trying to sound a warning.

"It's okay, Gerri," he said. "I'm bored out of my mind. It's like I'm hanging around waiting for my life to start. Like I said, I'm not doing anything."

"What about the headaches?" Gerri asked.

"They're not as bad," Greg said. "Don't worry about it."

"You know, you should lighten up," Nancy said to Gerri. "You're way too uptight for your own good."

Gerri wanted to strangle her.

That's how Greg ended up ferrying Kurt and Nancy out to the valley every day. For the first few days, they took the boys too, because Nancy was certain they'd all be hired as extras, herself included. Then she decided to leave them behind. She said she didn't want them missing any more school, but Greg said it was because Kurt had been asked not to bring them back, they were causing trouble, making noise and generally getting in the way.

As it turned out, Nancy didn't manage to get any work on the set but Greg did. He'd been hanging around watching, waiting for Kurt, when someone spotted him. He was just the right height for the North West Mounted Police uniforms they'd been able to get their hands on. Greg even had a few lines, although not in any recognizable language. The police were to speak a kind of gibberish that sounded to Gerri like a bad imitation of Swedish. The point was, Greg explained to Gerri, that the Indians couldn't understand the police or the Indian agents so the audience wasn't supposed to either. Using gibberish would force the audience to see things through the Indians' eyes.

The night before Greg's big scene, Gerri caught him practising his lines. He had only to shout the garbled equivalent of "Over here" and "I see smoke," but his short-term memory was so bad he was afraid he wouldn't be able to get it right. Gerri didn't know what he was worrying about. He could say pretty much whatever he wanted and who would know the difference?

One night when seven o'clock rolled around and the boys were still on their own, Gerri decided to invite them over for supper, just to make sure they had one good meal in them. The oldest boy was sullen and at first he said he wasn't coming.

"Well, can these two come then?" Gerri said.

"I don't care what they do," he said. "I'm not coming though." But then he showed up with his brothers.

"Mom said to stay with them," he said. "So that's what I'm doing. I'm the oldest, you know."

"Yeah, I know," said Gerri. She made them macaroni and cheese, and then she lit a fire in the fireplace and read aloud from an old book of fairy tales from her own childhood. The oldest pretended he wasn't listening, but Gerri knew he was.

When she finished the story, the youngest boy said, "My mom says Greg has a girlfriend."

"What?" Gerri said.

"A girlfriend," the boy said. "You know what that is."

"Yeah," Gerri said. "But I'm Greg's girlfriend."

"Not you," the boy said. "Someone else."

Gerri wondered what that was about, but she didn't bother pursuing it.

"Okay," she said to the boys. "Time for bed. You've got school tomorrow."

They didn't want her to come with them, although she offered. The oldest boy fished a key chain out of his pocket, one with a multitude of keys for all the locks.

"Are you afraid when you're alone in the house?" Gerri asked.

The youngest said yes and the oldest no, simultaneously.

Hours later, Greg, Kurt and Nancy showed up drunk. They all came into the house and when Greg sat on the couch Nancy sat on his lap.

"This doesn't mean anything," she said, staring right at Gerri. "Greg is like a brother to me, isn't he Kurt?"

Greg looked at Gerri and shrugged his shoulders. Kurt looked as though he could care less that his wife was sitting in another man's lap. Nancy was wearing a short black leather skirt and knee-high red boots. If Gerri had seen her on the street she would have bet her last dollar that she was a prostitute. Even now, she wasn't altogether sure.

"Have you got any beer in the fridge?" Nancy asked Greg.

Gerri left the room. Kurt followed her to the foot of the stairs.

"Where are you going?" he asked. "Party's just getting started. You can sit on my lap and we'll talk about whatever comes up."

Nancy laughed like a hyena.

"Fuck off, Kurt," Gerri said. "Go home and look after your children."

"Just asking, for Christ sake," Kurt said.

"Get them out of here, Greg," Gerri said, trying to stay calm. "Right now."

On her way up the stairs, she noticed that her hands were shaking. She was worried Kurt might follow her but he didn't. She heard Nancy laugh again, and then Kurt said, "That pretty much explains it, doesn't it?"

Later, when Greg came to bed, Gerri was still awake. She was too upset to sleep, having realized that Greg was now far away from her and what she thought of as a normal life.

Greg sat on the edge of the bed and said, "I guess I have something to tell you."

Gerri had the awful feeling he was going to confess that he'd slept with Nancy, but he didn't. He switched on the bedside light, and then he told her about Nina. He said he was having an affair with someone from Tacoma, Washington. He was sorry he hadn't told Gerri sooner but he had no memory of it. He'd found a letter, he said, and some photographs. Gerri tried to tell herself this was funny, like Mrs. Duncan putting eggs in the washing machine.

"You're not in love with her," Gerri said. "You don't even know her." She told him the story, all the details she remembered, even the mango and the DQ BON VOYAGE cake, and how she had put the candy box with the letter and photos in his drawer after the accident because she hadn't known what else to do with them. She should have told him before, she said, but there hadn't been a reason to. No further letters had arrived from Nina. Gerri was certain they wouldn't be hearing from her again. Greg didn't look convinced.

"Ask Martin," Gerri said. "He knows the whole story."

Greg began to get undressed.

"I know how I feel," he said.

"How's that?" Gerri asked. She was still trying hard to think this was funny.

"Like I'm in love with someone else," Greg said. He crawled into bed beside her. "I'm sorry," he said. "I must be an asshole." After he turned out the light he said, "I think I should move out. It's not fair to you."

Gerri didn't know what to say. This was so wrong. Greg needed help. He wasn't even seeing a doctor since he'd left Saskatoon. She waited a minute, trying not to panic, then said, "Let's not be hasty. Wait a while before you decide what to do. Maybe things will come back to you." Greg didn't say anything. "Promise me you'll wait a bit," Gerri said.

"Okay," Greg said, but there was no commitment in his voice.

The candy box found its way back onto the fireplace mantle. In the days that followed, in whatever time was left after Greg, Kurt and Nancy drove out to the movie location and back, Gerri caught Greg staring at the photos or sitting on the couch pouring over the letter. Once, Gerri found him at the kitchen table with a pen in his hand and a pad of paper in front of him. He'd written his own address and the date in the upper left-hand corner, but hadn't got any further than that. She found a long distance phone number on a piece of paper by the phone and when she checked she discovered it was a Washington state number. She called the phone company and asked for a review of long distance calls placed from their number, and was told that in the past two days a half dozen calls had been made to Tacoma. The first lasted four minutes. The rest were all under a minute.

Gerri felt sick. She had no idea what to do. She talked to Martin, but he didn't know either. He wondered if Gerri should call Greg's parents, but she didn't want to do that. They were so out of touch with who Greg really was, how could they possibly help? Then again, Gerri wasn't sure who he really was any more. Martin tried to talk to Greg again, to convince him of the truth, but Greg was suspicious. He didn't say so, but it was clear he thought Gerri and Martin were in collusion.

"What about the letter?" Greg always said. "You can't tell me that letter is a fabrication."

"Believe me," Gerri always said. "I was there. I took one of the pictures, the one of Nina feeding you cake."

It turned out that Greg was more inclined to believe Kurt than he was Gerri or Martin. He told Gerri he'd shown the letter to Kurt and Kurt had come up with a theory: Greg had met Nina and fallen in love with her, but her visa was about to run out and she was going to be deported. So the two of them had contrived for her to meet Sandy, and then Greg just happened to stop by Martin and Sandy's when Nina was there, and he found a way to drop the idea of the phony marriage plan, which he and Nina had already thought up. It was the perfect plan, Kurt said, because now Nina could write Greg steamy letters without hiding it from Gerri.

"Where are the rest of the letters then?" Gerri asked, and of course he had an answer, thought up by Kurt: Gerri was intercepting them. Kurt thought Greg should have his mail held at the post office.

"Please," Gerri said, "do that. Then you'll know there aren't any more letters." Greg said he might look into it, but as far as she knew he never did.

On the final day of shooting, Nancy said something that gave Gerri hope. She and Kurt were thinking about moving back to California. Hollywood was the only place Kurt could have a real career, Nancy said, and anyway, there was no hiding if you worked in the movie business, even in an out-of-the-way place like Saskatchewan. Television news teams had been visiting the set of the Big Bear movie and Nancy was pretty sure Kurt had been captured in some of the footage. They'd have to take their chances, she said. Maybe Kurt could work something out with the producer he'd backed out on.

This was good news. Gerri didn't care anymore what effect another move would have on the boys. She thought they were probably doomed anyway, just from having Kurt and Nancy for parents, and right now she cared only about Greg's recovery. She didn't see how she could possibly get him back to normal as long as he was hanging around with people whose version of reality was so skewed.

Just before midnight that night, as Gerri waited for Greg to get home from the wrap party, an ambulance pulled up in front of the Duncans' and took Mr., not Mrs., Duncan to the hospital. Before they left an ambulance attendant knocked on the door to tell Gerri that Mr. Duncan had fallen and broken a hip and Mrs. Duncan was refusing to come to the hospital with them. They would be contacting the home-care people, he said, but in the meantime Mrs. Duncan would be in the house by herself. Gerri knew the old couple didn't have any relatives in town (Mr. Coots had told her that) and so she offered to go next door and sit with Mrs. Duncan until someone arrived to care for her.

Gerri had no idea what to expect. She'd had a few conversations with Mr. Duncan over the back fence, but she'd never spoken to the old lady. She thought someone distraught and suspicious of strangers would answer the door, but instead, Mrs. Duncan greeted her as though it was the middle of day and Gerri had just dropped in for tea. She made tea, in fact, and served it in tea cups with a pattern Gerri recognized – green shamrocks; her mother had a vase with the same pattern. Mrs. Duncan put a plate of homemade cookies on a highly polished, antique-looking coffee table and, were it not for the fact that she didn't once mention Mr. Duncan and the broken hip, Gerri would have found it hard to believe there was a thing wrong with her. Gerri explained that she lived next door, just to make sure Mrs. Duncan knew who she was, and Mrs. Duncan said, "I know that. With the poor young man who had the accident. How is he?" Gerri didn't bother with the whole long story and said he was doing fine, and Mrs. Duncan expressed the reasonable opinion that motorcycles ought to be banned, they were too dangerous, no protection at all if anything happened. Gerri kept waiting for the old lady to get tired but she had plenty of stamina and plenty to talk about. It was almost two o'clock by the time the home-care nurse showed up, and Mrs. Duncan was still going strong.

As soon as Gerri got home and went up to the bedroom, she knew Greg was gone. His dresser drawers were open as though he'd grabbed clothes in a hurry, and things were missing that shouldn't have been. His toothbrush and razor. A backpack that had been propped in a corner. Gerri went downstairs and sure enough the candy box was gone. She immediately called Martin, even though it was the middle of the night, but he didn't know anything. She called Kurt and Nancy's and there was no answer. She began to understand. California. Washington. Greg had a car; Kurt and Nancy didn't. Kurt had no doubt convinced Greg he should head for Tacoma to look for his lady love, taking Kurt and his itinerant family with him. Gerri wondered how long Kurt and Nancy had been working on that plan; probably since he'd agreed to drive them to Fort Qu'Appelle and had become their personal taxi service.

There was nothing Gerri could do. Greg was a grown man. She'd just have to wait and hope that he survived a road trip with Kurt and Nancy and whatever happened in Tacoma when he got there.

Several days later, Gerri saw a Salvation Army truck out front, apparently taking away the Duncans' possessions, including their furniture. A man who looked like a younger version of Mr. Duncan seemed to be in charge. Mrs. Duncan was nowhere to be seen, but Mr. Coots was bustling around, cane and all, trying to be helpful. He and the stranger loaded a few boxes and suitcases into a U-haul trailer, and in no time they were locking the front door and shaking hands. When Mr. Coots saw Gerri was home he came over to gossip.

"How is Mr. Duncan then?" Gerri asked, fearful that he might have died.

"He's recovering," Mr. Coots said. "But the son from B.C. has put his foot down. They can't live on their own anymore, he says, and he's moving them out to the coast to live with him."

"Well, that's all right, isn't it?" Gerri said.

"I suppose," Mr. Coots said, "but he pretty much made the decision for them, and he wouldn't let them take their furniture because there's no room for it in his house. He called up the Salvation Army and told them they could have whatever they wanted."

Gerri was shocked. "You mean, he didn't even give them time to go through their own stuff? That's terrible."

Worst of all, Mr. Coots said, the son was leaving that very day with Mrs. Duncan because he had to get back to work, and Mr. Duncan would be staying in the hospital on his own until he was well enough to fly. "How's he going to get on a plane by himself with a hip replacement?" Mr. Coots wanted to know.

"Maybe the son will come back for him," Gerri said.

"They won't live long out there," Mr. Coots said. "It might be warmer, but that's not everything. We'll be reading their obituaries in the paper before you know it."

Gerri decided she'd better tell Mr. Coots, since he was here, that she hadn't seen Kurt and Nancy for days and that there was a chance they'd left town. She was somewhat reluctant to tell him, because she was holding out hope that they were still around somewhere and that Greg had not gone with them. Really though, she knew. Mr. Coots thought they ought to check the house in case something was wrong and anyway, he said, they owed him two months' rent. He was going to have to evict them if they were still there.

The house wasn't locked. Kurt and Nancy's various padlocks were all hanging open, and they hadn't bothered to turn the main deadbolt. The first thing Gerri and Mr. Coots saw when they entered was the cat. She rubbed up against their legs, begging for attention, so Gerri picked her up and carried her as they inspected the house, which Kurt and Nancy had left in an incredible mess. They'd taken almost nothing with them. A package of raw pork chops was stinking to high heaven in the kitchen sink along with a pile of dirty dishes. Sheets were still on the unmade beds. Even the boys' clothing and toys had been left behind.

Mr. Coots worked himself into a terrible flap over the mess and how he was going to get it cleaned up. He tried to talk Gerri into doing it for a month's free rent, but she had no desire to rummage through the debris of Kurt and Nancy's lives. When she turned down two months' free rent, he used her phone to call a cleaning company. He assured Gerri not to worry, he'd be finding new renters for the two properties; the owner wouldn't be selling, not just yet.

After he left Gerri called Miss Kershaw and told her she could come and get the orange cat, which had sniffed its way through Gerri and Greg's house and was now stretched out on the rug in the living room. Gerri had thought the house might cause it to have some kind of strange flashback to its previous life when it lived there with Miss Kershaw, but apparently not. It didn't look confused at all.

"They must have taken off in the middle of the night," Gerri said to Miss Kershaw when she called her. "What a mess. There was still food on the table. Even a carton of sour milk." She tried to sound upbeat and happy that the neighbours were finally gone.

Miss Kershaw said she would be there as soon as she could. She was coming from across town, where she managed a cable company branch office in a strip mall. She would leave as soon as she could get someone to fill in, she said, and take the quickest route, the bypass road, even though she didn't usually come that way because there were too many farm trucks and semi-trailers.

"I'm so happy, I can't tell you," she said. "I had almost given up hope. I thought she was gone forever."

When Miss Kershaw got there, she took one look at the cat and said, "But that's not Amanda."

"You've got to be kidding," Gerri said.

"Amanda has no white on her at all. She's completely orange."

Gerri looked at the cat. Her front paws were clearly white and she had a white spot the shape of a diamond on one side of her face.

Gerri could think of only one thing to do; she offered Miss Kershaw a drink. They sat side by side on the couch, each with a water glass half full of Scotch. The cat walked contentedly from one lap to the other, purring like mad. Gerri and Miss Kershaw didn't even try to make conversation.

Gerri absently reached for the mail on the coffee table in front of her. She hadn't opened it because it was all bills. Now she did. The phone bill recorded seventeen long distance calls to Tacoma, all of them under a minute.

"Christ," she said aloud.

Miss Kershaw, who smelled of Lily of the Valley, took a long swallow of her drink and said, "I think I'll go to the Humane Society and rescue another cat. That's where I got Amanda."

"You can have this cat," Gerri said.

"I don't think so," said Miss Kershaw. She gave no reason.

Gerri knew the sale of the houses was imminent. A week after the neighbours' flight and Greg's disappearance, Mr. Coots stopped by to tell her he'd sold all three properties to an insurance company that was planning to build its head office on the site.

"I thought the owner wasn't planning to sell just yet," Gerri said, even though she wasn't surprised and had already made plans to find an apartment for herself and the abandoned cat.

"A change in circumstances," was all Mr. Coots would say. It occurred to Gerri that there might not actually be an owner other than Mr. Coots.

The letter carrier came by as Mr. Coots was leaving and he handed Gerri a postcard. She could see that Mr. Coots was trying to get a look at it so she held it behind her back until he was on his way down the block. She was hoping the card would be from Greg, but it was from Nina. The message was blunt.

I'm in Mexico now with a guy named Juan. We're living on the beach and it's so cool I can hardly stand it. By the way, stop phoning my parents. My dad says he's going to call the FBI if you don't. Did you really think I was serious? Canada is too cold and besides it was a stupid idea. I thought you'd know that, but maybe you're a pathetic loser, I'm beginning to think so. Anyway, stop calling.

There was a stoneware teapot sitting on the floor in the living room. Gerri picked it up and fired it through the front window, sending shards of glass all over the couch and the carpet. She wasn't mad at Nina. She had no thoughts about her one way or the other. She was angry with Greg for not being there so she could show him what Nina had written and say, See.

The anger didn't last. Gerri held a match to the postcard and dropped it onto the fireplace grate. She sat on the couch and watched the evidence of Greg's folly burn down to ash. The orange cat hopped up beside her and then onto the back of the couch, curious about the hole in the window.

Acknowledgements

The author would like to thank the Canada Council, the Saskatchewan Arts Board and the City of Regina for their assistance during the writing of this book. For editorial advice, she would like to thank editor Barbara Kuhne, and Marlis Wesseler, Elizabeth Philips, Connie Gault, Marina Endicott. "Long Gone and Mister Lonely" and "Hawk's Landing" were first published in *Grain*. "Bone Garden" was first published in *Canadian Fiction Magazine*.

About the Author

Dianne Warren is the author of two previous story collections, *The Wednesday Flower Man* (Coteau, 1987) and *Bad Luck Dog* (Coteau, 1993). The latter book won three Saskatchewan Book Awards. Warren has also won the National Magazine Gold Award, the Western Magazine Award for Fiction (1993 and 1999) and the Regina Book Award. Warren is also a playwright and her play *Serpent in the Night Sky* was shortlisted for a Governor-General's Award. She has taught writing at the Banff Centre and the Sage Hill writers' workshops and until recently was an editor at *Grain* magazine. Dianne Warren lives in Regina, Saskatchewan.

Mount Appetite • by Bill Gaston
Astounding stories by a writer whose work is "gentle, humorous, absurd, beautiful, spiritual, dark and sexy. Gaston deserves to dwell in the company of Findley, Atwood and Munro as one of this country's outstanding literary treasures." – *The Globe and Mail*
1-55192-451-X • $21.95 CAN/$15.95 USA

A Sack of Teeth • by Grant Buday
This darkly humorous novel paints an unforgettable portrait of one extraordinary day in the life of a father, a mother and a six-year-old child in September 1965. "Buday's genius is that of the storyteller." – *Vancouver Sun*
1-55192-457-9 • $21.95 CAN/$15.95 USA

Small Accidents • by Andrew Gray
Twelve dazzling stories by a Journey Prize finalist. "Andrew Gray tells tall tales that tap into the hubris of the human condition … He expertly depicts the gore of human error and conveys a present as startling as a car wreck." – Hal Niedzviecki
1-55192-508-7 • $19.95 CAN/$14.95 USA

Pool-Hopping and Other Stories • by Anne Fleming
Shortlisted for the Governor-General's Award, the Ethel Wilson Fiction Prize and the Danuta Gleed Award. "Fleming's evenhanded, sharp-eyed and often hilarious narratives traverse the frenzied chaos of urban life with ease and precision." – *The Georgia Straight*
1-896095-18-6 • $16.95 CAN/$13.95 USA

What's Left Us • by Aislinn Hunter
Six stories and an unforgettable novella by a prodigiously talented writer. "Aislinn Hunter is a gifted writer with a fresh energetic voice and a sharp eye for the detail that draws you irresistibly into the intimacies of her story." – Jack Hodgins
1-55192-412-9 • $21.95 CAN/$15.95 USA